The

Beggar King

THE
BEGGAR KING

MICHELLE BARKER

thistledown press

Thistledown Press Ltd.
118 - 20th Street West
Saskatoon, Saskatchewan, S7M 0W6
www.thistledownpress.com

Library and Archives Canada Cataloguing in Publication

Barker, Michelle, 1964-
The beggar king / Michelle Barker.

Issued also in electronic format.
ISBN 978-1-927068-37-3

I. Title.

PS8603.A73567B43 2013   jC813'.6   C2013-900957-4

Cover and book design by Jackie Forrie
Printed and bound in Canada

Canada Council   Conseil des Arts
for the Arts   du Canada

SASKATCHEWAN
ARTS BOARD

Canadian   Patrimoine
Heritage   canadien

Thistledown Press gratefully acknowledges the financial assistance of the Canada Council for the Arts, the Saskatchewan Arts Board, and the Government of Canada through the Canada Book Fund for its publishing program.

Acknowledgements

This novel took approximately ten years from first draft to publication. A journey that long can only be realized with a lot of help and encouragement.

I am enormously grateful to the Canada Council for the Arts for the grant they provided. Thanks go to Sherrill MacLaren who showed me what it means to be a writer, and to Loranne Brown who set me on my way; to Ed Griffin, for his constant enthusiasm; to Dave Margoshes, for asking all the right questions; to Lynn Bennett, for her support in the early days; to Brenda Carre, who read my queries and synopses; and to Al Forrie, for saying yes. Liz Philips, editor and diviner — I am immensely grateful for her keen eye, patience, and wonderful sense of humour.

For several years Carolyn Rowell and I ran a writing workshop in the Eastern Townships of Quebec. Many of the scenes in the novel arose from the writing I did there. Carolyn read this manuscript more often than I can count. Without her advice and generosity it wouldn't exist. Tanya Bellehumeur-Allatt was a huge source of inspiration and, above all, of hope. To Brenda Hartwell, Marjorie Bruhmuller, Trisha Pope, Jerome Krause, and Marguerite Dunlop: truly, truly I have been blessed.

Above all, my gratitude lies with my husband and family. To Maddy, who read the manuscript in a breathless two days and asked for more; to Dallas, Sam and Harry for endless inspiration and comic relief; to my mother who would have loved it no matter what – and to Dan, for his steadfast love and tireless support. Anyone else would have given up on me years ago and told me to get a real job.

For Dan

"To light a candle is to cast a shadow . . . "
— Ursula K. Le Guin

One

THE FEAST OF THE GREAT LIGHT

"JORDAN ELLIOTT!" THAT RUMBLING VOICE COULD only belong to Mama Petsane. "Get down off that roof, or ye'll fall and break yer legs and then we'll have to wheel ye around in a donkey cart."

Jordan laughed but did not come down. He shaded his eyes, looking for Ophira, but in the alley below he saw only the round old woman, an apron tied across her sky-blue feast robes. "Tell Ophira I'll see her at the palace grounds," he called.

"If yer lucky," cried Mama Petsane, waving her wooden stew spoon at him. "Don't be bringing any love potions, neither. Feed 'em to the goats. Maybe they'll stop nipping at yer back side."

Jordan's face coloured. It had been a few years since he'd concocted those potions, but he didn't realize anyone had known about them. Then again, Mama Petsane was one of the Seven Seers of Cir. The seers knew everything, and they were especially protective of their adopted daughter. The last thing Jordan wanted was for Ophira to hear about his childish experiments. He'd been hoping she might come outside to watch him jump the roofs, but now, with Mama Petsane here, he was rethinking that plan. Mama Petsane was bound to embarrass him.

Pulling up his feast robes to free his legs, Jordan set off at a run and leaped onto a neighbouring roof several feet away. He received the shriek he'd been expecting from Petsane. The jump was less than graceful. Even though the robe, woven from spun mellowreed, was almost as light as silk, he wasn't used to its length and bagginess.

Today was the annual Feast of the Great Light, the most celebrated day in the Holy City of Cir and its provinces. It was also Jordan's birthday. He had agreed to meet his father for the ceremonies atop the mountain and he intended to enjoy himself along the way.

Jumping across roofs and patios and sneaking up private staircases was Jordan's preferred method of reaching the golden palace at the mountain-city's summit. Sometimes strangers chased him with straw brooms, and once he nearly tripped on a giant lizard sunning itself in the midday heat, but usually he was alone with the birds up there.

Gathering up his robes again, he took the next rooftops at full speed, relishing the feeling of strength in his legs and the way the warm summer air whooshed by him. He was fast. His good friend Donovan had suggested that the year — which would be named that afternoon and always after a bird — should be named after Jordan. The year of Jordan Elliott.

His father hated when he travelled by rooftop but the truth was, it was perhaps the only thing he was good at. Today he was fifteen. That left one year before he would have to declare his vocation and take his robes. Roof-jumping didn't qualify.

"If you spent more time at your studies, you might discover that talent of yours," Elliott T. Elliott often said. It wasn't long ago that Jordan would have attended to his father's advice, but over the past year he'd stopped listening. Elliott had ideas about Jordan that fit him as poorly as these stupid robes.

He stopped to catch his breath. From where he stood he could see all the way down to the Balakan River which surrounded the city and rendered it an island. Yellow sasapher flowers grew wild along its banks. The twelve magical bridges connecting the city to the mainland glistened in the sunlight. Or rather, eleven of them glistened. One of the bridges — the Mystic Corridor — was invisible. Beyond them shimmered the alluring reds and gleaming yellows of the mainland city of Omar, a glaring contrast to the Holy City's whitewashed stone.

Jordan picked a handful of pink flowers from a stranger's rooftop garden and scurried up the last few steep stairways.

When he finally reached the summit, he remembered his mother had promised to bring him cakes for his birthday. Tanny was a palace cook, and it was widely acknowledged that she made the best sasapher cakes in all of Cir. There was no sweeter taste to Jordan than sasapher. It was not just lemon: it was lemon with a history, lemon with mud on its feet and courage in its belly. He knew his mother would be frantically busy in the kitchen today, but she would steal the time to come find him.

Jordan turned his back on the palace and its enormous domed temple and headed towards the gardens and pathways that surrounded the feast day's centre of attention — the mysterious, blackened holy tree.

Near one of the fountains he spotted a tall grey undercat wearing blue feast robes decorated with gold-threaded runes, his hat upturned and hopeful as he recited a traditional story with flair. "Draw near, friends, and listen to the tale of our Cirran tree," he cried. His furry hands flew out to his sides and his long whiskers jittered. "It was first struck by the power of the Great Light on a night of true-full moons. It burned, but was not consumed."

The undercat winked at him and Jordan realized it was Sarmillion, a friend of his father's. "Jordan," he called. "Tell me why the tree burns."

"I dunno," he mumbled. "Something to do with magic."

"It is a warning, young rogue, of the dangers of strong magic. I'll tell your father you've been shirking your schoolwork," the undercat said with a twinkle in his eye. His gaze flitted to the flowers in Jordan's hand. "Phinius," he said. "Flower of the sages. That's a rather bold choice for a boy with sticky fingers."

"I resent that accusation," Jordan said with a laugh.

He kept walking, scanning the crowd for his mother's short but solid silhouette and flour-dusted clothes. She would be wearing her small white apron embroidered with the Cirran crest — a dove set in a circle — and her face would be flushed from hours of baking.

Ahead of him stood the majestic, charred tree. Bordered by grass and a colourful mosaic of stone pathways, the tree wore feast day ribbons in its branches. Three brave yellow finches sat upon the highest tips observing the procession of blue robes below. Occasionally one of them would take off and soar with abandon above the heads of farmers and belt-dancers, as if it too were celebrating.

The tree was already surrounded by hundreds of offerings of flowers. On the feast day you weren't supposed to look at it as you came close, but Jordan couldn't help raising his eyes to study the twisted blackened bark and the long branches that made him think of outstretched arms. How could a tree burn without being reduced to ash? Once a year when the moons rose true-full and midnight crept towards the world, everyone gathered — some near the tree itself, others from rooftops or out their windows — to see it burst into sudden flame and then just as abruptly go out.

He placed his stolen bouquet at the foot of the magical tree, and then found a patch of grass where he could sit and wait for his parents — and, he hoped, Ophira. The air was alive with conversation and murmured incantations. The faithful set down their flowers with their heads bowed. Three more finches lit upon the branches, and then something beneath the birds caught Jordan's eye.

A small older man with a hooked nose and dark eyes stood brazenly before the tree, staring at it. He must have sensed Jordan watching him, for he turned and gave him a smile that made Jordan shudder. The man's lips were drained of colour, and his pale skin made Jordan think of candle wax. Those nearest to the tree didn't seem to notice him. The pilgrims farther away, couldn't they see him reach towards the finches and snatch one? Didn't they hear the terrible crunch as he squeezed the tiny bird to death and then tucked it into his pocket?

The man rested his hand on the dark surface of the tree. Something sparked, and Jordan smelled ash. Then, before his incredulous eyes, the man stepped into the air beside him and disappeared. In his place, one small black feather drifted down and settled at the base of the tree. Without thinking, Jordan picked it up and put it in the pocket of his feast robes. He stumbled back to his patch of grass, trying to process what he'd seen.

"Happy birthday, Jordan."

He startled so badly at the sound of Ophira's voice that she asked, "What is it? Are you all right?"

Jordan studied her pale face and blue eyes that were trained on him. He glanced back at the tree. "I . . . nothing. It's nothing." Jordan had been certain that he'd seen the man. Now he wondered: what had he seen?

Ophira was wearing her blue feast dress, with white ribbons in her long dark hair. She had bent to adjust a sandal, her body as graceful as a belt-dancer's.

"You managed to escape your grandmas for the afternoon," Jordan said, swallowing what he'd really wanted to say.

"I expect they'll track me down before long," she said easily. Everyone called the seers grandmas, even though they weren't. They were just old.

Ophira laid a hand upon his arm. "Look — Arrabel is coming. She's going to name the year."

High Priestess Arrabel had entered the ceremony accompanied by four of her crimson-robed mystery keepers, one of whom carried the immense and sacred Book of What Is in both hands. Jordan's father had once told him this was the only occasion in the entire year that the precious Cirran book of spells and incantations left the Meditary.

Something about Arrabel made her beautiful, though Jordan could never figure out what it was, for her nose was long, her forehead high and her chin pointed. Perhaps it was the stillness that shone through her like a lantern, or maybe it was just her kind-heartedness. There were others in the palace whose mere presence made a person feel like a servant, but Arrabel was not like that. Even the farrier felt chosen when she spoke to him. Today her blonde hair was pinned up, her priestess robes an intricate arrangement of beads and buttons and the feathers of countless birds.

A hush descended as the mystery keepers edged away from Arrabel. Her eyes were closed, her arms thrown wide, her face angled towards the cloudless sky. The breeze lifted wisps of her hair.

"Do you figure she's already decided which bird will name the year?" Jordan asked softly.

"Oh yes," said Ophira. "She's been studying the sky for months."

One of the mystery keepers opened the Book of What Is and in unison the keepers recited an incantation to the Great Light. As they spoke, light flashed from the book's pages in tiny sparkling points.

"Now the wind will pick up," Ophira said. "Listen — the keepers are calling the birds."

Jordan was thankful to live in the Cirran part of Katir-Cir that honoured the great mysteries. Mystery did not cross the snow-tipped mountains that divided the lands of Cir from the coldly rational provinces of Brin. He thought of the magical burning tree. He liked the way a mystery teased you, like a locked door.

The mystery keepers' chants fell to a hum, and went silent. Then, in a tone both calm and commanding, Arrabel said, "I declare this to be . . . the year of the magpie."

There were cheers as the sky thickened with the black and white birds. Ophira's forehead wrinkled and she stared at the grass. "The birds of thievery," she said.

"Is it a bad omen?" Jordan asked.

"A warning, maybe. Magpies are known for stealing the eggs out of other birds' nests."

The mystery keepers closed the book and began to walk back towards the palace but Arrabel stopped, as if she'd been struck by a puzzling idea. Her eyes searched the gathering, her expression grave. When Jordan realized her gaze was on him, he gave a short bow and said, "My lady." By the time he'd straightened, she had walked on.

"What was that about?" Ophira asked.

"I have no idea."

"Bells and billy grain," came a wrinkled cry. "There you are, 'Phira!"

Jordan sighed. It was Mama Manjuza, a hunched woman concealing a face as wizened as an overripe mango behind her seer's veil. She gripped Ophira's arm and pulled her away, saying, "Girl's gotta see to her grandmas now, Jordan. Off ye go."

Ophira shot Jordan a look of regret, gave a small wave, and departed with the old woman. Jordan scanned the people for his father's face and found him beside a small koi pond offering family friends good wishes for the New Year. Elliott squeezed his shoulder and whispered, "Happy birthday, son," and Jordan smiled.

"Have you seen Mom?"

"I expect she's here somewhere," he said. But when they went searching for her in earnest, they couldn't find her.

"Go on ahead to the contests," Elliott said. "I'll bring your cakes. Just be home for dinner," and he gave the customary Cirran sign of greeting or leave-taking, pressing three fingers to his forehead with a short bow. Jordan made sure none of his friends were around and then gave the quickest bow possible and hurried off.

As he made his way past trumpeters, jugglers and merchants, he noticed the crowd had swelled. By now the underrats had arrived — Jordan spotted two in trench coats, and several others wearing extraordinary silver silk suits. They had already imbibed too much mug-wine and were trying, without success, to pick people's pockets. Nearby, a woman swatted one of them with her basket.

But that was normal for a feast day celebration. What was unusual was the number of foreigners. Not just Omarrians or farmers from the provinces who attended the celebrations every year, but unfamiliar people, dark and quiet, hanging back from the others. They did not offer greetings as Jordan passed, and when by accident he bumped an older man and apologized, the man answered in a thick unrecognizable accent. Perhaps they were from the south. The land of Ut was rarely traveled because of the heat and sheer desolation of a desert journey. And then a jester popped up before him wearing a hat formed entirely of shoes, each of which proceeded to hop off his head and walk away, and Jordan laughed and forgot about the strangers.

He passed the hammer throw and the wrestling ring that had been set up in one of the larger courtyards, and continued until he reached the archery fields, a colourful conglomeration of flags and targets. The Cirran flag flew in every direction, and with the breeze it seemed as if the doves themselves would take flight. Jordan spied some of his school friends already taking turns with the bows. Anyone was allowed to shoot before the official contests began. When they saw him they waved him over.

"Take a shot, Jordan," they called. "Donovan's already hit the bull's-eye twice."

Everyone knew Donovan would take the dark blue robes of a novice Landguard next year; his aim was unsurpassed. It made Jordan jealous to think of it. Not that he wanted to be a Landguard; he just wished for a recognizable talent, an uncomplicated path towards the future. All of his friends knew what they were going to be. A few were born to be scholars, and one was going to his uncle's ranch in Cirsinnia to work in the horse stables. But Jordan could not follow in his father's footsteps. Carving tools felt awkward in his hands and he tended to use too much force, cutting too deeply with the chisel and ruining the bowl or bird sculpture.

He sighed and fixed his eye on the concentric circles of the target, nocked the arrow and pulled. He had the strength for this art, but not the aim. When his arrow landed in a haystack, his friends hooted.

"You're supposed to hit the parchment, Jordan."

He grinned. "I was aiming for the haystack."

A series of trumpet blasts announced the beginning of the real contests. Everyone moved aside, and Jordan saw the commander, Theophen, leading the palace Landguards towards the field. With his hair streaming behind him and his head so erect and proud, he reminded Jordan of a lion. A jagged scar ran the length of his left cheek. It gave him a stern bearing, but most folks knew he had a kind heart. Donovan would be lucky to train under him.

Two boys struggled to bring in the enormous ceremonial bow and presented it to Theophen. In other regiments the commander shot first, but Theophen passed the honour on to his second-in-command. He would shoot last. The target was placed an impossible distance away. One after the other the Landguards shot. They were well trained and reasonably accurate and their shots earned respectable applause. But when Theophen picked up the bow, everyone went quiet.

A tall man with a long black beard had come to stand next to Jordan. "Is he a good shot?" the man asked in a heavy accent.

"The best," said Jordan, "Watch." One, two, three quick arrows were released, each scarcely aimed it seemed, and each a precise bull's-eye. The spectators roared with delight and Jordan felt some interior needle swing as surely as the needle of a compass. The way all eyes were on Theophen; that was what Jordan wanted, to stand at the centre of an admiring crowd.

"Hmm," the stranger said. "Is the high priestess as talented with a bow and arrow?"

"High Priestess Arrabel is not allowed to use weaponry." Jordan was about to add, "But everyone knows that," when he realized the man had walked away.

There were horseshoe games and a distance race from one end of the mountain plateau to the other, and then a challenge to see who could throw the weighted ball farthest. When the trumpets announced the palace feast, Jordan took leave of his friends and made his way home. Something was bothering him; something wasn't quite right about the day, but it was like trying to recall a dream. He could grasp one corner, then another, but when he tried for the third the whole thing fell apart. Finally he gave up, remembering that sasapher cakes awaited him, and he hurried towards home.

When he arrived, Elliott was placing small lit lanterns in every window of the house. The glass chimes were already hanging by the front door, a traditional ward against dark magic. Jordan could smell chicken roasting on the fire outside, but there were no cakes.

"The feast has probably kept your mother occupied," Elliott said when he saw the disappointment on Jordan's face. There was a tone of concern to his father's voice that hadn't been there earlier.

Jordan knew this was the busiest time of year for Tanny. She would work until midnight helping with whatever tasks arose. Tomorrow at breakfast she would tell them all about who had sat next to whom around the enormous banquet table, and which snippets of conversation she had caught as she rushed to deliver yet another platter of food. She would speak of High Priestess Arrabel's grace and how gallant Commander Theophen was, and Jordan would find himself wishing once again for something more in his life, something nameless and great and exciting . . . and unknown and impossible.

He went into his bedroom and gratefully exchanged his feast robes for the short pants he usually wore. That evening he and his father ate their dinner on the rooftop patio because the spectacle of the burning tree was more magnificent when viewed from afar. After the meal, Elliott lit his sasapher pipe and Jordan chewed on a stalk of mellowreed. They sat back in their chairs as the heat of the day rose from the stone around them. The summer breeze smelled of fried fish and cardamom, the Balakan River flowed in the distance, and somewhere nearby came the music of a flute. When the two moons rose like yellow eyes in the sky, their edges shone with an orange hue that happened only once a year and made them true-full.

"The Twins," Elliott said, and proceeded to tell Jordan the old tale about how a thousand thousand years ago the moons had once been twin sisters named Lucinda and Maelstrom.

It was a tale Jordan knew well. The sisters had lived back when magic bloomed freely across the lands of Katir-Cir, the good sort that came from the Great Light and delighted everyone with innocent enchantments. Elliott spoke of Lucinda's talent for magic and how ordinary lumpy Maelstrom had no gift for it. He told of the day Maelstrom discovered that magic had an underside — the undermagic, which few spoke of, because naming something gives it life and few wanted such dark magic to live. The source of this shadow magic was a great candle that awaited its king, a sorcerer of formidable power whose spirit was greedy for more.

"They would call him the Beggar King," said Jordan's father, "for he would be inclined to want."

The Beggar King came to Maelstrom, and they left to seek this power. When Lucinda found out, she begged the Great Light to hide the undermagic, hide it away where neither her sister nor this sorcerer could access it. And the Great Light heard her prayers, and the undermagic disappeared, its vulture guardians put to sleep. To end the sisters' dispute, the Great Light transformed them into twin moons obliged to rise and set in tandem. Jordan could see even now that one moon was slightly darker than the other.

"Some folks call it the undermagic moon," Elliott said, "for Sister Maelstrom likes to remind us of the darker ways of the world and how she longs to see them return to Katir-Cir."

As for the sorcerer, he was never heard from again. Some believed he died; others claimed he had been cursed with a half-life of eternal restlessness, never to be granted his true desire.

In the distance Jordan heard the shouts of the younger children who must have still been waiting on the Common for the arrival of the Beggar King. The annual ritual was always ushered in by a Heralder walking the streets of Cir, calling, "Beware the beggar who would be king." As soon as the Beggar King appeared, they would chase him down the mountain and across the Bridge of No Return.

Of course it wasn't the real Beggar King. There was no such thing. It was usually the scholar, Balbadoris, who agreed to play the part. The Beggar King had merely become the name given to dark corners and long shadows and the underside of things that didn't otherwise take to naming. It made everyone feel better to get rid of him once a year.

Jordan felt now as if he were caught in some in-between place: too old to don his black cloak and horns to scare away the Beggar King, but too young to spend the night at the Omar Bazaar. He longed to be old enough for that sort of adventure but his father had forbidden it. And while Donovan had bragged about going, Jordan knew his parents had obliged him to stay home, too.

He thought of the ugly vulture disguises that some of the children would be wearing, and how the parents' torches would flicker in the darkness. He imagined the whoops and shouts down the mountain as the Beggar King ran down, down, then across the bridge and into the enchanted cedar groves in Somberholt Forest. No one knew quite what happened in there, but scholars believed the deer were involved in his transformation. Deer were revered throughout Cir for their healing magic.

After this ritual, the younger children went to bed and the older children and adults would settle in to view the burning of the holy tree. It would begin with a crack, which would be followed by a burst of flames, and then — silence. This was supposed to occur somewhere around midnight but it never failed to catch Jordan by surprise.

Jordan and his father had grown quiet, both of them gazing up the mountain towards the holy tree, though it was still too early for the burning. And then Elliott straightened and said, "Listen."

A heavy stamp of footsteps came down the road, together with children crying and a general grumble of unhappiness, and Jordan realized he hadn't heard the whoops he'd been expecting. His father leaned over the patio railing and called out, "Ho, there, what's the trouble?"

"Strange goings-on," an older man replied, shaking his head. "Children waited a full hour for Master Balbadoris in his Beggar King garb."

"Never showed up," said a woman in a kerchief. "The Heralder got hoarse from calling. It ain't right to disappoint the young ones like that. It just ain't right."

Jordan and Elliott exchanged puzzled glances.

"That's not the least of it," said another man, a child at each hand. "Group of Landguards all dressed in black shows up on the Common and orders us to leave. Scared my boys half silly with their sticks and daggers. They got no right doing that."

Elliott and Jordan drew away from the edge of the roof.

"The Landguards don't wear black," said Jordan.

Elliott scratched his head and relit his pipe. "No. And I don't recall them ever brandishing their daggers at children, either."

The sound they heard next began as a rumble that grew quickly louder until the shouting and mayhem were unmistakable. Near the palace, flames burst into the sky. At first Jordan thought it was the holy tree, but when the fire didn't go out as it was supposed to, he knew something was wrong.

"Sweet sasapher!" said Elliott as another group of people dashed past their house yelling, "The barracks are on fire!"

"Brinnians. It's the Brinnians!" others cried.

Jordan's chest tightened. "What about Mom?" he said. "What if she's in trouble?"

The same thought was written across Elliott's face. The street had become a rushing stream of people pushing and scattering in every direction. From the palace came the clashing sounds of battle.

"Stay indoors!" shouted someone. "The streets are not safe!"

Jordan rose and reached for his sandals. "I don't care. I'm going up there. She might need our help."

Elliott grabbed him by the arm. "You'll get yourself killed." He eased Jordan back onto the chair. "We'll wait until morning. She'll be back by then, you'll see."

Jordan refused to go inside, and eventually fell into an uneasy sleep.

When he awoke, he was surprised to find it was morning and he was still on the rooftop. His father sat red-eyed and wide awake beside him. Two large green lizards had perched themselves near the edge of the roof, enjoying the early sun.

The air smelled of ash. His mother had not come home.

Two

The Morning After Mug-Wine

The inside of Sarmillion's mouth felt like an old carpet. He peeled one eye open and then the other. Mice alive, where was he? A tacky fern motif decorated the stone walls around him. He'd fallen asleep on an orange couch — orange! A couch button had left an indentation on his furry cheek, and on the low table beside him sat two empty mug-wine glasses. Yes, his headache spoke of mug-wine, far too much of it to be exact.

He sat up, rubbing his head and straightening his whiskers. Holy slag, was that the time? And it was the morning after the feast day. He let out a soft groan. *Time is the great burglar.* Just when you weren't paying attention, it snuck up on you and then you spied the burlap sack slung over its shoulder, filled with hours you hadn't even noticed were missing.

Master Balbadoris was expecting him this morning. There were tales to transcribe and parchments that needed illustration. Lately inspiration had been leaving Sarmillion behind, though Balbadoris never accepted that excuse. "Hard work, underkitty," he'd declare in his gravel-dry voice, and then he'd mumble about how he'd never met an undercat who had grasped this concept, and Sarmillion would bow his head and try not to listen but those damned pointed ears of his didn't miss a word.

He peeked at the stack of parchments sitting on a side-table, addressed to Minerva Wigglesnip. *Who?* How many glasses of mug-wine had he had? Blast, he'd slept in his feast robes, as well. He'd have to change back in his apartment, then sneak into Balbadoris's chambers and hope that the lecture on hard work wouldn't put him to sleep.

He slid two furry feet into gold palace-issue sandals and tiptoed towards the front door, hoping not to wake said Wigglesnip. Just as he was opening the door, he heard a high-pitched, "Honey Pie!" Quickly now, and he closed the door with a soft click.

Behind him came a shriek. "You're leaving? You . . . you cat!" Sarmillion bristled as he hurried away. It was the ultimate insult. Those four-legged, impossibly small and silent creatures hadn't a sense of style among them. And to think they were his ancestors? Disgusting.

He stepped out into the morning Cirran sun that glared upon the city's famed whitewashed stone. While tourists might have found it enchanting, Sarmillion could guarantee they were not tourists with hangovers.

Head bowed, he fought his body uphill all the way to the palace, trying to ignore the bongo drums playing in his stomach. He glanced up the main road that led to the Meditary — who wanted to cope with fresh-faced mystery keepers with their incense and incantations after such a night? Instead he slunk along a weedy side road that led to a small gated courtyard to which he happened to have the key — namely a sharp fountain pen he kept in his pocket for such occasions. The courtyard backed onto the living quarters of the old scholar Mimosa who was half-blind and hadn't heard a thing since the year of the peacock. Sarmillion loved Master Mimosa; his apartment had long served as the undercat's secret passage into the palace at inconvenient times such as this one.

And so we face yet another day when you won't be working on your masterpiece, twittered that little voice inside him that drove him near-insane.

"No," Sarmillion snapped back, "it appears we will not write poetry today."

As usual.

"Oh, do shut up," Sarmillion growled as he stole across the coarsely woven Circassic rug in Mimosa's living room. *How provincial.* It seemed the scholar wasn't home. Sarmillion opened the door that led onto a cold stone hallway, then scurried to his apartment at the end, turning a brass key in the lock and slipping inside.

He hadn't mentioned his new hand-knotted Omarrian rug to Balbadoris. He took off his sandals and stood enjoying its luxurious softness. And then he looked around. It took his eyes a minute to register what he was seeing. Parchments were scattered across the floor. A vase full of sasapher flowers had been knocked over, water and yellow petals splattered on his desk. Embroidered pillows lay hither and thither, scribe's robes were flung across the divan, and the delicate wooden crane that Elliott T. Elliott had carved for him had been split clean in half.

"Someone has broken in," he gasped. Who would do such a thing? And why? While Sarmillion was a great coveter of valuables, only the new rug was worth anything and it was still here. But at least this would make an excellent excuse for his lateness.

He splashed cold water onto his face, changed into fresh robes, added a dash of cologne to that sweet spot between neck and collarbone, and then a dab of scented oil to slick back the head-fur. Now he was ready to face the morning. Picking his way through the confusion, he decided he'd clean up later and headed out the door.

He mounted the two flights of stairs to Balbadoris's study and knocked with a crispness of purpose he didn't feel. There was no answer. Sarmillion called, "Master Balbadoris?" and pushed the door open, but he could see for himself no one was there. Worse, the study was in the same state of disaster as Sarmillion's apartment. "In the name of the seven seers, what is going on here?" He let out a long groan at the sight of his work strewn across the room, and decided he would seek out the scholar first and break the bad news to him. Perhaps Balbadoris was in the library.

No sooner had Sarmillion shut the study door when a scullery maid named Trina came running towards him. Every morning Trina snuck two sweet nutty-buns from the kitchen and delivered them to Sarmillion with a cup of strong coffee, but today she carried only a small cloth sack.

He snickered. "What's happened to my nutty-buns?"

"Embers 'n ashes, Sarmillion, do ye not know?" Her face was pale and her body as jittery as a frightened squirrel.

"Know what?"

"Brinnians've taken over the palace and oh, Great Light, the battle was most fierce. They took away High Priestess Arrabel and Master Balbadoris and . . . feirhart, ye should not be here!"

Sarmillion took hold of her scrawny shoulders. "Slow down," he said. "What do you mean, Brinnians? What Brinnians?"

"Soldiers. A group of 'em fought with Theophen and his men last night. They set fire to the barracks. Scores of Landguards are dead. And there was no burning."

"No burning? What are you on about, woman? You just said there was a fire."

"Goodness, feirhart, I meant the holy tree. It didn't burn. Where were ye all night?"

"I'd rather not talk about it." The girl was deranged. It wasn't possible that the tree hadn't burned. "Tell me, Trina," he spoke with deliberate calm, "where has Master Balbadoris gone?"

But she just kept shaking her head. "One of the keepers's been murdered. Mind how ye go, Sarmillion. Don't let 'em catch you."

Sarmillion grasped Trina's small cold hands. "Tell me, did this all happen before or after Balbadoris crossed the Bridge of No Return?" Sure, that was it. The old man had decided to spend the night in Omar with the keeper and some of the others, though Sarmillion could hardly imagine stuffy Balbadoris with his long white hair, tapping his yellow toenails to a raucous tavern song from the Rubber Band.

Trina pulled away from the undercat. "No, feirhart, I told ye, the tree didn't burn. There weren't no crossing of the bridge. Master Balbadoris weren't dressed up like the Beggar King. He was wearing his feast robes when they took him. Master Sarmillion, yer wasting precious time. Get yer belongings and go."

With that, Trina hurried off, her small quick footsteps fading down the hall as Sarmillion retreated into the study and shut the door.

"But what about the banquet?" He scratched at his furry head. "Who carved the mutton roast? Who got to stomp on the sherry glass this year?"

He stared at Balbadoris's desk and for the first time noticed that the scholar's long blue sasapher pipe was sitting there — and on the floor lay his walking stick. Balbadoris never went anywhere without either.

Clearly someone had been looking for something in here. But what? It would take too long to sort that out. Sarmillion picked up his canvas parchment bag and began gathering his work from the floor, and then stopped and sank into an armchair. This was his life. He couldn't just leave it behind. Where would he go? What would he do? He was a scribe, for crying out loud. He hadn't a single marketable skill besides the magic he made with ink and parchment.

Sarmillion knew he should get up, pack the parchments he cared most about, salvage Balbadoris's pipe — but instead he watched specks of dust drift in the sunlight that shone between the heavy velvet drapes.

"Which great scholar would use his walking stick as a perch for songbirds?" he remembered Balbadoris asking him. Sarmillion rarely knew the answers to these sorts of questions. They would come randomly, without any seeming purpose, though Sarmillion understood what the scholar was up to — he wanted to make sure the undercat was keeping up with his work, not hanging about in taverns or cavorting with women.

"Master Wickellhelm," Sarmillion murmured into the silent room. That was who would set his walking stick across the benches of the Common for the birds to sit upon. Sarmillion had done an illustration of the scene in a parchment for children.

There was a knock at the door. As if he'd been expecting it all along, Sarmillion answered it. Before him stood two tall men dressed entirely in black, with berets upon their heads and daggers at their belts.

"The emperor will see you now," one of them said, speaking Cirran with a heavy tongue.

"Who?" croaked the undercat, as the soldiers grabbed him by the arms and led him away.

Three

A MURDER OF CROWS

NEITHER JORDAN NOR HIS FATHER COULD eat breakfast. They sat together in the reading room, shutters closed to the light, staring at the cold grate in the fireplace. Both still wore the rumpled clothes of the night before.

Elliott stood. "I must do something. I'm going to the palace."

Jordan rose, too. "I'm coming with you."

"You'll stay right here. We have no idea what's happened. I won't put you in danger." He exchanged his feast robes for the dark brown robes of a carver and strapped on his tool belt.

"You plan on carving a serving bowl along the way?" asked Jordan.

"Don't be a fool," said his father and Jordan straightened in surprise. Elliott never spoke to him that way. "I'll send feirhaven Merralee to watch over you until I get back."

"I don't need a guardian," Jordan snapped, but Elliott had already walked out the door.

Jordan was left standing in the silent, darkened room alone. Was his father scared? His tools were the only things he owned that resembled weapons.

Jordan put on his sandals and went upstairs to the roof. There was no time to waste; the widow Merralee would be here any minute and she'd want to give Jordan at least three rambling accounts of the night's events. He took the neighbouring roof in one leap, and then scurried down a set of stairs that led into an alley. The cries of the previous night still rang in his head — Brinnians and barracks on fire, talk of Landguards in black. His mother might be in danger. It would be a cool day in Ut before he sat around and did nothing about it.

The main street was so clogged with travelers returning to their hometowns after the feast day that Jordan almost went back up to the roofs, but he wanted to hear what people in the streets were saying. Nervous chatter passed him like cold currents of air. Everything was wrong. The Beggar King had not been chased across the Bridge of No Return this year. The holy tree hadn't burned. No one had seen Commander Theophen anywhere.

Jordan tried not to think about his mother's round freckled face or her easy smile, or of how she couldn't scold him without laughing. The morning was already warm and sweat trickled down his neck. He was so lost in thought that he didn't notice the clop-clop of footsteps in unison until he was almost run down by a group of marching men. They were dressed in black uniforms, complete with tall black boots. In their belts they carried short sheathed daggers; in their hands, long black batons.

He pressed himself into a doorway until they had passed, and then stood staring after them.

"Landguards," said an older man who had appeared by his side.

"Those weren't Commander Theophen's guards," said Jordan.

"No, indeed," said the man. "Haven't you heard? Most of the palace guard was slain. The ones who survived were taken away. Arrabel, too." The man's eyes were wide and kept flitting up and down the road. "The streets are no place for a boy today." He lowered his voice. "Those guards are itchin' for trouble. You should get yourself home."

Jordan had no intention of going home but he didn't want to meet up with those black boots again. Arrabel and her people had been taken away? Where? By whom? Jordan couldn't imagine anyone forcing Theophen to act against his will. But maybe Theophen was dead. He looked around for a staircase, some way up onto the roofs.

It took over a dozen roofs and staircases (not to mention shimmying up two sturdy drainpipes) to reach the flattened palace roads at the top. He rested for a minute at one of the fountains, his breathing hard. Up here the air smelled even more strongly of ash and he could see in the distance where the ruins of the barracks were still smouldering. He made his way carefully towards the palace grounds. His sandals had scarcely moved from cobblestone to grass when he noticed something odd about the holy tree. It took his brain a second to catch up to his eyes, but when it did his mouth went dry.

The tree was still surrounded by flowers and coloured with ribbons, but now something else was there, too. A rope, tied to one of its majestic branches, with a lifeless body hanging from it.

A man's body.

He wore the robes of a mystery keeper, but Jordan couldn't stomach a closer examination to figure out who it was. A murder of crows was gathering on the branches where yesterday the three yellow finches had perched. It was only a matter of time before they would peck at the body.

"You! Boy!"

Jordan startled at the harsh tone. A man in black strode towards him. His black shield bore the Brinnian coat of arms: the hawk, its wings outstretched, carrying a red battle-axe in its beak.

"What are you doing here?" the guard bellowed in an unfamiliar drawl. "Go home."

"But . . . " Jordan stammered.

"Now!"

"My mother," he said, his voice trembling. "She works in the kitchen."

"Then she's gone," the man answered, and rapped his long stick on the mosaic stone path near the tree. "Leave now, or I'll have to arrest you."

Jordan ran towards one of the roads that led away from the palace, but as soon as the guard was out of sight he circled into an alley that he knew from experience would lead him back to the golden building. It was the way he took whenever he snuck into the kitchens to visit his mother and beg a snack from her.

The back routes to the palace were overgrown with mellowreed and sasapher. A few chickens pecked at the plants, and the tall sunflowers he passed hummed with bees. In fifteen minutes he was standing before the unshuttered windows of the enormous kitchen. No smells wafted through the air, no spoons clanged upon giant pots. Jordan climbed through and landed easily on the shining tile floor. It was a morning for surprises, for there, at the stove, stood Ophira in a white dress and embroidered slippers with a tall silver bottle in her hand. They stared at each other for a moment, and then they both smiled with relief.

"What are you doing here?" he asked her. "Where are your grandmothers?"

Ophira glanced at the bottle in her hand and seemed unable to make her mouth work. "They were here. When the tree didn't burn last night they were worried, and then Mama Appollonia had a terrible vision with her glass eye, so they all insisted on coming to the palace to find out what's going on."

On the counters were pots with meals half-cooked, vegetables still uncut, and a leg of mutton sitting bloody on a baking dish. Jordan spied a small plate with squares of sasapher cakes upon it, the edges crimped in the pattern his mother liked to use, and held onto the counter to steady himself.

"Jordan, these people are dangerous," said Ophira. "You should go home."

He blew out a lantern that must have been left burning all night. "People are saying it's the Brinnians."

"All I know is, there's trouble."

"Have you seen my mother, Phi?"

Ophira shook her head. "Anyone who was in the palace last night has been taken away, but we don't know exactly who was there, and we don't know where they're being kept."

Jordan's father had made the wooden tool his mother used for her cake edges. It was sitting on the counter. Jordan picked it up, laid it back down. "Why would they have been taken?"

"I don't know any more than that. That's why the grandmas came up here. You know how Mama Petsane gets."

Jordan nodded, remembering how she'd waved her stew spoon at him yesterday.

"The whole lot of them — except Grandma Willa, of course — shuffled up the road this morning and tried to force their way into the Meditary. They figured no decent man would harm a bunch of old ladies. But these aren't decent men. It's the first time I've ever seen the grandmas back down."

"So they made you sneak into the palace, instead."

"They're a little too old to climb through windows, Jordan."

He studied the silver bottle in her hand. "What do the grandmas expect you to do with that?" The words were scarcely out of his mouth when from outside they both heard the pronounced sound of boots upon stone.

"Now we're in for it," Ophira whispered. She grabbed Jordan's arm, led him out of the kitchen and down a long hallway of cupboards and storerooms. They climbed a short staircase and headed left along a hall lined with tapestries, then left again down another where the coat of arms of every land in Katir-Cir was displayed on the walls. The sounds of conversations drifted from open windows and beneath closed doors — strange inflections of speech, and foreign words.

"How do you know your way?" Jordan asked in amazement.

"I've been here before," she said.

Ophira didn't go to school like other children their age. She didn't do anything the way other people did, which was somewhat understandable, given her family circumstances. When you were raised by seven spinster sisters who liked to shine the edges of the future on their saffron robes, your life was bound to be different. Though they weren't seven anymore; a family feud had seen to that. Jordan glanced at the graceful curve of Ophira's neck, and quickly looked away.

As the halls grew quieter, they slowed their pace. Jordan knew Ophira was up to something — the grandmas wouldn't have sent her into such danger without good reason — but he also knew she wouldn't tell him what it was until she was ready.

"Have you ever heard of someone disappearing?" he asked.

"People slip away sometimes, Jordan. Usually there's something shady behind it, a secret lover or some bad business. But your mother hasn't disappeared. She's been taken away. There's a difference."

"I'm not talking about my mother, and I don't mean slipping away. I mean disappearing. You know — now you're here, now you're not."

She stopped walking. "Jordan," she said. "People don't disappear."

"I've heard they do." He thought of that sickly man and the feather he'd left behind. Jordan hadn't imagined it, he was sure he hadn't.

"Who told you that?" Ophira challenged.

"It's just what I heard." What would Ophira say if he told her the truth? She would laugh, that was what. She would think he was a fool. She began walking again and Jordan followed her down more twisting corridors until he was convinced they were walking in circles.

"Disappearing is not common magic," she said. "It's not magic at all."

"What do you mean? What is it, then? A gift?"

Now the halls were getting darker and colder. "Don't you know your old tales?" Ophira didn't wait for Jordan's hesitant *yeah*, because she knew he skipped more school than he attended. "It was only during the years of the undermagic that people used to disappear, but that would have just been the tip of an undermagician's skills. They did a lot of things they shouldn't have, before the undermagic was put to rest once and for all. No one has disappeared since then, Jordan, and no one ever will."

"Why? What's so bad about disappearing?" It didn't sound dangerous to Jordan in the least. In fact it seemed a rather convenient skill to possess.

"It puts you on the wrong side of the world. The dead side." She tilted her head and looked at him. "You're keeping a secret. What is it?"

"Oh, and you with your silver bottle," Jordan sputtered. "You're not keeping any?"

"There are things I can't tell you."

"Why not? I thought we were friends."

"We are. Best friends."

More than friends, he thought.

They walked until they reached a place where the hallway branched into several different directions, like an overgrown tree. Ophira hesitated, counting archways, when once again there came the hollow sound of boot steps. She pointed to the darkest of the halls and said, "That one leads out."

"Are you sure?" asked Jordan. He didn't relish the idea of getting lost down here.

"Yes. Only . . . " She shifted uneasily. "It's forbidden to go that way. You mustn't tell anyone I brought you here. High Priestess Arrabel would be furious. Walk until you find a wooden door with a stubby handle. It's the back door of the library archives. No one uses it. It shouldn't be locked . . . I don't think."

Great.

"Once you're inside, go through to the very end. You'll find a narrow window that leads onto an out-of-the-way courtyard."

"Wait, can't you come with me?"

She gazed down the hallway in the direction they'd come. "I . . . have to go. Don't come back to the palace," she said as she backed away from him. "Promise me."

"But my mother . . . "

"I'll see what I can find out. Go, now, before the Brinnians find you."

Before Jordan could ask any more questions Ophira had skittered out of sight, and he was alone. The sound of boots was coming closer. He took a breath and stepped into the dark, empty hall that Ophira had indicated.

There were few torches and no signs of life. Jordan half-wondered if this was the way to the burial chambers. A wooden door with a stubby handle — that was what he had to find. But he saw now that every door he passed was wooden and stubby-handled. There must have been fifty of them down this long hallway. Ophira hadn't said how far he should walk. He would have to try all of the doors. He began checking the handles, only to discover that every single door was locked.

The hallway ended at a piece of brass set into the stone wall. This, at least, could not be a door, for it came only to his waist and had no handle. He considered his surroundings. He couldn't imagine why it was forbidden to come this way; he did, however, understand why a person might not want to come here. The floor and walls were covered in a thin sheen of frost, and it was unnaturally quiet, as if everything nearby had died.

He pressed his hands against the brass plate to see if it might give way. With a start he realized it was warm. He could feel engravings beneath his fingertips, and knelt to study them. They were unfamiliar shapes. He thought of his father, who had a fondness for ancient script — he might be able to read the runes upon this door, but Jordan couldn't. Elliott . . . he would be home by now. The widow Merralee would have told him she hadn't seen Jordan. He would be worried. Blast it anyway, he should never have come up here.

Jordan traced the script with his fingertips, as if somehow these shapes might have an answer to his predicament. Slowly, slowly, his eyes closed and his breathing calmed. From somewhere came a shadow, perhaps of a man, though he couldn't be sure. The shadow was calling to him in a strange language, an old language. Jordan seemed to know the words to respond and as they came out of his mouth, something opened.

He could not have explained what it was — not a door or even a window. More like a passageway, or a possibility.

When he opened his eyes, the brass plate was ajar, as if indeed it were a door. He stared at it, dumbfounded. Perhaps this was a way out. He had to remain on his knees in order to see inside. But there was no inside to speak of. It didn't lead out, but it wasn't a room either.

He leaned forward. There was something unusual and electric in the air, the way it felt outside when a storm approached. There was power, and all Jordan could think of was *glorious darkness*, and it was dizzying and he wanted it, he wanted to hold it in his hands. Something sounded around his head, like the flapping of a thousand wings.

And then he came back to himself in a jolt and backed away, slamming the brass plate shut. He ran to the first wooden door he could find, wrenched on its handle with all of his strength until the door came open with a lurch that threw him to the floor. Picking himself up quickly, he sprang forward and shut the door behind him. He leaned against it, breathing hard. His hands were shaking.

The room in which he stood was stacked from floor to ceiling with scrolls. He'd found the library archives. Into one wall was cut a small door that must have led to the larger part of the library, but Jordan moved instead to the back of the long room until he spied the opening that Ophira had generously called a window. It was so narrow that he had to press his head to one side in order to squeeze through, and his ears scraped against the stone sill.

Once outside, it took Jordan a minute to get his bearings. He had landed in a small weedy courtyard surrounded by a low stone wall, over which he scrambled into yet another larger enclosure. He crossed it at a clipped walk, letting himself out through a metal grated gate, and then took the rest of the route home at a run.

When he burst through the front door, his father was sitting in an armchair resting his head in his hands, the reading room darkened.

Elliott looked up with a frown. "Where have you been? Feirhaven Merralee said . . . "

"They've been taken somewhere," Jordan interrupted, hurling himself into the chair next to his father. "High Priestess Arrabel, Mom, I don't even know who else. There are Landguards with daggers and sticks and tall black boots. One of Arrabel's mystery keepers. . . . " He couldn't continue. The thought of the hanging man and the hungry crows above him filled Jordan with dread. He bowed his head and closed his eyes.

Elliott's large rough hand was on Jordan's back and he leaned against it, exhausted. When at last he straightened, his father was watching him.

"There's going to be a ceremony in the Meditary tonight."

Jordan's forehead wrinkled. "What kind of ceremony?"

"I don't know . . . "

"But where have they taken Mom and the others? When will they come back?"

"We'll go to the Meditary tonight. We'll find out what's happened. Surely," Elliott said. And then softly, again, as if to convince himself, "Surely someone will know."

Four

SMOKE AND CEREMONY

THAT EVENING THEY JOINED A THRONG of Cirrans making the long climb up the uneven stone road to the plateau at the top of the mountain. No one regarded the holy tree, even though the feast day was over. People kept their eyes down. There was no music, no conversation, no ribbons or fancy dress. Jordan wore his short pants and Elliott his brown carver's robes. Those whose sons or daughters had been members of Theophen's guard were dressed in plain grey mourning garb.

Jordan and his father followed the solemn crowd and crossed the courtyard gardens to the eastern archway that marked the entrance to the large domed temple known as the Meditary. Two guards were positioned there. The customary bowl of cleansing water, into which everyone dipped their fingers before entering, was gone. Elliott began slipping off his sandals but one of the guards tapped the ground with the end of his stick and barked, "Shoes on."

Jordan was bending to unfasten one of his sandals but his father held him back. "Do as he says."

Jordan peered through the archway. Inside, Landguards were clomping around on the marble floors in their boots. Elliott nudged him into the large round room.

Gone were the small colourful kneeling carpets. The central font, which had always glowed with the orange of a firestone, was covered by pieces of wood. Burning torches lit the temple with unnatural brightness. Elliott's lips were pressed into a thin stern line. Around them people spoke in hushed tones, their faces pale and eyes widened.

Ophira stood with three of the seers, all three older women wearing their veils and saffron robes. Jordan knew them by their shapes. The shrunken Mama Manjuza leaned upon the tall girl's arm for support. Behind the veil were wise eyes and an old-apple face, as well as long hairs upon her chin. To the average person, Manjuza seemed harmless. But anyone who knew her wouldn't be fooled by her frail-old-lady act. Once she'd hexed a merchant for selling wormy tomatoes, and it had taken five years before he'd produced a good crop.

Next to her stood the sturdy Mama Petsane, arms crossed and legs askance as if steadying herself for a fight. She hadn't brought her stew spoon, but she still looked as if she were just waiting for someone to say the wrong thing so she could thump them with it. The third could only be Mama Bintou, for she was holding her knitting.

When Ophira saw Jordan, she motioned for him and Elliott to come over. As they approached the women, Jordan and Elliott bowed, pressing three fingers to their forehead. "May the Great Light shine upon you," they said.

"And upon your family," replied Ophira and the grandmas.

"Shame on you, Jordan," growled Mama Manjuza.

"Take off your sandals!" said Mama Bintou.

"Show some respect," added Mama Petsane.

Each of the old women was barefoot, their sandals beside them on the floor. Jordan glanced at his father who was already surreptitiously removing his, then at Ophira whose eyes were fixed upon the Brinnian Landguards that stood stiffly against the walls, watching the gathering crowd.

"You don't be listening to them black-booted boobies," Petsane said. "They think they know what's right for Cirrans. Bunch of clod-hopping donkeys, and in our Holy City."

"I knew it all along," said Manjuza. "I knew it would happen."

"Ach, you don't know nothing," muttered Petsane.

"Two years ago I warned our high priestess," said Manjuza. "I say to her, that mountain range ain't gonna keep the peace between Cirrans and Brinnians forever."

"Yeah, yeah, you be right, as usual," said Petsane with a loud sniff.

"I hear they paid a sorcerer to make their path," Mama Bintou said, her eyes roaming the room. She clutched her wool and needles in one hand but it was only for show. She was searching for a mind to read.

"That couldn't be, Mama," said Elliott. "Brinnians don't believe in sorcery."

"Brinnians believe in whatever gets the job done, and don't you think otherwise," snapped Mama Petsane. "They're gonna stomp on our Cirran ways because they can."

"They got the bigger boots, eh?" said Manjuza. She laughed and then began coughing.

"You should quit smoking that sasapher, Mama," said Ophira.

Jordan edged closer to her. "Did you hear anything about my mother?"

"All the grandmas say she's with Arrabel," Ophira replied.

"Where have the Brinnians taken them?"

Ophira busied herself with a fraying pocket. "We don't know."

"Aye, what's she doing here?" grumbled Bintou, pointing with her needles to a small older woman who stood across the room alone. Her grey hair was in a tumble and she wore a long stained coat and rubber boots.

"Sweet sasapher," Ophira said to Jordan. "It's Grandma Willa."

Willa had parted ways with her seer sisters many years ago, having given up prophecy for the utterly non-magical pursuit of door-making. Most of the sisters thought her mad and wanted nothing to do with her.

"Look how she march around this place like an Uttic fishwife," said Petsane. "Boots! In the Meditary. Just imagine!"

"Where's her robes?" said Manjuza. "And how come she goes out without her veil?"

"Fancies herself a real door-maker now, I reckon," said Bintou.

"Ach, she can make all the doors she wants," said Petsane. "Once a prophet, always a prophet. Don't matter how fast she runs from it, it's gonna catch her sooner or later."

Ophira shushed them and pointed to the northern archway. The chatter in the temple gradually stilled as a tall man strode in and stood before the central font. He had long black hair, a beard that ended in a point midway down his chest, a long nose and dark hooded eyes. He seemed to be smirking. Jordan grabbed Ophira's arm.

"I've seen him before."

"That's not possible," said Ophira. "No Brinnian has ever crossed those mountains. We wouldn't even know what one looked like."

"No, Phi, that man was at the archery contests. He stood beside me." Great Light! The coup had been taking place right before Cirran eyes and no one had realized it. Had Jordan unwittingly made things worse by answering the man's questions? Tonight he was wearing black robes — normally the robes of a sorcerer — that fell open to reveal a jewelled breastplate. In one hand he gripped a golden staff. Yesterday he'd seemed like any other pilgrim.

When he snapped his fingers, Landguards surrounded the font. Jordan couldn't see what they were doing but then Ophira gasped, "That's cedar wood! He's setting fire to it."

"That couldn't be," said Jordan, but when he strained to see, there were flames and smoke and the smell of burning. The tall cedars of Somberholt Forest were filled with the Great Light's healing magic. Those trees were never felled. Jordan often stole away into the forest and lay at the soft mossy base of the great cedars, staring up at their invisible crowns. Invariably he would fall asleep, and dream about the birds pulling clouds across the sky.

"Good evening." The man spoke in a rich, deep voice. Everyone was listening. "My name, in case you haven't heard, is Rabellus, King of the Brinnian Provinces. And as of last night, ruler of the Brinnian Empire." He paused. The only sound in the room was the crackle of the fire.

"Too long have Brinnians lived surrounded by the forbidden riches of Cir and her provinces," declared Rabellus. "We have offered trade and fair exchange, and your high priestess has spurned us. Why? To protect you? No, friends. To blind you to the reality of progress. But I come here to bring you good news. The tyranny of the Cirran priesthood has ended. Arrabel's Landguards were not as mighty as she thought. Those who did not perish in battle waved the white flag of surrender."

Surrender?

"They've been imprisoned far away from here," Rabellus continued. "It seems they did not want to serve the new Brinnian Empire."

"Long live the empire!" shouted the guards.

The Cirrans shifted restlessly, and here and there a muffled protest could be heard. "Empire!" one fellow scoffed.

"Let us begin your Brinnian education," said Rabellus. "You people have been fed lies about the workings of this world for too long." He waved his staff in the air. "But I come here to tell you the truth. The Great Light is a myth. And last night, finally, it was proven. There were no flames upon your so-called holy tree. All along it was the high priestess's charade, a display of smoke and ceremony to keep the Cirrans in their place. It was the priesthood who blocked passage into Brin. You've been prisoners in your own land. You have lived as blind folk, but we Brinnians have come to give you back your sight."

The protests grew louder, though they were quietened in an instant by the guards rapping their long sticks upon the marble floor.

"We welcome Cir and her provinces into the Brinnian Empire. We welcome you Cirrans as our own." Rabellus threw his arms wide. "Behold, your emperor!"

"Long live Rabellus," cried the guards. Everyone was stunned into silence.

And then a tall man stood and cleared his throat. The Cirrans knew him from his blue beaded robes as the chief healer, Malthazar. Elliott laid a hand upon Jordan's shoulder as if to support himself.

"Cir and her provinces have always been independent and free," Malthazar said in a warm tone that had comforted families for years. "We are guided by a priest or priestess, one of our own, chosen by the power you claim does not exist. Many of us live by the mysteries you deem a charade. You cannot impose Brinnian rule upon us. You do not honour our traditions. You do not understand the Cirran ways."

"Bravo, Malthazar," Mama Bintou said quietly, as three guards moved in on the healer.

Rabellus raised one hand. "Leave him." He turned his attention back to the assembly. "Cirrans, tell me, have you seen this Great Light? And pray, what has become of your burning tree? It seems to have stopped working." He let out a snort. "Any circus fire breather could do as much."

The entire room seemed to hold its breath.

"Your holy tree has been visited by crows, the birds that feast on death. And I understand Cir is a land that loves its birds." Rabellus waved over one of the guards who carried a large book. "Behold," taunted Rabellus, "one of your so-called mysteries." He took the book and flipped roughly through its fragile yellowed pages until he came to the one he was after. No sparks of light issued from the parchment in his hands.

"Prayer for the Feast of the Great Light," he read as if he were bored. "Blessed is the Great Light, light of all lands of Katir-Cir, light of our path. We pay homage to the holy tree, light of our darkness, lamp to the world."

"The Book of What Is" was the phrase that raced around the room as everyone recognized the holy words. The Cirrans were spellbound. Every land in Katir-Cir possessed such a book, though its content and usage varied from one place to another. But there was one thing common to them all: they were each symbolic of their land's very identity.

Elliott whispered, "How could he have gotten his hands on that?"

Rabellus had stopped reading. "There are no mysteries. As of this moment, you are Brinnians." Without warning, he threw the book into the fire.

"No!" yelled several people at once. Malthazar bounded towards the central font, but this time Rabellus did not call off the Landguards.

"Put him in prison," he commanded. They seized the healer and dragged him, shouting and struggling, out of the Meditary.

For the first time Jordan noticed just how many guards there were in the room. More must have arrived while Rabellus had been speaking. The Cirrans were sorely outnumbered.

"You see that?" shouted Mama Manjuza. "Ye don't need magic or skill to destroy mystery. Ye just need muscle."

"Bravo, Mr. Mucky-Muck," called Petsane. "You and your black-booted boobies are doin' a fine job."

"Who said that?" Rabellus bellowed. But no one would ever have suspected shrunken Manjuza and fat Petsane. The guards strode right past the veiled women, unable to find the culprits.

Elliott's face was drawn, his jaw clenched.

"It couldn't have been the real book," Jordan said. He touched his father's arm and found that Elliott was trembling.

"Oh yes, it was," said Mama Manjuza. "I saw the wax seal on the cover."

Rabellus's arms were raised, golden staff in one hand. "Let there be fire!" he proclaimed, and the guards cheered. "Let there be feasting!"

Two Landguards appeared with long skewers of some kind of meat. Then more guards carried in a small deer trussed to a stick. When they placed the sacred animal onto the font flame, Jordan gasped, and a woman nearby fainted. The Meditary filled with the acrid smell of its burning flesh. People pushed towards the eastern archway, covering their mouths and nostrils with their hands. Jordan was about to follow when his father stopped him.

"We must try to understand," Elliott said. "It may be our only way to find Tanny."

A few Cirrans took pieces of skewered deer flesh and placed them into their mouths, chewing hesitantly at first and then with greater relish.

"How could they?" Jordan asked.

"It only takes a single act to make the unthinkable possible," replied his father.

"'Tis the work of the Beggar King," said an older man nearby. "Didn't cross the bridge on Great Light's Feast, now, did he? The evil wasn't chased away. And what've we got ourselves now?"

Mama Manjuza wheeled around to grip his wrist with her strong age-spotted hand. "Foolishness!" she spat. "You make evil into a man and ignore the truth. Every one of us got the darkness in us sure as we got the light."

"Not just the Brinnians be killers," added Mama Petsane. "Not just the Cirrans be good." She moved towards the archway and Manjuza followed, steering Ophira away.

Jordan's breath had quickened and he almost gagged at the smell of roasting deer flesh. He eyed the exit, but his father had now stopped to speak to an undercat who wore the emerald and black zigzag robes of a scribe. Jordan recognized the grey of his furry face, the sly golden eyes, and the way he spoke with his hands fluttering about. It was Sarmillion, scribe to the great scholar Balbadoris.

Sarmillion was the reason why Elliott T. Elliott possessed so many beautiful volumes of the old tales, for the undercat often made copies for Jordan's father. They would sit together in Elliott's reading room, talking late into the night over tall glasses of billy beer, their faces aglow with candlelight. Jordan had overheard them, sometimes discussing their work, sometimes arguing over ancient runes.

"I don't know what's become of your wife," the undercat was saying into Elliott's ear. He was taller than Jordan but not as tall as Elliott, and so had to strain on his toes in order for the larger man to hear him. "I wasn't here last night," he continued. "I was out — with a friend." His shoulders sagged as if he was embarrassed and Jordan noticed he, too, had taken off his golden slippers despite the guards' command to leave them on. "Few of Arrabel's people remain. That scoundrel Rabellus wants me to stay on as his scribe but I can't bear it. I'll be gone before morning."

"Rabellus said Theophen and his guards surrendered," said Elliott.

"Ha!" cried Sarmillion. "That's one way of putting it. Another way is to say that the Brinnians offered Theophen a deal."

"Theophen would have given his life to protect this city," said Jordan. "What kind of deal would he have accepted?"

"One like this," said Sarmillion. "Give up, or we'll kill everyone who's hiding in the palace. Including the high priestess."

Including my mother, thought Jordan.

"Thank goodness Theophen wasn't too proud," said Elliott. "It must have been hard for him to back down."

"Indeed," said Sarmillion. "And now they've been taken away, and no one knows where. It is wickedness; it's an outrage. He chose our feast day for his coup."

"The one time when no one would be on their guard," said Elliott. He looked up at one of the rounded windows. "Where will you go?"

The undercat sighed. "Omar, perhaps. Some folk are headed north to Circassic but that's too far for my tastes. I intend to fight back." He pressed a pointed tooth against his bottom lip. "I fear the worst for our old tales," he said, his voice cracking. "I shall smuggle as many as I can out of the palace library."

The library. Jordan's thoughts turned to that strange brass door he'd found near the library archives. He scanned the Meditary for the wild-haired grandma who was now a door-maker but she must have left. Maybe Sarmillion would know more about that door.

"Can I bring the parchments to you?" the undercat was saying to Jordan's father.

"Of course. It would be my pleasure to protect them." Elliott hunched towards him. "I can't help but wonder how that Rabellus character ever got hold of our Book of What Is. You told me the high priestess keeps it under lock and key."

Sarmillion coughed so hard he was nearly choking. It took him a minute to compose himself. "Brinnians," he hissed. "Long have they wanted to control Cir. I can't fathom how they managed to cross the mountains."

Elliott shook his head. "Not everyone will want to chase them away, you know. Some are ready to abandon the traditions. The Brinnian ways will appeal to them."

"Well! Do you know what the Brinnian word for 'foreigner' translates to in the Cirran tongue? Underling. Cirrans aren't fools. Even the ones with a modern bent will sense their loss before long. And no one will put up with such brutality." Sarmillion's whiskers curled into a frown. "I shall keep my ears open for any news."

They took leave of each other in the traditional way, and then Sarmillion touched Jordan lightly upon the cheek. Jordan was surprised. The undercat had always been friendly but never affectionate.

Jordan attached his sandals and followed his father out of the Meditary and across the palace courtyard. Neither of them dared to speak until they were on the cobblestone road leading down the mountain.

Finally Jordan tried to say what was on his mind. "Do you think, I mean, is it even possible that they're — ?"

"We have to believe they're all right, Son," Elliott said. "They're all right, and they'll come home."

Jordan's mother had often said that while it was Elliott's sharp tools that cut wood, it was his voice that smoothed them into works of art. Jordan took comfort in that gentle tone now.

"What will happen to Malthazar?" he asked.

"I don't know. But the high priestess named the year well. Year of the magpie."

The twin moons were still full — though not true-full anymore. They looked like two round eyes, watching Jordan. And then something struck him. "Has Maelstrom's moon gotten darker?"

Elliott squinted up at the sky. "Maybe it has."

"Do you think it means something?"

"Who can say?" said his father. "These are dark times."

"You told me people call it the undermagic moon," said Jordan. "But the undermagic could never come back to Katir-Cir, could it?"

"Anything can happen if we allow it."

Jordan glanced back at the holy tree that hadn't burned on the Feast of the Great Light. Its branches were black against the dusky sky — its branches, and the dark outline of a hanging body, had transformed the mystery of this beautiful tree into menace.

Five

LADY DESTINY

SARMILLION HAD ALWAYS FIGURED HE COULD tiptoe through life without ever waking Lady Destiny, but she must have heard about the raucous nights of mug-wine parties and decided it was time for some payback. Or maybe she just wanted to test his mettle. Mettle, sure. Rabellus and his men had scarcely mentioned hanging before Sarmillion was pulling out the key kept in a hidden compartment in Balbadoris's study and leading them to Arrabel's onyx chest, which he'd unlocked with trembling hands. An important detail, that: his hands did tremble when he gave up the precious Book of What Is. He'd been aware of the enormity of his treason even as he was committing it.

And then last night there was Mars, one of his closest friends, telling him, "Ye should stay in Cir, underkitty. It'll be the best means of defeating the Brinnians. Only way inside the palace now will be to work there and we're gonna need all the information we can get."

Mars was staying on as palace gardener. He had nothing to feel guilty about. The hunchback would never have given up the priceless book, not even if they'd tortured him.

53

"No, can't stay, can't stomach this regime, got to get out," Sarmillion had said to Mars. He intended to get as far away from this life of parchment and ink as he could. It would be the only way for him to sleep at night.

"Tragic, his burning the Book of What Is," Mars had said, and Sarmillion had replied, "Oh yes, tragic. Don't know how it could have happened." It had taken every bit of Sarmillion's willpower not to howl with anguish. There was no telling how great a loss this might be. Some of the prayers and spells were known to Arrabel alone, and she might be dead. Would the magical incantations even work now that the book was destroyed?

At first light Sarmillion packed his belongings into a canvas bag, including Balbadoris's sasapher pipe. He took up the scholar's walking stick, and then turned his long brass key in the door to his apartment one last time. He crossed the tatty rug in Master Mimosa's apartment, went through his private weedy courtyard and out the rusted metal gate, pulling it shut with a gentle squeak. That was the sound of the past, ending. And even though it seemed as if he was pulling a long sack of years behind him as he tramped down the steep Cirran streets, he felt an end as surely as if he'd written it himself after the hard work of a manuscript was done. *The end.*

When he arrived on the open-air cobblestone Common, a knot of enthusiastic Cirrans was talking to Mars who was already dressed in his gardening overalls and carried a long pitchfork.

"We'll form the resistance!" cried one.

"We'll thwart every slagging project Rabellus starts," said another.

"We won't let him get away with nothing!" hollered a third.

Sarmillion's whiskers twitched. He sensed action, heroism, fame and fortune. "I'll join you," he said. "What can I do?"

Mars eyed him up and down and fingered his canvas bag. "So ye've decided not to stay," he said, with a short nod of his bald head, and Sarmillion prepared himself for an outburst of scorn. Instead the gardener addressed the others. "This underkitty's got a way in or out of just about anything. Our group of Loyalists has got itself a burglar and a spy."

Sarmillion clapped his hands. "From scribe to burglar in one morning. Who would have guessed?" and they all laughed.

"Burn your robes!" one of the men shouted, and it occurred to Sarmillion that if he was no longer a Cirran scribe, he might wear real clothes. Imagine, a silk smoking jacket. Mauve. Sarmillion had always fancied a smoking jacket: cocktail hour, candlelight, and a good long pipe of sasapher. The colour would set off his grey fur beautifully.

"Embers and ashes," he said, pulling the robes up and over his head. "Let the rebellion begin!" He threw them to the ground in a heap and someone lit a piece of parchment and tossed it onto the fabric and there was a poof and the zigzag robes went up in flames.

"I will not be a scribe for the Brinnian Empire," he roared, one furry hand punching the air. "I remain loyal to High Priestess Arrabel and the Cirran mysteries." *Liar*, hissed the voice in his head, but Sarmillion ignored it. "Long live the priesthood. May the Great Light shine upon you all," and the crowd that had surrounded the undercat and his little bonfire cheered. Sarmillion noticed the tanned skin and dark curly hair of the Elliott boy among them.

Suddenly there was a whistle and the call of "Landguards" from someone who'd been watching. An older man in work boots hurried to stamp out the fire and Sarmillion eased himself into a group of Cirrans and made his way off the Common wearing only a pair of silk pants and sandals.

Mars grabbed him by one arm and fixed him with those eyes that shone such a bright blue in his weathered face. "Are ye going to Omar, then?"

Sarmillion nodded.

"Listen well," he said quietly. "We'll need to find out where they're keeping Arrabel and the others. Keep yer eyes and ears open, underkitty. Omarrians talk, specially in their taverns. And I expect them black boots will be about, as well. Stay out of trouble, now."

"You know me," said Sarmillion.

"'Tis exactly what worries me," said Mars, but the way his bushy eyebrows rose and fell, Sarmillion couldn't help but smile.

As the undercat set off on the road to Omar, Jordan caught up with him.

"You'll get yourself arrested acting like that," he said, though Sarmillion noted with pleasure that the boy's green eyes were warm with admiration.

Sarmillion puffed out his furry chest. He could become the self-appointed saviour of precious Cirran parchments before Rabellus destroyed them. He could steal them. Burglary could be his redemption.

"My boy," Sarmillion intoned, "We're going to fight this Brinnian rogue. We're calling ourselves Loyalists. We will — " he stopped. "Why aren't you in school?"

"No time for school." Jordan had that same gleam in his eyes. "I'm going to be a Loyalist, too."

Sarmillion swatted the air. "Oh, absurdity. Oh, recklessness. You shall do no such thing. Your father would never forgive me. Besides, you need an education."

"I'm getting one," said Jordan.

The road sloped downwards and they followed it for several minutes without speaking.

"Do you know anything about a brass door near the library archives?" Jordan asked.

Sarmillion's whiskers drooped into a scowl. "That door is forbidden. It's no place for a child. And how ever did you hear of such a thing?"

Jordan coughed. "A scullery maid showed it to me."

Sarmillion studied the boy, who immediately focused upon a hideous display of porcelain rooftop ornaments, and then the undercat understood. He could sniff out a lie as easily as a piece of fried trout. "What sort of mischief have you been dirtying your fingers with?"

"Nothing. I told you." But Jordan still refused to look at him.

Sarmillion put an arm around his shoulder. He admired anyone who had the courage to follow the dark and twisting labyrinth that led to that door. A person could get lost. And there were spiders.

"You didn't touch it, did you?" he asked. "It's enchanted, you know."

"Enchanted?" Jordan said and pulled away.

"Your maid forgot to mention that, I suppose," said Sarmillion. "Scullery maids know their nutty-buns, may the Great Light shine upon 'em, but when it comes to enchantments their only education is whatever they learned on their grannies' laps. Once long ago Master Mimosa touched that door, I'll have you know, and two weeks later his great uncle dropped dead of a heart attack. I'm telling you, it's a hazard. It should never have been put there, but there's not a thing anyone can do about it now." He grunted. "Next you'll be telling me you opened the blasted thing."

They walked in strained silence for another minute and then the boy asked, "Does anyone know what those runes say on the outside of the door?"

"Indeed," said Sarmillion. "They say, 'This door does not open for fools, rascals or teenaged boys. Period. All fools, rascals and teenaged boys who find themselves in front of this door should take themselves home immediately and douse themselves in cold water and then perform ten years of penance for their stupidity.'"

"It doesn't really say that," said Jordan.

"I forgot, you're wise beyond your years," said Sarmillion with a good-natured chuckle. "No, it doesn't say that. But I'm under palace oath to keep certain secrets." *Like the secret of the Book of What Is, for example.* The thought came unbidden, and he was quick to stuff it back down where it would keep quiet. "In Arrabel's time there was always a Landguard posted at the entrance to that hallway. You wouldn't have gotten within a hundred feet of that door."

"Why? What's behind it that's so dangerous?"

Sarmillion wagged a finger at him. "I told you, I'm sworn to secrecy, loyal to Arrabel and all that." He cringed inwardly, for a memory had come to him all at once, the way bad ones always do, as if they've been called by one of those high-pitched whistles only dogs can hear. It had all been foretold, his treason, long ago and when it had had little meaning, by Willa — in the days when she'd still been a seer.

He'd been fifteen, Jordan's age now, and his father had taken him to her to determine if he might truly have the writer's gift of tale-spinning. Willa had taken one look at him, just one, and declared, "Liar! Traitor!" which had scared the fur off Sarmillion's teenaged self. But his father had been elated.

"We have a writer in the family," he told all the neighbours.

Sarmillion had all but forgotten the incident. But now, as he fled the scene of his own traitorous crime, he realized he had fulfilled Willa's prophecy.

Besides, hadn't he snuck down that very hallway once in his life when the fellow guarding it had slipped away for his nightly nip of mug-wine? The truth was, Sarmillion had gone to seek out that door specifically to read the ancient runes he'd heard had been set into them. He'd never forgotten them; blast it anyway, he'd absorbed the words through his fingertips until they'd sunk into his blood, and wasn't that why the door-maker had done it? Of course it was.

Beware this door, beware your soul! May this door never be opened, or the beggar shall be king. Think twice and thrice, for if it be opened, this door can never again be shut.

Now he remembered another one of Balbadoris's questions. "How would one rid the world of the Beggar King if ever the circumstances arose?" the old scholar had asked him.

"If the circumstances arose?" Sarmillion had scoffed. "But they never would. How can you rid the world of an idea?"

"By drowning it in the River of the Dead," he'd hollered. Oh, Balbadoris's ire had been great that day. He did not share Sarmillion's view that the Beggar King was merely a metaphor. But there it was. Sarmillion had considered it silliness then, and he thought it so now. Even if there was such thing as the Beggar King, a person would have to be dead before arriving at the River of the Dead (hence, the name) and so would not be much use as far as drowning was concerned.

The sound of the river brought Sarmillion back to himself. The Balakan River ran grand, clear and wide, spanned by the twelve bridges which connected the mountain-island city with the rest of Katir-Cir.

"Can I come to Omar with you?" Jordan asked.

"You most certainly cannot. And if the Great Light knows what's what, there won't be a single bridge in Cir that will grant you passage. Now, go back up that road and get to school. Learn something that will make your father proud."

He leaned towards the boy and confided, "A Loyalist needs to know his history if he wants to fight with the sharpest weapons." Then Sarmillion gave a gallant bow. "May the Great Light shine upon you."

But something must have occurred to Jordan, for his forehead wrinkled and he asked, "What robes will you wear? What will you do?"

The undercat shrugged. "I won't take robes under Brinnian rule. I shall live by my wits, boy, and stout glasses of mug-wine." It sounded impressive, but in reality Sarmillion didn't have a single idea what he would do now, and he wasn't convinced his wits were sharp enough to earn him even a place to sleep.

He gripped Balbadoris's varnished oak walking stick and set his foot upon the stone Bridge of Resolve, which admitted him immediately.

Six

SPELLS FOR BOYS

JORDAN GAVE SARMILLION A SAD WAVE as the undercat embarked upon the stone bridge. But as soon as he was out of sight, Jordan moved towards the same bridge. He was going to Omar to find a door-maker named Willa and ask her about a brass door that should have been guarded, but wasn't. Jordan grimaced. He hadn't just touched it, he'd opened it — and hadn't Sarmillion told him about Master Mimosa's great uncle who had died just because the scholar had touched the door? What if Jordan had doomed his mother? Great Light, what had he done?

He approached the Bridge of Resolve with a determined stride. But as soon as he tried to put his foot down on the stones, he felt a force like a giant hand push it back and knock him to the ground.

"Slag," he said as he got up, rubbing his backside.

Each of the twelve bridges connecting Cir to the mainland possessed a particular wisdom which people had no choice but to respect. You were granted passage upon the bridge that best reflected your state of mind. It forced you to think every time about why you were entering or leaving the Holy City. Practically speaking, it sometimes meant you had to walk for miles before you found a bridge that admitted you. Sometimes it meant not crossing at all.

Jordan moved on towards the bridge he used most often when skipping school to spend the afternoon in Somberholt Forest — Ne'er Do Well — but to no avail. He sped right past Amethyst, which required complete tranquility to cross, and past the Bridge of No Return, which no one ever used. Finally he reached the Undetermined Walkway, but it was hopeless. He was stopped in his tracks by an invisible force so strong he felt as if he'd smacked right into a wall. The distant shimmer of the Bridge of Many Happy Returns was so out of synch with his mood he didn't bother checking it. Now what?

There was nothing for it but to go all the way back and try Peril. As he made his way once again past the tar-black Bridge of No Return, something made him stop. But no, surely it would be futile to try this bridge. And yet, if he didn't, he would spend the rest of the afternoon trekking from one bridge to the next, and then it would be time to go home.

Jordan knew only one thing about this bridge: no one ever used it except Balbadoris, once a year on the Feast of the Great Light, when he dressed up as the Beggar King and had scores of children chasing him towards it. But he'd always come back, so the name couldn't mean what it suggested. *It won't admit me.* Still he hurried towards it, as if his feet knew something he didn't.

Not a soul was about this morning. Most people were probably still stunned by Emperor Rabellus's performance in the Meditary the night before. So no one gasped as Jordan took hold of the black wooden handrails of the Bridge of No Return and hoisted himself up onto its slanted entryway. No one cried out in shock as he took one step forward, and then another. He walked as if in a trance.

Halfway across, Jordan realized where he was. He realized with this horribly sensible adult reason that had begun forming inside him, which told him if he made it to the end of the bridge he might be doing something irreversible, something he would regret forever.

He spun around and ran back the way he'd come. This time he knew the Undetermined Walkway would grant him access, and it did. As he crossed, he glanced over at the black bridge and while the sensible adult told him he'd made the right decision, the teenager in him couldn't help but tingle at what might have happened if he'd stayed on it.

Once across the bridge, he found himself on a path with three choices. Before him was the entrance to Somberholt Forest, a place he knew well. To one side was a path that led to the bridges on the Omarrian side. And to the other was the footpath that led into Omar and, of course, to the bazaar.

This was not the first time he'd crossed to the Omarrian mainland, but on every other occasion he'd lacked the courage to veer towards the bazaar. His father's warnings of drunken underrats and dirty-dealing merchants had scared him enough to limit his truancy to Somberholt's cedar grove. But today he did not head into the trees. Today he set his feet towards Omar and, with his eyes averted from the adults who might ask why he wasn't in school, he walked.

While the Holy City's buildings were made uniformly of whitewashed stone, Omarrians painted their homes and shops in brilliant reds, blues and yellows. Crossing the Balakan River felt like entering a different country.

The bazaar was Omar's most infamous attraction, stretching like a maze from one end of the city to the other. As Jordan wandered in, he overheard two men arguing over the price of a goat. Nearby, some kind of meat sizzled in a sauce that smelled of pepper, and several women were shrieking about a snake that had fallen out of somebody's basket. A flash of yellow slithered past Jordan's feet, making him jump back. Chickens and goats sauntered by the canvas-partitioned stalls as if they, too, were browsing the merchandise. Merchants called to customers about the best prices for porcelain figurines or sasapher pipes, while in the background there was the erratic hammering of tradesmen. He closed his eyes and breathed it all in.

"Trinkets," called a man in a striped suit. "Almost free." Nearby came the jittery music of several twangers accompanied by a single flute. Jordan had heard about the wild women belt-dancers who moved with the travelling musicians, selling woven belts scented with cinnamon. He'd heard that sometimes the dancers took strangers with them for the night and that when you came home you couldn't speak for a whole week.

Jordan concentrated upon the distant sound of hammers, following their irregular clanging until he arrived at a great rusted metal archway announcing Trades Alleyway. Open sheds and doorways lined the long winding road. Dust hung in the air, and the noise, the banging and pounding, was deafening. There were blacksmiths and cabinet makers and a man who made chairs, stacked one upon the other on a perilous pile, atop which sat, inexplicably, one red hat.

Finally, at the end of the alley, he spied a small placard announcing, 'Willa, Maker of Doors that Open and Shut.' A wooden shed stood behind it, surrounded by the greatest number of glass chimes Jordan had ever seen in one place. In the gentle breeze they sounded like a symphony of falling coins.

He poked his head into the shed and called, "Hello?"

One inadequate lantern gave off a dull yellow light, revealing a space made of rough wood, with sawdust on the floor and cobwebs strung across the ceiling. A scrawny pigeon rambled out into the sunlight. Jordan waited, but no one came. He was about to leave when a sudden movement caught the corner of his eye, startling him.

"I don't do spells for boys no more," someone said in a low voice.

Before him stood a stooped woman with the hurricane hair he remembered from the Meditary. Her grey eyes were set far apart and seemed to see more of Jordan than he would have chosen to show.

"That's not what I came for," he said, taking a step inside.

"Why, then? You ain't here to buy a door."

The way she held her hammer — upright, in one strong hand — made her look dangerous. Jordan shifted his weight, considered leaving. It felt as if she was looking right through him.

"Out with it — what sort of foolery have ye got yourself into?"

"Do you know about a door in the Cirran palace?"

"There's over three hundred doors in that place. Ye can't expect me to know 'em all."

Jordan swallowed hard. "This one is made of brass. It doesn't look much like a door, actually. It doesn't even have a handle."

Willa stiffened. She knew exactly what he was talking about.

"Well, then, if it ain't got a handle, it ain't a door," she said matter-of-factly. "Now, I got orders to fill, and I reckon ye got a mind to waste my time. Go home to your mama and find something useful to do."

Jordan's jaw tensed. "I can't go home to my mother. She's been taken prisoner by the Brinnians. I snuck up to the palace to find out what happened to her and the Brinnian Landguards showed up, so I ran. I found this door, and it is a door. Please, if you know anything about it, could you tell me? Because my friend said it's enchanted and I don't want my mother to die, and I touched the door and then it opened."

She put down the hammer. "Eh?"

"I didn't mean for it to open," he sputtered. "I just touched the runes and — "

"Who were ye with?"

"No one."

"Ye did it yourself?"

"Yes," said Jordan.

She went to the shed door and slid it shut with a thud, making it even darker inside. As she tramped towards him, she looked at him with those hammer-force eyes. "Sit," she said. "Tell me what happened."

Jordan settled himself onto a pock-marked wooden bench, resting his forearms on his thighs, and struggled to find a way to describe it.

"It was like a vision," he began, and told her about speaking a language he didn't know, which he believed was what had made the door open — or maybe not. "It was an opening in a different way," he said. "Inside me, sort of." He grimaced in frustration. He told her about the shadow. He didn't mention that it looked like a person. He no longer felt sure about any of it. It all sounded so silly now that he put it into words.

When he had finished, she smacked her lips and said, "Ye been eating anchovies?"

"No. Why?"

"Indigestion. Does funny things to the head."

Jordan leaned back so hard he almost fell off the bench. "I didn't imagine this. It felt like something was calling out, like it was waiting for the person who knew the words, and I don't know — with my hand on the runes, I knew them."

"All right, then. Say 'em to me."

"I can't. I don't remember them."

"Well," said Willa, crossing her arms with a snort.

"I know it makes no sense," said Jordan.

"Damn straight it don't." Willa scratched at the rough fabric of her beige work robes with dirty fingernails. "I told Arrabel to set guards by that door," she said to herself. "I told her it wasn't safe."

"They're probably in prison," said Jordan. Something welled up in his throat but he forced it down. "What sort of enchantment is it? Is my mother going to die now?"

"Don't be a fool. Ain't no enchantment, not like that anyhow. That's naught but a silly palace rumour." She was studying his face. "How old are you?"

"I turned fifteen on the Feast of the Great Light."

She smiled. "Only a few days ago. Pray, tell me, what is yer gift?"

"I don't know. I mean . . . "

She nodded. "Not to worry, boy. Some gifts take longer to declare themselves. Usually they're the special ones. But you," she wagged her crooked finger, "ye'd do well to find something in the meantime."

Find a gift? "It's not like that. You've got to be good at something. You have to have a feeling for — "

"Find something," she said. "Don't matter what."

"But why? There's still a whole year before I choose my robes."

"For protection. That door ain't meant to open. Certainly not for a boy who's still in his short pants."

Jordan gritted his teeth. "Then how did it happen?"

"I can't rightly say. Maybe ye got a sense for spirits."

A night gift. His skin went cold. He may have wanted a gift, but he certainly didn't want a night gift. Those with night gifts were into creepy things like talking to spirits or ridding a home of ghosts. People were afraid of them. He was afraid of them.

Willa just shrugged. "Can ye see into the future?"

"No," said Jordan.

"You ever have communications with the spirits?"

He laughed nervously. "Not that I know of."

She sighed. "Night gifts normally declare themselves very early. By yer age, you'd know if ye had one. I reckon it ain't that at all." For a moment she was quiet. "'Tis what makes the great gifts dangerous — they take their time coming out. Folks what got 'em think they got nothing. Most don't have the patience to wait it out, so they take up a labouring job like farming, or they set up a stall in the market, or they take to drink." She picked up a chisel and examined it, as if for rust. "Too bad, but it happens. 'Tis an empty time, the waiting, when you're like a passage that wants walking through. Makes the underside of this world sit up and take notice. That could be why ye opened that door."

Jordan was silent. A great gift? Could he dare to hope for that much?

"Some say Arrabel didn't know what she been about till she was nineteen at least. All she showed was a love of birds, not one thing more. Dark world tried to lure her into sorcery. Almost had her, too, if ye believe the scholars."

The High Priestess Arrabel? Jordan frowned in disbelief.

"All I'm saying," Willa continued, "is ye got a sense that others don't, and it could get ye into trouble if ye don't get busy doing something on the living side of the world. Cuz it seems the dead side's got its eye on you."

The dead side. He made as if to stand, but then Willa started talking again.

"Tell me, what bridge did ye use to cross into Omar today?"

"The Walkway," he mumbled.

She put down the chisel. "The Walkway was yer second choice."

Jordan could hear the chimes from outside, and the tradesmen and merchants who were handling their affairs — their normal, everyday, living concerns.

"No one steps foot upon the Bridge of No Return 'less something allows it," said Willa. "That's two handfuls of bad business, now."

Jordan remembered the strange man he'd seen, and then didn't see. He couldn't bring himself to confide in Ophira, for fear of losing her good opinion of him, but maybe he could speak to Willa.

She was watching him. "Ask yer question, then," she said. "I ain't got all day to sit here while ye crap yer pants with worrying."

Jordan focused on the cracks and knot-holes in the shed walls as he told her about the man at the holy tree, about how this man had killed a songbird and taken something from the tree, although Jordan wasn't sure what. "And then he disappeared."

As soon as he'd finished, Willa's face went saggy, as if her skin had suddenly become too heavy. "What did he look like?" she said in a hoarse whisper.

"He had pale skin and long greasy hair and — "

"Then he's back," she almost spat. "I thought if I gave it up, it would be enough. I thought it was just me." Her eyes were very dark now, almost opaque, and she seemed to have forgotten he was there.

"Feirhaven?" Jordan said, and then more loudly, "Willa!"

She startled, and then held up a trembling hand. "You stay away from that man. Do ye hear me? He has nothin' to offer you. Promise me ye'll stay away."

"But . . . I only saw him from a distance. We didn't speak. Do you know him?"

Willa scowled towards the far corner of the shed, scratching her head so hard that sawdust flaked from her hair and onto the ground. "Ain't no virtue in being a fool, boy. He's been itching to come back and he's got just enough of the undermagic to do it. You stay away from that man and ye steer clear of that door. Beware the beggar who would be king!"

Jordan's eyebrows drew together. "What?"

"He's a scoundrel beyond reckoning, a danger that reaches all the way to the vultures themselves. The undermagic has no place in our world. Its power is too great. Beware the beggar! He's coming!"

Vultures and undermagic? Jordan stood. "I think it's time I got home," he said, though Willa was now speaking in another language altogether.

As he eased himself towards the shed door and slid it open, his eyes fell upon the work she had been doing before he'd arrived. A door lay flat upon sawhorses, swirls of metal and coloured glass set into the wood in ways he hadn't imagined possible. He turned back to look at her, but she was sitting on a footstool facing the far wall where a variety of tools hung from long rusted hooks.

"Forgive me, feirhaven," he said quietly, and went outside.

The sudden bright sunlight, combined with a pungent smell of goats, made Jordan feel faint. As he wandered out of Trades Alleyway, he thought of his mother and how she had left him so abruptly. No one but his father was waiting for him in Cir, and the streets of the Holy City were filled with patrols of heavy-footed Landguards.

This was madness, worrying about visions from doors and men who disappeared, Jordan thought as he made his way back through the bazaar. There was danger right at home, and he had better put his mind towards it. Willa's advice had been straightforward enough: find something to do, and then do it. Maybe he did have a great gift, though he couldn't dare to think that way. But what he could do was to develop some useful skill that might keep him out of trouble.

He reached the edges of the bazaar where dirt-smeared urchins tended undernourished horses, and baggy-suited traders sold cheap souvenirs. These were the merchants who would chase after customers, their prices falling until you hesitated and they knew they had you. His father hated them, and then just the thought of Elliott sitting alone in the darkened reading room with his shoulders hunched made Jordan pick up his pace.

"Present for yer mama?" called an older woman. "Come on now, wouldn't yer mam like a nice new apron, or a bonnet for her hair?"

"Belts!" cried a man as if he were announcing a word of great wisdom. "Belts! Cheap! Three bronze groder. Alright, my finest belt for two. Two bronze groder."

Jordan shook his head and kept walking. And then a quiet voice behind him said, "Perhaps we're looking for a gift."

The way the man said that last word made it seem as if he didn't mean an Omarrian souvenir at all, but rather a gift in the Cirran sense, a talent upon which a person built his life. Jordan stopped.

The man who had spoken was smallish, with long grey hair — or was it black? — and he wore dark tattered robes. His face was so pale he looked ill. When he fixed Jordan with fervent eyes, Jordan recognized him as the one who'd been at the holy tree that day — the man Willa was calling the Beggar King.

"Are we inclined to want, then, young feirhart?"

Clearly he was not a merchant. He had no stall, no goods to sell.

"No," Jordan said, remembering Willa's warning. "I don't want anything."

"Are you sure?" and his smile revealed stained teeth. Jordan noticed a tuft of yellow feathers sticking out of the bulging pocket near his chest, and at once he shivered.

"I'm sure." He edged away and set off again towards the bridges.

"But you've just had a birthday," said the man from behind him.

At this Jordan wheeled around. "How did you — " But he was speaking to thin air, for the man was gone. Again. Although this time Jordan couldn't be sure if he'd really disappeared or had simply stolen away.

He was near the twelve bridges now. The sound of the Balakan River rushed in his ears, but he found himself running instead into Somberholt Forest. He sank to the soft mossy ground and rested his back against one of the enormous cedars. The light was softer in the forest, the wind evident only in the slow movement of branches. As he watched the gentle exchange of light and shadow, his breathing slowed, and the panic seeped away. There was a deer in the distance, her soft brown gaze directed at him. *You should run,* he thought. *This world isn't safe for you anymore.* And she slipped into the protection of the shade.

Slowly Jordan rose and left the forest. He eyed the black Bridge of No Return. Why had it allowed him on? Passing it at a determined pace, he set his foot instead upon the uneven and carelessly nailed planks of Ne'er Do Well. His mind spun with marching Landguards and Sarmillion drinking mug-wine, and Willa who'd allowed him to think he might be destined for something greater than picking corn in a sweltering Cirsinnian field. *It's a powerful gift,* came one thought. *You could be great,* came another.

It was only when he'd finally arrived home and breathed deeply of its safe smells of wood chips and sasapher that he relaxed. He could hear the rasping of sandpaper as his father worked in the courtyard out back. Jordan would have time to wash the scents of Omar from his skin and hair before facing him. Erasing the afternoon from his memory would be harder. That man in his torn and dirty robes — just the thought of him made Jordan's skin crawl.

Seven

Dark Moon Rising

As the days and weeks and months passed, Jordan found his mother's empty chair at the kitchen table the hardest thing of all to bear. At least Elliott had put away her sandals that always sat beside the front door. The chairs and tables accumulated dust. The windows stayed shuttered for days at a time. Jordan and his father ate too many meals of boiled cabbage and crusty bread. They took turns watering Tanny's herbs and flowers, but it wasn't long before most of the plants shriveled and died. Only the stoic peppermint and wild-evergreen ivy managed to survive.

On Jordan's bedroom wall he had pinned up a map of the lands of Katir-Cir. Every night before bed, he stood with a candle in one hand, his eyes moving slowly from the top of the map to the bottom. *Where are you? Where have they taken you?* The light flickered uncertainly.

He didn't sleep well anymore. Often at night he would sit on the rooftop patio and watch the sister moons, and the moons would watch him. It was the darker moon that had captured his attention of late. Strange ideas came to him on the rooftop. He imagined having the power to make the Brinnian Landguards vanish in a puff of smoke. He thought up the words to possible curses, dreamed of evaporating potions and vaporizing oils.

Sometimes he fantasized about collecting all the Brinnian flags and setting fire to them on the Common, or defacing every likeness of Rabellus with black horns. He thought of enlisting a couple of school friends in his plans, but when it came down to it, he didn't.

He tried desperately to imagine himself in robes. He could see the ceremony and all the people in the audience, but he could never quite glimpse the colour of the homespun fabric he would wear.

By daylight, as often as he could, he visited Mars at the Balakan Gardens that bloomed along the riverfront. It was from here that Mars quietly led the Cirran insurrection. With his hunched back and gentle ways, he was the last person anyone would suspect of sabotage.

"I hear the Loyalists might try calling up the undermagic to get rid of the Brinnians," Jordan said to him one day.

At this, Mars's great eyebrows rose into bushy arches. "Who's been feeding ye such nonsense with yer supper? That would be like sending in the cobras to manage yer toad problem. Ye'd have no more toads, to be sure, but then what would ye do about them snakes?"

Jordan didn't have the courage to tell the gardener this was one of his rooftop ideas. It had come to him one night while he'd been gazing at the twin moons. "But it would work, wouldn't it?"

"Blast, Jordan. That depends on what ye mean. Is the undermagic strong enough to rid our city of Brinnians? 'Course it is. But ye can't wash yer hands of dark magic as if it's horse manure. It don't come off."

"Let me join up," he begged. "I want to be a Loyalist."

But Mars only tilted his weathered brown head to one side and laughed. "Jordan Elliott, ye can't be a rebel. Ye got school to attend and robes to be taking."

Robes. He thought about them listlessly. Some of his friends had already taken theirs. One boy was now a carpenter's apprentice, and a girl he knew had left last month to be apprenticed to a healer.

"A shoemaker's helper wouldn't be such a hardship, would it?" Elliott asked one night. And in the next breath he said, "I'll call upon Uncle Eli in the provinces. I think he's still looking for a shepherd."

One day Jordan was buying onions at the market when a tall woman in saffron robes and a veil came to stand beside him. Her shape wasn't entirely familiar but he recalled that one of the seven seers was about the same height.

"Hello, Grandma Mopu," he said.

"No, Jordan, it's me."

Ophira? "What happened to making potions?" His legs felt wobbly.

Ophira held her arms at the elbows. "It didn't work out."

"It's the grandmas, isn't it? They make you wear the veil."

"Of course it's the grandmas."

Jordan gaped at her as if she were an apparition. The veil was made of thinly spun mellowreed that covered her head entirely, sheer enough only to hint at her face.

"Why won't they let you do what you want?"

"Jordan, must you know everything?"

He leaned towards her. "They want you to replace Willa, don't they?"

Her only answer was to squeeze his hand.

Seers never married. If they tried, something terrible would befall their fiancé. Jordan remembered what had happened when Grandma Mopu had tried to marry. Her beloved had been a fisherman, tragically drowned. Most people had called it an accident, but Ophira had told Jordan the truth: it was the curse of second sight.

"What about you?" she asked. "Do you have an idea yet which robes you'll take?"

As if it was up to him. Robes were not something you chose. They chose you.

"Oh, sure," he said, "I'm going to be a mystery keeper." When Ophira didn't respond, he added, "Anyway, who needs robes? We're Brinnians now." Jordan walked away without taking his onions.

No longer did songbirds sit upon the holy tree's branches. The dead bodies that hung there became so commonplace no one bothered to mention them anymore. The emperor had issued a decree that the customary feast-day celebrations for the Great Light this year would be replaced by Brinnian festivities involving roasted deer, dried dung for smoking, and mug-wine. There would be no flower ceremony at the holy tree, and no Beggar King to chase across the Bridge of No Return.

The last time Jordan had been to Somberholt he'd heard Cirran tunes being sung as they worked the saws on the giant cedars. He'd seen Cirran arrowheads red with the blood of deer. And on the Common, Cirran folk gallivanted about dressed like underrats, with velvet outfits and flashy buttons and all manner of shiny jewelry.

One night after dinner his father set down two hot mugs of lemongrass tea and sat across from him. "Your instructors tell me they see you in class more regularly these days."

Jordan shrugged. "Nothing better to do." He waited for the lecture that was sure to come. *An education is the foundation of all the blah blah blah.* But Elliott just sipped his tea and gazed at the shuttered window.

"I've been thinking," said Jordan. "I might not take robes."

Elliott picked at something brown that had hardened onto the table. "Tradition and ritual are the mainstays of our world, Jordan. They hold great power. If you don't take robes, it's another victory for the Brinnians. Is that what you want?" But all the fire in his voice had been doused.

Jordan left the room, taking the stairs two at a time up to the roof where he could be alone.

The setting sun had lost its merciless heat, though he could still feel the warmth rising from the roof stones. He stood and listened to the day empty itself of working sounds. The smell of cooking fish wafted through the air. Leaning over the railing, he surveyed the city he loved. The sun glowed red, casting a glorious pink onto the Cirran stone, and in the east the twin moons began to rise.

Jordan stared at the two round yellow moons glaring back at him as if they were the eyes of some great creature, one bright, one just a shade darker. What the Cirrans needed was inspiration, someone to remind them of who they were. He studied the darker moon in particular. It had more shape to it somehow, more contour and possibility.

Soon he wasn't looking at the moons anymore. He was imagining the white Cirran buildings without Rabellus's likeness painted upon them. He could see the holy tree covered in flowers and then later, beneath the true-full moons, he saw it burst into flames.

Suddenly he knew what to do. He knew where he would do it, and he knew when. For the first time ever, he looked forward to his sixteenth birthday. The next morning when he awoke, he went around the house and opened all the shutters to the rising sun. He ran up to the market on the Common and stole two freshly baked nutty-buns and a hunk of goat cheese, brought them home and set them on the table. He was pumping water into the kettle when his father appeared in the kitchen doorway rumpled with sleep.

"What's got into you?" he asked.

Jordan smiled. "Breakfast," he said with a grand wave of his arm.

As the days passed he had only to glance at the Brinnian coat of arms and think of the hawk's meaning: "Do not rest until your objective has been achieved."

Eight

THE COBRA AND THE MONGOOSE

SARMILLION SUCKED HARD ON HIS PIPE of dried dung, one hand jammed into the pocket of his smoking jacket. A breeze blew steadily off the Balakan River into the open-front bar, making the torches dance and bringing the mingled scents of tar from the boatyard and fried food from the nearby restaurants.

Sarmillion's eyes were focused on the centre of the room, the so-called pit that gave the Omarrian bar its name. At this hour the pit was roped off to prevent fools and drunkards from doing something they'd regret. Mug-wine and billy beer were secondary here. The Pit was a gambling den. You came here to play, or you stayed home. For sheer excitement it beat a stack of dusty parchments any day.

In the corner of the room sat one of the members of the Rubber Band, a tall thin man named Binur who played a mean twanger and had some talent as a flutist. He also had a sense for snakes. That was how he'd described it to Sarmillion the first time the undercat had come here.

"It's a whole dance thing, ye know? Ye fix its eyes with yours and ye play the music and ye sort of move the way it moves, and it works, ye know?" And he'd asked if Sarmillion wanted to try, and Sarmillion had eyed the cobra coiled in its wicker basket and said no, thank you, he didn't think he had a sense for snakes at all. Besides, he always bet against the snakes and he had a feeling they knew this and were only waiting for him to get that flute in his hands before they took their revenge.

Now the peculiarly intoxicating flute music was dying away and Binur eased himself into the crowd that had formed around the pit. The cobra froze and for a second Sarmillion felt sorry for him. Probably all he wanted to do was slither home and go to bed, but the show had to go on.

Into The Pit strode Jack-Jack, an underrat who kept himself shaved right down to the pink skin. In his spare time when he wasn't drunk or breaking into people's homes, Jack-Jack was a mongoose trapper.

"Here's Mojo!" he called, holding up a mongoose in a metal cage, and everyone cheered.

Every mongoose he brought in was called Mojo. Mojo number forty, or whatever it was, would probably be dead within the hour. Most often the mongooses were the winners in these fights, but this cobra was an uncommonly feisty contender. This would be his fifth mongoose, if he succeeded. Sarmillion was probably the only one in the bar who had put his money on the mongoose tonight. Not even Shasta was betting on it, and she usually shared his soft spot for underdogs. She stood beside Sarmillion, wearing high heels and a short skirt, bright blue colour around her eyes, the rhinestones on her long underrat tail glittering in the torchlight.

With its small pointed head and long body, the mongoose seemed more like a furry pet than a predator, especially when compared to the swaying, spitting snake. There had been fatalities in The Pit. You had to stay on your guard in this game, even as a spectator. Just because the animals started out behind the ropes didn't mean they stayed there. Sarmillion had never

81

seen a cobra attack one of the patrons, but he'd heard stories. He gripped his stubby dung pipe and backed a safe distance away from the commotion.

A lot of folks came to The Pit for the blood and action, and of course for the chance to win big coin.

"Got your money on Mojo, eh, Scribbler? Eh?" said Jack-Jack.

"I am a great believer in brains over brawn," responded Sarmillion.

Jack-Jack set the mongoose cage onto the dirt floor with a clatter, and unlatched the door. "Brains over brawn, ha, that's funny, I hope that bartender's got some free drinks for ye there cuz you're not gonna have no slaggin' money left, eh, Ex? Eh?"

Ex approached the bar with his slow, cool underrat stride. He was tall and thin, and wore a black bandana and a long black goatee. He looked like a lead twanger player in one of those hard core bands that toured the Circassic port town taverns.

"Free drinks, yuh," Ex said.

Sarmillion puffed on his pipe, making the dried dung glow and sizzle. When would he hit bottom? This had to be it, hanging out with underrats, betting on cobra fights, working for Piccolo. He'd promised himself he'd spend every morning writing poetry. He would be halfway through his masterpiece by now if he'd started when he had intended to. Certainly he wouldn't be here, eye to eye with a spitting reptile.

Well, he had one eye on the reptile. The other was trained on the beaded doorway. One of two people could walk through it at any moment. He was hoping it would be Grizelda, a white Persian undercat who painted her claws red and had this way of rolling her 'r's that made Sarmillion's stomach do back flips. She often showed up here on Saturday nights.

He hoped to see Grizelda, but it was also possible Piccolo might walk in. Piccolo was expecting a black velvet sack bearing the weight of silver Cirran candlesticks that Sarmillion hadn't been able to get hold of just yet.

The mongoose had begun his game of strike and retreat, tiring out the cobra, biding his time, waiting for the perfect opportunity to kill. He was smart, and he was faster and more agile than he looked. But would he be a match for this snake? Slowly the cobra moved around the pit's perimeter. Every time he drew close to people's legs there was a collective "aah" and the sound of shuffling as the spectators edged away and then back again.

Sarmillion hunted for a stool to perch on at the bar, but they were all taken. He kept feeling something slithering around his legs, but it was only Shasta's bejeweled tail. She had her paws on a leather-clad underrat named Marco who stood on the other side of her. Marco liked to play with knives and he had this way of not paying attention while he was doing it that made Sarmillion nervous.

The beads jingled and Sarmillion swiveled and saw two Brinnian Landguards stagger in. They held each other steady and almost stumbled into the pit ropes before someone guided them back to relative safety.

Now here might be a stroke of luck. While Sarmillion had been charged to eavesdrop on any Landguards that showed up in the Omarrian taverns, he'd discovered that most of them were tight-lipped and kept to themselves. Sneaking into the palace was proving to be unfeasible. Every time the Loyalists had attempted it, they'd been caught. Many were in prison. A few had been hanged. The upshot was that no one had found out anything about High Priestess Arrabel and the other prisoners.

"You make a decent Elderberry Blaster in this place?" one of the Landguards shouted to the bartender above the hollering crowd.

"I gots mug-wine and billy beer — bloody or not," said the bartender. "Them's your choices. Place your bets and take your drinks," he said with an icy glare. Sarmillion glanced at the mongoose darting in and out of people's legs, and then edged his way towards the Landguards.

"I'd put my money on the mongoose tonight if I were you boys," he said. He took a deep breath. "Buy you a drink?"

The two exchanged a look, and then shrugged. Sarmillion called for mug-wine, and the bartender took their bets.

"Off duty tonight?" asked Sarmillion as the mugs of greasy brown liquid slid across the bar towards the Landguards' burly hands.

The rounder, pock-marked Landguard burped and said, "Gonna have to work double time round that Cirran feast day, so the Emp give us some extra days off now."

"Before things heat up, like," said the taller thinner Landguard, who had a particularly long face and protruding front teeth. The unfortunate combination gave him the appearance of an idiot. It was this that buoyed Sarmillion's confidence.

"I suppose all the men have to do a tour of duty guarding the Cirran prisoners, huh?" he asked casually.

"Yeah, what a pain in the butt that is," said Pockface with a groan.

They're alive, thought Sarmillion. *But where? Where are they?*

There was an eruption of boos as the snake struck out at the mongoose and missed. Sarmillion winced.

"I hope you haven't lost us our coin there, undercat," said Buckteeth.

Sarmillion gave a sly smile. "I've got a feeling about the mongoose tonight. I think he'll get his man, so to speak." He pretended to take a sip of his drink as the two men gulped theirs.

"Tastes sort of meaty," said Pockface.

"You get used to it," said Sarmillion. "So, what's so bad about guarding the prisoners? You get to travel."

"Damned hot down there," said Buckteeth. "Nothing to do. Skunked if I know why the Emp sent them to the desert. We're the ones gotta go down and watch 'em there. He gets to stay in that fancy palace."

The desert. It could only mean one thing: Ut. This was bad news. Ut was a vast land that was notoriously hard to cross because of the challenges of weather and distance. There were nomadic tribes that knew how to survive in such conditions, but none of them was Cirran. Or Brinnian, for that matter. Brin was, for the most part, a land of cold snowy winters. Sarmillion wondered how the guards were handling the heat. Perhaps the prisoners were being held near one of the coastal towns.

"When you come back from that desert you got sand in places where sand ain't meant to be, if you catch my meaning," said Pockface, and Sarmillion pretended to think this was hilarious, banging the table and calling for more drinks. He felt something at his feet and startled, thinking it might be the cobra. The mongoose scrambled across his two-toned leather shoes and darted back towards the snake. *You go, little fellow.*

"I hear Elion is lovely in the winter," said Sarmillion. He waited for the response with the tensely alert patience of a mongoose. And just as Buckteeth opened his mouth to answer, Sarmillion felt a hand on his arm and looked up to see the greasy hair and bulbous red nose of his boss, Piccolo.

"Sorry to break up the party," he said, elbowing his way between Sarmillion and Pockface. He plunked his forearms onto the sticky counter, his gut pressing against the bar, and the bartender handed him a Bloody Billy.

"On the house," he said, and Piccolo grunted.

"Who's winning?" Piccolo pointed to the pit with his grizzly double chin.

"Anyone's call tonight," said the bartender.

"So, Scribbler? You got something for me?"

Sarmillion's stomach clenched. The last thing he wanted was for those guards to find out he'd once worked as a palace scribe. He turned his back to them and lowered his voice. "I'm working on it."

"Working on it? Working on it would mean you're hangin' around the place waitin' for the lights to go out. Working on it would mean ye gots the key in yer pocket, or better yet, the loot in yer sack. What the hell, underkitty, work harder. You don't wanna gets yer name in my big books, now, do ye?"

Sarmillion cleared his throat. "Of course not, feirhart. You'll have your ... items by tomorrow afternoon. My word. I'll bring them by your tavern."

"I know where ye live, underkitty."

"Indeed you do, feirhart."

"I'll hunt ye down."

"I know that, feirhart."

Suddenly the room exploded in boos and cheers. The mongoose had struck and the cobra was dead.

"Your lucky day, I reckon," said the bartender, as the Landguards slapped Sarmillion and each other on the back.

Piccolo fixed him with his dark piggy eyes. "I'll see you tomorrow, underkitty. And I'll tell ye this: tomorrow, it's my lucky day. Eh? Eh?" He laughed and his chest rattled with phlegm and he coughed and spat onto the dirt floor. Sarmillion grimaced in disgust. His hands shook as he gathered his winnings into a velvet sack.

The Landguards drained the last of their drinks. They were steadying themselves when the beads jangled and in strode Grizelda. Sarmillion cursed her timing because he knew he couldn't stay. He gave her a wave and a wink and as she purred past he took in the rosewater scent of her and whispered, "Buy you a drink later?" and she said, "Later I might not be here," and he said, "Wait for me?" and she said, "Are you worth waiting for?" and he said, "You bet I am," and her red-painted claws skimmed his cheek. "I'll wait," she said.

The Landguards stumbled out the door and into the fresh night air. Sarmillion slowed his pace to theirs.

"So, where are we off to now?" he asked.

"We're staying just around the corner," said Pockface. "The what's-it-called."

"Here On Inn," Sarmillion said. "Try their pickled herring for breakfast. It's the best in Omar." Blast Piccolo. His conversation with the Landguards had been picking up momentum. *Strike and retreat. Here goes.* "Riverboat leaves from here down to Utberg, I hear," he said. "Gets you down south in ten days' time. Nice ride, folks say."

"Who'd want to go there?" said Buckteeth. "The place is a dead zone. Nothing but clay huts and dust and a couple of straggly trees. Talk about getting ripped off on leave. Emp can't put us up in a fancy resort in Elion? No, he's gotta send us five miles away from the damned prison camp for R&R. Utberg — steaming goat dung, that's what I say."

So the prison camp was five miles from Utberg, was it? There it was. The cobra was dead.

"Brinnian coast resorts are cold even in the summer," Pockface was saying. "Man, we come to Ut, we want palm trees and pretty girls and all the Elderberry Blasters we can drink."

Buckteeth began describing the girls he was particularly interested in, but Sarmillion wasn't listening. Utberg was about as far away from the Holy City as you could get. At least now they knew what they were up against. He would meet with Mars tomorrow and give him the news. They could dispatch spies immediately to Utberg to assess the situation. It might be the beginning of redemption for the Scribbler.

He'd done his duty this evening — perhaps he'd make a good spy after all. Now a white Persian undercat with red-painted claws awaited him and he wouldn't have to think about Utberg or Piccolo's blasted candlesticks until tomorrow.

Nine

PRIVATE REBELLIONS

JORDAN STRUTTED THROUGH THE CIRRAN MARKETPLACE, his pockets filled with stolen tomatoes. On this day, in the year that bore the Brinnian designation 1329, it was finally his sixteenth birthday. He did not deserve to feel so happy. Sometime this month he would have to take his robes, and he still had no idea what his gift might be. But today he would fulfill a different purpose.

Beyond the market, Jordan passed one of the enormous portraits of Emperor Rabellus that had been painted onto building walls all over the city. Jordan hated that smirk, those hooded eyes scrutinizing you whenever you walked by. Checking to make sure there were no Landguards, he faced the likeness and crossed his forearms in a curse.

Today was the first anniversary of the Brinnian coup. It was also the Cirran Feast of the Great Light, but there was no question of holding a traditional celebration. It was forbidden. Besides, the Brinnians were using the Meditary that night for another one of their Fire and Feasting parties that some Cirrans planned to attend. For those who were disgusted by the scent of once-sacred deer roasting in their once-sacred hall, there was nowhere to go except the Common.

Rabellus had doubled his Landguard patrol, expecting trouble. Jordan's jaw tensed: he would personally ensure that the emperor was not disappointed. When he'd confided his plan to Sarmillion, the undercat had pretended to disapprove, but the way his whiskers had jittered Jordan could tell even he was excited about it.

Finally he reached the Alley of Seers, a crooked narrow passage made up of the attached stone homes of the Seven Seers of Cir. Each door was painted a different colour, though according to Ophira, the dwellings themselves were connected by back stairways and hidden doors and rooms you'd never guess at. Jordan had never been farther than Mama Petsane's kitchen, and it was at her bright blue door that he knocked this morning.

"Ach, come in already, Jordan," she called from the other side of the door. As Jordan entered, he was met with the fragrance of countless herbs simmering in one of Petsane's famous stews. The smell made him think of shade trees and Cirsinnian pastures just before harvest.

"Good morning, Mama," he said, flashing her a grin and producing, with a flourish, a tomato in each hand.

Mama Petsane stood before the big black woodstove in the kitchen, a green apron around her waist, her head bare. She waved her long-handled stew spoon in the air with a grimace. "Where'd you get those, boy?"

"I grew them in my garden," he said with a wink, and won for himself one of Petsane's rarest gifts, a brown-toothed, big-gapped smile.

Mama Manjuza, who had been seated at the kitchen table, rose awkwardly and took the tomatoes from Jordan. "At least he brings something worth stealing," she said.

"You sixteen today," said Mama Petsane. "Big day, uh?"

"Big day, no robes in sight," Grandma Mopu piped up from the divan. Mopu was a tall woman with long teeth and a horse-like face. She was the one whom everyone called the Monkey-Maker, on account of her tendency to make fun of things. It was amusing, as long as you weren't her target. While Petsane and Manjuza giggled at this comment, Jordan's face fell.

"Maybe I just won't take any robes," he said. "I'm not obliged, you know. Lots of people aren't bothering with them anymore."

"Yeah, maybe you just be a tomato thief for the rest of your life," said Petsane.

"Your father will be so proud," said Mopu.

"You all know which robes I'm going to wear." Jordan hadn't meant to whine. He cleared his throat. "Why won't you tell me?"

"Maybe we don't know," said Manjuza.

"Maybe we already told you but you don't listen," said Mopu.

"Maybe I don't have a gift," he said. He stood beside Mama Petsane and lifted the lid on the stew. Petsane tapped his hand with her wooden spoon.

"Sit, Jordan," said Mama Manjuza, gently patting a wicker kitchen chair. Jordan came and sat across from her.

"You be good with goats?" she asked.

"No. They chase me and bite at my shorts."

"You ever try carving, like your father?"

"He says I was born with two left hands."

"But you sure be good at dreaming away an afternoon beneath the cedars," said Petsane, her large backside facing them as she attended to her stew.

"Yeah, but there are no robes for that," said Mopu, shuffling over and sitting down. While all of the seers were obliged to wear their saffron robes whenever they left the house, at home Mopu insisted upon wearing a multi-coloured dress because, as she claimed, she was good at everything.

"What you gonna do to celebrate your day?" asked Grandma Appollonia from her worn rocker in the corner of the large room. Jordan turned to see which side of Appollonia had spoken. It seemed she was squinting at him with her good eye. The left eye, made of swirled blue glass, remained fixed straight ahead. That was the one you wanted to watch out for. Strange things happened when she spoke from that side.

"He's gonna get a haircut," said Mopu. This was a perpetual threat amongst the grandmas who all agreed Jordan's mop of curls was far too unruly.

Jordan laughed. "No way." Then he said nonchalantly, "I don't have any plans."

The kitchen fell silent as the four old women glowered at him.

"Don't you dare," said Mopu.

"What?" said Jordan, struggling to keep his face neutral.

Manjuza stood and waved her cane at him. "You do it and you be the next one hanging from that tree, Jordan. It would kill your father. You're all he has in this world."

Jordan focused on the empty staircase and wondered what was taking Ophira so long to come down.

"Ach, Manjuza, forget it. Ye know he's gonna do it no-how," said Petsane. "Anyway, I saw it first."

"Now that's a load of dried dung," said Manjuza, slamming the kitchen table with the flat of her hand. "All the Cirrans say Mama Manjuza sees farthest."

Mopu pushed her chair away from the table. "Yeah, yeah, you all see so far, but none of you can see what you're doing to this family. Bunch of blind old farts."

"Don't you be starting on that Willa business again," grumbled Petsane.

Jordan could sense he was about to get caught in the middle of a storm, so he went to sit in the empty chair next to Appollonia. Her glass eye was open but her good eye was closed, and she kept up a steady snore.

Then she snuffled and murmured in a sleepy voice, "Little boy in too-big shoes."

"What was that?" asked Jordan.

Appollonia stared at him with her disturbing blue-glass eye, almost as if she were wide awake. "Little boy in too-big shoes, he find his gift. Oh, wretched gift."

Jordan jostled her shoulder. "What do you mean? What did you just say?"

Her good eye blinked open. "Eh? Why you wake an old woman when she be napping?"

The other three seers were chuckling and coughing about something between them. When Jordan looked up, there was Ophira at the top of the stairs in her saffron robes — unveiled.

"Go," Petsane waved at Jordan with the spoon. "Take her for a walk to the river. It's yer birthday."

Ophira came down the stairs, stepping lightly in her embroidered slippers, and Jordan rose.

"Pick me up some billy grain for our biscuits," Petsane said to the girl, making a show of placing a silver groder on the table and glaring pointedly at Jordan. "She's gonna pay for it, so keep yer sticky fingers in yer pockets. And put yer veil on!" she cried as Ophira pushed the front door open.

Jordan followed her out and shut the door behind them. "What's up with Mopu?"

"Oh," said Ophira. "It's about Grandma Willa. You know how Mopu cares for her. Poor Willa has fallen into complete disgrace since she showed up last year in the Meditary with her head bare — and in rubber boots."

"So it doesn't have anything to do with this?" Jordan tugged at the sleeve of Ophira's saffron robes. "The seventh seer of Cir? You're taking Willa's place, aren't you?"

Ophira struggled to speak, as if something were caught in her throat. "I can't talk about this with you, Jordan. Yes, I'm the seventh seer of Cir, now. That's all."

That's all? It was quite enough. Jordan didn't speak until they reached the extensive gardens that lined the riverbank walkway around the entire Holy City. The Balakan River was wide and long, the waters dividing around the mountain-island that was the Holy City of Cir before they continued past Omar and south into Ut. Jordan loved the sound of the rushing water and the way the river's breezes carried the Balakan Garden's fresh scent of flowers. Low boats passed now and then beneath the twelve bridges, bearing cargo or passengers from the provinces. Sometimes you could hear the singing of the oarsmen below deck. He settled himself on a stone bench, and Ophira joined him.

"I hate this birthday," he said. "Everyone expects me to decide the rest of my life, when I can hardly make up my mind about what to eat for lunch."

"You're lucky to have a real birthday," she said.

"What do you mean? Everyone has a birthday."

"Not me. The grandmas just chose the day they found me on their doorstep."

"Do they really not know who your parents were?"

"Sometimes they talk of a Circassic healer and a wandering belt-dancer when they think I can't hear them." She paused, as if lost in thought.

Everything about Ophira was a mystery to Jordan. So were love potions, and love itself. Lately he'd been struck by the idea that the world around him was merely a backdrop. The stone buildings, the river and trees, they weren't the real things. It was what was behind them that was important, the things you couldn't see.

He gazed at Ophira's veiled face. "Would you take it off? I feel like I'm talking to you through a wall."

She hesitated. "I'm not supposed to. The grandmas . . . well, they worry."

Jordan let out a snort. "About what?"

"About you. You know what happened to Mopu's fiancé. It's not just a superstition."

"I think I can take care of myself," he said, fighting the blush that threatened to creep across his face. "Anyway, what are they going to do about it?"

Ophira shrugged. "Mama Petsane has threatened to make a paste of billy grain and mug-wine to glue the veil to my head." She bent forward and let it fall into her lap. For the first time Jordan noticed how pale her face appeared against her hair, and how her blue eyes were ringed with dark circles.

"You look so tired," he exclaimed. "Aren't you sleeping well?"

"I'm needed at night," she said.

"What do you mean?"

She shook her head. "There are things I can't tell you." She glanced down at the pile of yellow fabric in her lap. "It's my fourth one," she confided.

Jordan's eyebrows rose.

"I threw the first one into this river. The second I shredded with Petsane's carving knife and I cut eye-holes into the third."

Jordan burst into laughter.

"The grandmas didn't think it was funny. Well, Mopu did."

"Who would ever suspect you of being a rebel?" He thought of the grandmas. "How do you manage to keep anything from those old women?"

Ophira's lips were pursed, as if she were guarding something, but her gaze was as clear as ever. "You have to make a place in your mind for secrets, a corner where they wouldn't think to check." She watched the tall mellowreeds swaying in the breeze. "I put you there sometimes."

What did she mean? Ophira's long elegant hands were curled in her lap, and Jordan wondered if he would regret what he was about to do. He decided he was past caring. He took one of her hands in both of his and held it gently. *Please don't pull away.*

She grinned. "You do know it's hopeless, right?"

"Superstitious nonsense," he mumbled.

"The grandmas are right to be afraid for you." But she kept her hand in his.

Mars came hobbling towards them along the riverbank walkway, carrying a long hoe. The way the gardener's body curved, like the plants he tended, he seemed to be made of dancing. Whenever Jordan saw his bald head, weathered brown face and bushy grey eyebrows, he couldn't help but feel happy.

Mars bowed slightly and whispered, "May the Great Light shine upon you."

"And upon your family," Jordan and Ophira responded quietly. The traditional Cirran greeting was now dangerous enough to get anyone who spoke it arrested.

"'Tis yer birthday. The year of your robes," Mars said to Jordan. "What will ye take?"

He grimaced. "I don't want to talk about it."

Mars's smile was warm. "What does your father say?"

Jordan let out a long sigh. "I think he's finally given up hope that I'll become a scholar, and of course there's no honour in being a Landguard now. He thinks I should take ecru robes."

"Grove-keeper," said Mars.

"Yeah. Rabellus will send me into Somberholt to cut cedars, not keep them."

Mars studied him. "You'd do well to heed yer father. Being sent to do somethin' and doin' it are two different birds now, aren't they? Think of the thirteenth bridge."

In the distance Jordan and Ophira could see charred planks of cedar. The twelve bridges that connected the Holy City to the rest of Katir-Cir had been erected by magic. But Emperor Rabellus and the Brinnian guards were losing patience with these bridges. They wanted to build a thirteenth bridge out of cedar that anyone could cross whenever they liked. Eight times Rabellus had conscripted a group of men to construct the bridge; every time it had been set on fire in the middle of the night.

"Have the Loyalists been working on the thirteenth bridge?" Jordan asked.

"Aye, in a manner of speaking," said Mars. "Ye could do some good."

Ophira's eyes had a mischievous twinkle to them. "I think he's hoping for a more glamorous task."

"Ah," said Mars. From behind his back he produced a bouquet of tiny yellow flowers and handed it to Jordan with a bow. "Something like this?"

Jordan's eyes widened. "Holy slag." They were sasapher flowers, the official flower of the Holy City.

Mars tapped him playfully with the end of the hoe. "You got a mouth as foul as the underrats, boy."

"Where did you get those?" Brinnians were unaware of the tendency of sasapher to infuse endurance into those who smoked it. Probably they wouldn't have believed it anyway, though they had been contending for months that dried dung was cheaper to produce for smoking.

Mars leaned towards them. "I'm under strict orders by Emperor Rabellus to pull up all the sasapher and destroy it, but I never was one for strict orders." He fixed Jordan with his bright eyes. "Sarmillion tells me ye got promise." He gestured towards the bouquet with his chin. "You'll be in a great heap o' slag just for having them flowers. You'll be in two heaps for what yer wanting to do with 'em. Don't do it unless yer sure ye won't get caught, ye hear?"

Jordan nodded, but as soon as Mars had limped away Ophira gave him a stern look. "The grandmas told you not to. Don't you listen to anyone, Jordan?"

He smiled but didn't reply.

Ten

WALLPAPER UNIVERSE

WITH THE SASAPHER FLOWERS TUCKED INSIDE his shirt, Jordan took his leave of Ophira and made his way alone up the long steep road towards the hanging tree. That was what most Cirrans called it now, though Mars didn't approve.

"We're the ones letting Rabellus hang innocent folk from its branches," he'd said during one of Jordan's visits to the riverside gardens.

Today, on his birthday, the Feast of the Great Light, Jordan would sneak up to the tree, recite the customary prayer and place the flowers beneath it. He was doing this for his mother. He was doing it for the tree, which needed reminding that some Cirrans had not forsaken tradition. And he was doing it for himself, the boy who had no gift.

It was late morning and the day was already warm. Lizards lined the rooftops, and the white-washed stone walls blinded Jordan with their reflected light. Although there were Cirrans milling about the Common, it was unnaturally quiet. Jordan squeezed past a donkey laden with straw and then past a group of scholars in their emerald robes. Having a secret made him feel as if his whole body was humming. He walked a little faster up the cobblestone road, and couldn't help but smile.

All too soon the tip of the golden palace came into view. What if they caught him? Rabellus would not hesitate to hang a teenager if the offense were serious enough, and this one would be. Jordan stopped. He was tempted to just go home.

He noticed a man standing in the shadow of a nearby doorway who seemed oddly familiar. He wore ragged robes, darker than the brown of a carver, but not quite the black of a sorcerer, and while he carried himself like an old man, he did not in fact look old. His skin was pale, his hair long and straggly, grey from one angle and yet not from another. He had the long hooked nose of a bird.

"Greetings," the man said, but then he didn't follow it with, "Rabellus is great," or even a discreet, "May the Great Light shine upon you."

Jordan could not afford to take any chances, so he ignored him and continued on his way. But the man kept up with him.

"Where do we go?" he asked.

"Nowhere," said Jordan.

"And yet we go there at a determined pace."

Jordan slowed. "Where I am going is none of your business, feirhart."

"Have we not one groder to spare for a poor fellow?" he said, resting a pale, scrawny hand upon Jordan's shoulder. There was a musty smell to him, like a closet that had been closed for too long. Jordan backed away from him.

From one angle the man had blue eyes, from another brown. Were those wrinkles around his eyes, or not?

"I'm sorry, feirhart, but I have no coin," Jordan said. Had he any, he would have given the man one just to make him go away.

"A gift for one who has none," the man said quietly.

Jordan froze. "What did you say?" The way he said gift, it made Jordan think of that day so long ago in the Omar Bazaar, of that man who was not a merchant, the one who'd known of his birthday. Was this the same person?

The man held his hands together as if cupping something precious. "A gift. Perhaps you fancy one? For we are inclined to want, are we not?"

"I thought you had no groder," said Jordan.

"Ah, but I do not speak of coin."

"I don't care much for trinkets," said Jordan and walked away.

"I offer something far greater, young man," he called. Jordan was about to ask, "What?" but when he turned around, the man had already gone. He tried to recall his face, but it slipped away, like water running through his fingers. He frowned and kept moving.

Finally Jordan reached the plateau at the top of the mountain. The palace's main courtyard, which had always been open to the public in Arrabel's time so that people could go to the Meditary whenever they pleased, was now closed off and guarded. The hanging tree was some distance away from that courtyard but still close enough for a guard to notice someone approaching. Not even mourners whose loved ones had been hanged were allowed to come pay their respects to the dead.

Jordan's heart was pounding. He should just call the whole thing off.

Then, out of the shadows appeared Sarmillion, dressed in a mauve smoking jacket, black silk pants and two-toned leather shoes. With his slicked-back fur, pierced ear and sunglasses, he looked more like a gangster than a scribe.

"What are you doing here?" Jordan said.

"I came to watch out for you," said Sarmillion, "you being a Loyalist now and all."

Jordan threw his shoulders back. "Really?"

Sarmillion removed his sunglasses. His expression was grave. "This isn't like stealing tomatoes, old friend. You won't be able to run fast enough if they see you."

"I know," said Jordan.

"Some of the others argued that you should let yourself get caught," said Sarmillion. "Let them make a martyr out of you. But I told them to go get stuffed. Don't let them take you." The undercat placed a gentle hand upon Jordan's forearm. "We've had news. Arrabel and the others are being kept down south, near Utberg."

Jordan's chest tightened. "Are they all still alive?"

"We don't have details, but we've sent spies to scope it out, along with courier hawks to bring the news back as fast as possible. If they capture you, Jordan, you could make things a lot worse for your mother. "

Jordan gave a short nod. Everything suddenly seemed too bright.

Near the main courtyard, a commotion had erupted. A man in dark robes stood before the guards, yelling and shaking his fist, claiming he'd been robbed. Cirrans had begun to cluster around him.

"Robbed, my eye," scoffed Jordan. "I met that fellow a few minutes ago. He asked me for a groder." *He offered me a gift.*

Sarmillion gave him a push. "It's the very diversion you need. Run, friend. Speak the invocation as you go. Don't linger at the tree. Go!"

Jordan focused upon the great blackened oak and raced towards it. "Blessed is the Great Light, light of all lands of Katir-Cir, light of our path." The words came out in huffs with his breathing. "We pay homage to the holy tree, light of our darkness, lamp to the world." His feet reached the mosaic stone pathway set in meandering patterns along the approach to the tree. "Thankful are we for the many mysteries of this world that keep us seeking wisdom. Guide us upon the paths we're meant to take," and he almost choked on the words. "Why have you given me no gift?" His tortured cry burst in upon his recitation.

Now he was close enough to the charred trunk to see the knots and furrows that gave it the look of a wise but angry man. There was no point in checking behind him to see if that man was still arguing with the guards. Jordan stopped, pulled the sasapher flowers from inside his shirt, and brought them to his face to inhale their strong lemon scent.

A body hung from one of the branches. Crows surrounded it, and one had perched on the dead man's shoulder. They had already taken the man's eyes. A wave of nausea washed over Jordan.

"Get," he hissed at the birds. In a flurry of wings they took to higher branches. "May the Great Light have mercy upon you," he murmured to the dead man.

Then he resumed his feast day prayer. "Let our eyes remain open to small wonders. Let our hearts remain a dwelling place for spirit. Let our . . . "

"You there!"

His hand shaking wildly, he placed the yellow flowers at the base of the tree. "Some of us still remember," he said, then faced the group of black-clad men running towards him. Two of them had drawn their daggers. For some reason he thought of those finches that used to dance upon the treetop.

Run! But he just stood there.

And then a different voice, a man's, said, "The world is merely wallpaper. You've known that all along. Hide behind it. Here is your gift. Take it, and save yourself." Somehow Jordan knew what to do. He pulled at the edge of the tree trunk as if it were a doorway. A great rushing sound around his head made him think of the wings of a thousand birds, and then he stepped out of the world and disappeared.

At first it seemed as if he was simply hiding behind the tree, but he could sense it was more than that. He was hiding behind the air behind the tree. It was dark and musty and his own heavy breathing sounded in his ears. He examined his shadowy surroundings and saw a narrow dirt path. And then one of the shadows moved.

"Greetings," said a voice Jordan recognized, and he tensed. It was that fellow he'd met earlier. "I have waited such a long time for you. You have accepted my gift, then."

"This? You did this?"

"Now you have a talent to be reckoned with," and the old-young man flashed a crooked smile at him.

Pandemonium had erupted in the world Jordan had left behind — Landguards yelling and waving their long black sticks in the air, a crowd of Cirrans talking and pointing with excitement towards the tree — but it all came to him from such a distance. He could see and hear it, yet he was no longer a physical part of it. If the world was only wallpaper, then he had stripped it back to see what the walls of this house were really made of.

"Where's that boy?" one of the Brinnian guards cried over the cheering and applause.

"You let him get away!" said another.

"Someone better go after him. If the emperor finds out . . . "

"Shut your mouth. Find the boy."

"And if we don't?"

"Find someone. What about that beggar? Arrest him. Where'd he go?"

And the old-young man standing next to Jordan laughed. "See how it is with us? We have the power now. They'll never catch us, Jordan Elliott. Do you see?"

Us? Jordan flinched. "How do you know my name?"

"I know what's worth knowing." The man winked at him. "Return to the world at a safer location. Tell no one about the Beggar King," and he was gone.

Jordan stood very still. *Beggar King?*

A guard ground his boot into the delicate sasapher flowers that Jordan had placed beneath the tree. Jordan turned his back on the scene and felt his way along in the dark, all the while crossing the plateau between the hanging tree and the palace. As he walked, he could hear Cirran onlookers spreading the news of what he'd done. An elderly man gestured wildly with gnarled hands about the sasapher flowers. A woman hid her beaming face behind a notice for the Fire and Feasting party.

Finally Jordan reached the edge of the city. He curled his fingers around the air, heard the loud whoosh of wings in his ears, and appeared back in the world directly behind Sarmillion.

"There," he said, grinning. "I did it."

Sarmillion wheeled around. "Embers and ashes, boy. How . . . ? I thought you were done for. I thought . . . but then you were gone. And now here you are." He grabbed Jordan by the arm. "We must get you away from here. They'll be searching for you. Rabellus will want your head."

"Where can I go?"

"We'll take the back routes down the shadow side of the city and then cross into Omar. You can stay with me for a while. I'll see what I can do about protection."

"But my father . . . "

"I'll get a message to him."

Omar. Jordan hadn't been there since he'd met with Willa the door-maker almost a year ago. He hadn't realized that perhaps he'd been avoiding it. Perhaps he'd been afraid. Of what, he wasn't sure.

"They'll love you in Omar," Sarmillion said.

"What do you mean?"

"Omar is where many of the rebels have been hiding. There'll be lots of sympathy for your cause. Mice alive, you'll be a hero."

"Really?" Jordan stood up straighter.

They made their way quickly and carefully down the north face of Cir, the darker, more hidden side of the mountain. Sarmillion was watching Jordan with wary eyes.

"We'll need to talk," was all the undercat said as they hurried from one bridge to the next in an attempt to cross the river. Finally they both embarked upon the only bridge that would grant them passage: Peril, a rickety affair made of worn rope and rotting wood.

Eleven

THE LIFE OF A THIEF

AS JORDAN AND SARMILLION ENTERED THE Omar Bazaar, goat meat sizzled and flutes competed with mandolins over the hollering of merchants and their customers. There were baskets of different coloured beans, glimmering displays of knives, leather belts, hand-knotted rugs, and donkeys pushing everyone out of the way.

"Read your palm?" said a woman in a dark veil as they passed, her silver bracelets jangling all the way up her arms.

"Hey, Sarmillion," breathed a white Persian undercat with red claws, glittery whiskers and a black sequined dress. "Will I see you later?" The 'r' of later seemed to stretch into next week.

Jordan couldn't hear Sarmillion's reply. "You know her?" he asked.

"Grizelda," Sarmillion said with a sly grin.

They passed stall upon stall of malachite headdresses, fuchsia jackets and indigo shawls. Jordan inhaled silk perfumed with sandalwood, and saw the wind take a dress and transform it into a flower. The air seemed to be alive with flowing cloth. And then Sarmillion veered into a hidden alley and pushed through a pair of swing doors.

Jordan rested his hand on the tavern doors. He'd often imagined the music and sweet smells in a tavern, the fun with friends — though of course Elliott had forbidden it. But his father wasn't here.

It took Jordan's eyes a moment to adjust to the bluish haze of pungent dried dung smoke that hung in the air. A couple was having coffee at a small round table, and near one wall a group of young men slumped against each other as if they'd been sitting there since daybreak. The darkness seemed unnatural in midday, like a sick room.

A sweaty-faced man appeared behind the bar and called, "Hey, Scribbler!" He smiled at Sarmillion, revealing crooked teeth. His hair was long and thin and pasted to the sides of his head. He had a red nose and a round belly, and though he nodded and simpered, his squinty eyes seemed to be calculating what he could get from you.

"Piccolo," said Sarmillion with a bow, as they approached the bar.

Piccolo banged a glass onto the bar counter, filled it with billy beer, threw in a shot of tomato juice and set it before Sarmillion. "Bloody Billy for yer friend?" he asked the undercat in a phlegmy voice. "Or maybe he'd prefer fruit juice."

"He'll take a Bloody Billy," said Sarmillion.

"I'm not thirsty," Jordan said sharply.

"Watch yourself," Sarmillion murmured. "We may need him." He opened a leather satchel and passed Piccolo a silver necklace adorned with glittering blue stones.

"Nice job," Piccolo said, handing back a small velvet sack that clinked with coins. "For yer troubles, feirhart."

Three tall stringy men had entered the bar and went to sit upon stools at the far end. Each took up a twanger made of sticks and rubber bands. The men had long pointed beards and wore tall hats, striped pants and long jackets.

"The Rubber Band," said Sarmillion. "We're in luck."

But instead of playing, the three musicians set to arguing.

"You've been coming in a beat too soon."

"You're flat."

"I'm never flat."

"I'm never early."

"Slag, Binur, you're always early."

Piccolo called out, "Sing Sarmillion's song, boys!"

"F-sharp?" one of them asked.

"Why not?" the others answered and they began a monotone off-key twang, stomping slowly in time to the beat.

> *"Oh, the life of a thief is the one I choose,*
> *I've got two-toned shoes and nothing to lose,*
> *I'm two steps down the river.*
> *Check your silverware,*
> *Hide your coin.*
> *Kit's been here, your purse purr-loined.*
> *Find him? Ha!*
> *Bind him? Bah!*
> *He's two steps down the river.*
>
> *Oh, the thing with a kitty when I sing this ditty*
> *I've got scribbler's blues, and a mislaid Muse*
> *I'm two steps down the river.*
> *Lost — your golden bells,*
> *Gone — your jewels,*
> *Kit's got keys and prying tools.*
> *Find him? Ha!*
> *Bind him? Bah!*
> *He's two steps down the river."*

Sarmillion looked as if he wanted to disappear beneath the bar but Piccolo hooted and clapped along.

"Wrote it himself, that undercat did," he announced. Then he turned to Sarmillion. "You bring me a laddie for some work?" He pointed towards Jordan with his chin. "Or is this just nuisance I sees at my bar?"

Sarmillion opened his mouth, but it was Jordan who spoke. "I won't work for you." He glared at the greasy older man.

Piccolo's laugh was sharp and dangerous. "You will when yer hungry, laddie. Eh, Sarmillion? We all knows what it's like to be hungry, don't we? That dark hole in the belly that just don't get smaller no matter how much you wishes." He winked at Jordan. "You're a proud one, are ye? Just like yer paps." Then he left the room, passing through the swinging doors that led into the kitchen.

Jordan straightened. "What did he mean by that? That man doesn't know my father."

"Piccolo knows everyone," said Sarmillion. "You'd better hope your father never made an enemy of him. He keeps a ledger — a brown leather folder he calls his big books — a record of every wrong that's ever been done to him. And he pays them back, one by one. He never forgets the face of a man who's crossed him."

"I'm not crossing him," Jordan said. "If I have to steal a tomato or two to feed myself, that's one thing. But I won't be indebted to someone like him."

Sarmillion's eyebrows rose. "Perhaps you don't understand the magnitude of this situation. Every Brinnian Landguard is hunting you down. You won't be going home for a while — maybe not a long while. Piccolo's the sort of fellow who can offer you protection. He knows the right people. He has the

power to make a Landguard look the other way. But he expects
something in return. When he offers you work, you take it."

Jordan shrugged. "I won't work for him. I'm a Loyalist. I plan
to do something important. Something glorious." He looked up
to see Piccolo standing before him.

"A Loyalist, he says. Now there's a rag. Loyalists know better
than to announce theirselves to the world, ye damn blatherskite.
Ye still got yer slaggin' milk teeth. Don't worry, I'll teach ye your
occupation before long." He set a plate of steaming food before
Jordan. "There you are, now. Fresh fish, bit o' scrambled egg,
slice o' bread, fine tomaties. On the house."

Jordan didn't need anyone to tell him this meal wasn't free.
It was a down-payment on the job Piccolo would ask him to
do as soon as he'd finished eating. "I'm not hungry," he said,
pushing the plate away.

Piccolo's face went red. He coughed, spat onto the plate of
food, then said to Sarmillion, "Tell yer friend he'll be paying for
his meal whether he eats it or not."

Sarmillion opened his velvet sack, took out a gold coin and
placed it on the bar.

"No, undercat, I don't want yer coin. I want his."

"I don't have any," said Jordan. "But you already knew that."

"Well then, my bootless little measle, we have ourselves a
problem. See, I made ye a meal. I wants my coin."

"Come on, Piccolo," said Sarmillion. "It's his birthday. A
round of Bloody Billy's for everyone, my treat."

Piccolo kept his eyes trained on Jordan. "Ah," he said with
a smirk. "Sixteen, are ye? A man, now. Big man. Loyalist man.
Too good for the likes of us simple folk, eh? Your mule-brained
papa was the same. And that sweet young Tanny, wasn't she just
smitten by the skinny carver. Never had a real man, I reckon,
or she would'a fancied me instead, eh?"

Jordan slammed his hands onto the bar. "I don't need to take this from you."

For an instant he panicked. *You did it once. Why not do it again?* For he had something Piccolo would never have. He thought of the modest vocation that he might have been stuck with: keeper of the cedar groves. Just the sort of thing a boy with no gift could be expected to settle for. But he'd been made for a greater purpose; Willa had been right about that. He reached behind him, pulled apart a corner of the air and waited for the rushing sound of wings around his head. Then he stepped out of the world.

If the tavern had seemed dark and dank, it was nothing compared to this echoing passageway he entered for the second time that day. He rubbed his arms to keep warm, and breathed through his mouth to avoid the smell of rotting meat.

"Greetings," came a voice from behind him.

Jordan wheeled around. There was that fellow emerging from the shadows, more like a shadow himself than a man.

"I see you're making good use of your gift," he said.

"It comes in handy," said Jordan. He tried to make sense of this new place, though the light was poor. "Where are we?"

"On the dead side of the world, of course."

"Don't be ridiculous," said Jordan. "Only spirits walk on the dead side. Everyone knows that." Had Willa been right? "The dead side's got its eye on you," she'd said. But how could it be? He was alive.

Behind him Sarmillion was dancing around in confusion as Piccolo thumped his meaty fists on the counter and yelled, "Where is he? You bring that dog's body back in here and make him pay for what he done. I don't like the look of him. Got too much of his own mind and not enough respect for his elders." See? There was life, Jordan could hear it.

In the background came the twanging of the Rubber Band as they sang something about a young rebel who that very morning had made the hanging tree bloom, and he realized with a start it was a song about him.

The shadowy man was staring at him.

"Everyone knows the dead side is for spirits, do they?" He let out a high-pitched laugh. "What everyone knows is a far cry from what is, wouldn't you say? Everyone knows there's no such thing as the Beggar King. Everyone knows a boy cannot disappear. That's why no one will believe these things, even when they see them with their own eyes. They'll search for every possible explanation, and deem impossible the ones that do not please them. They will believe anything except what is. Human nature works in our favour, does it not?"

Jordan shifted his icy feet. Why did this man keep saying we and us?

Just then a group of underrats burst into the tavern and sashayed towards the bar, rolling their hips and swivelling their shoulders, their long tails making lines in the dirt floor.

"Oy!" called a shaven underrat. "You got enough jars o' mug-wine to feed a thirsty lot of rodents?"

"Aye, Jack-Jack," said Piccolo, "for rodents with coin I gots a barrel-full."

"Show the man, Shasta."

Tottering in her high heels, the underrat named Shasta leaned towards the bar and pulled a velvet sack from somewhere inside her skimpy blouse, dumping several bronze coins onto the counter.

Piccolo smiled. "My mood's improving already. The Scribbler here did me a dirty."

"Confound you, Piccolo," cried Sarmillion. "You know I meant no harm."

"What dirty?" asked Jack-Jack.

Piccolo poured glasses of brown mug-wine. "Brings me the son of the scallywag that took my girl, and then he don't even let me get my due." He fixed Sarmillion with his small eyes. "I don't want yer fancy explanations, undercat. I want my coin for that meal. You tell that little toad he's in my big books now right alongside his warty-faced father."

"What boy?" asked Jack-Jack. "Who is he? Who's he work for?"

An underrat dressed entirely in leather leaned forward, his outfit squeaking as he moved, and said, "Shut up, Jack-Jack. The man's talkin'."

"That Elliott boy. He don't work for me," Piccolo said with a growl. "But he's gonna." He turned back to Sarmillion. "You tell him, Scribbler. I wants a word with him."

"Yes, of course," said the undercat with a small bow. "And in the meantime, feirhart, please accept this gold groder in payment for the food."

Piccolo pocketed the coin in silence.

"The Elliott boy? He's the one what stood on the black bridge," said Jack-Jack. "Ain't he, Piccolo? Ain't he?"

Jordan startled. He hadn't realized anyone had seen him. And he'd never made the connection between being granted passage on that bridge and meeting this man who called himself the Beggar King. He checked behind him but the strange fellow was gone.

The leather-clad underrat slapped Jack-Jack on the side of the head with a mug-wine coaster. "For the love of dried dung, how ye figure the man's gonna know who was on that bridge? 'Twas at least ten twin moons ago."

Sarmillion put down his glass. "What bridge? What are you talking about?"

"Bridge of No Return," said an underrat wearing a trench coat, his teeth made entirely of gold. "That be the Beggar King's bridge."

"I know what bridge that is, Sardine," said Sarmillion. He took a great gulp of his Bloody Billy. "No one's been on it since Balbadoris was taken."

"Elliott boy was on it," said a tall, thin underrat, nodding so that his goatee jumped up and down. "Yuh, we sees him with our own eyes. Cirran kid, wearing his shorty pants."

"Ridiculous," huffed Sarmillion. "Jordan Elliott would never have been granted entry onto the Bridge of No Return. And if he had, he'd have been a fool to accept it."

Sardine let out a long burp. "Not our fault the kid's a dullard."

"Nope," said the underrat with the goatee.

"Old Willa's been saying the Beggar King's coming," Shasta said. "I'd say 'twas him what let the Elliott boy on. I got eyes for that sort of thing."

"Shasta's got eyes for anything in pants, eh girl?" said Piccolo, and he clapped, enjoying his joke. Shasta lowered her head and Jordan felt sorry for her.

"Ain't just anyone who can see spirits," she muttered. "But I can. I saw one by the river that day, watching. Just sitting and watching. "

"Mice alive," cried Sarmillion, clearly forgetting the company he was with. "I've never heard such nonsense in my life. Don't any of you read Cirran literature?"

"Ain't none of us can read, save Marco, and he only do it real slow," said Sardine.

"Well," said Sarmillion, "here is your lesson for the day. The Beggar King is a metaphor, not a real person; a way of thinking about darkness. The only one who ever crosses the Bridge of No Return is the scholar Balbadoris who dresses in black robes on the Great Light's feast day as part of a ritual for cleansing the Holy City of evil. But you wouldn't know anything about cleansing. I'd wager the lot of you hasn't seen a warm bath in months."

"Nope," said Jack-Jack with a howl of glee. "Ain't no one ever chased us outta town for no rit-u-al cleansing."

Jordan, who was listening from far away, found himself drifting as if the underrat's words had created ripples in time that could touch other ripples from other conversations. He heard his father say, "Tradition and ritual are the mainstays of our world."

"Your Cirran books is wrong," said Shasta. "The Beggar King is real, and he's coming. He's been calling out to folks. I reckon someone'll answer him sooner or later."

Calling out? Answering? What could she mean? Perhaps this hadn't been such a great idea after all, accepting a gift from such a man. And yet, thanks to his new skill, Jordan had shown Piccolo — just like he'd shown those Landguards at the holy tree. He shivered.

"They say he's a sorcerer," said Shasta. "Knows all the black spells."

"Bet he's Brinnian," said Jack-Jack. "Eh, Marco?"

"Blasted bells!" Marco cried. "Brinnians don't hold with neither cloaks nor spells. Don't you know anything?"

"Well I'm just betting the fella's Brinnian," sputtered Jack-Jack. "Got a feeling about it. It's like Mojo. Eh, Sarmillion? Sometimes ye just get a feeling about a mongoose. Eh?"

Jordan heard Sarmillion sigh. The undercat tapped a stubby yellow pipe with dried dung, lit it, and left the tavern with his head down. Jordan followed, making his way along the dark path.

For a little while he trailed Sarmillion, finally emerging into the living world of the bazaar from behind a canvas partition. The light and warmth that rushed back to him were such a relief he forgot the circumstances under which he'd disappeared, tapped the undercat on the back and said, "Hey, there you are."

"You!" Sarmillion snarled. "You're coming with me."

Twelve

A Trickster Called Glory

HE HAD DISAPPEARED. HADN'T HE? SARMILLION was certain that was what he'd seen, and yet his mind fought it. *Boys do not simply disappear, no matter how much you might wish they would.* But he resolved not to speak of it to Jordan right away. Sometimes things needed time to simmer, like a good fish stew. Simmering brought out the flavour of the herbs and spices, and then you knew what was what.

"Blast you, boy," he sputtered, forcing Jordan to keep up a good clip beside him. "Have you lost your wits? You call yourself a Loyalist but let me tell you, they don't employ fools and what you did back there with Piccolo was imprudent, to say the least. If you want to accomplish anything useful you'd best start using your head. Oh, impulsiveness. Oh, short-sightedness. What am I to do with such a child?"

"I'm not a child," Jordan grumbled.

"No? Then stop acting like one." Sarmillion's jaw was tense and he felt a headache coming on. "What's going to happen now when the Landguards knock at Piccolo's tavern? Do you think he'll say he's never seen you before? You're on his slag list now. He'll betray you the first chance he gets."

The undercat turned down an alley overgrown with black snakeweed and then doubled back onto the main street. He pulled Jordan behind him into a doorway and waited. If someone had been following them, he'd know it. Their breathing sounded loud to his ears.

"I'm sorry," Jordan said. "I just don't like him."

"Who says you have to like the man? This is about your survival...to say nothing of the entire Loyalist cause. You could do things — great things. But first you'd better learn when to keep your mouth shut." He peered around the doorway, then nodded to Jordan and they continued walking.

"So you mean I should have used Piccolo," said Jordan.

"The way he would use you. Yes." *The way he uses me.*

"My father wouldn't do that," Jordan said, and the undercat thought he sounded a little self-righteous.

"Welcome to Omar, boy. This is the way things are done. You don't like it?" He threw his arms up in frustration. "Then you should have taken your tree-keeping robes when you had the chance."

"It's a little late for that now, isn't it."

"Indeed," huffed Sarmillion.

They proceeded for several minutes in silence.

"So what should I do?" the boy said finally, gaping at Sarmillion with wide scared eyes.

"I don't know yet." Sarmillion gentled his voice. "For now, you'll stay at my place, and I mean stay. Indoors." He led Jordan up a spiral flight of wrought-iron stairs to the undercat's apartment. He'd never heard anyone speak to Piccolo like that before. He hated to admit it, but Jordan had courage. A fool's courage, perhaps, but courage nonetheless.

They stopped at an elaborate door constructed of swirling metal rosettes that were filled in with stained glass.

"Who's that in the middle?" Jordan asked, pointing to the carved face of a woman with unkempt hair and crazed eyes.

"That's Lady Destiny," said Sarmillion.

"I've never heard of her."

"She'll catch up to you when you're older. She always does." He unlocked the door and stood aside. "Welcome to my humble quarters," he said, and was pleased to see Jordan's face go slack as he crossed the threshold. Sarmillion knew the Elliott home well; he'd spent many an evening with Jordan's father in the reading room. Compared to this opulent setting anyone would say their home was dark and narrow and smelled of cabbage.

Here were beaded curtains and colourful silks hanging from the ceiling, window after window opening out onto the bustling bazaar, candle sconces and tapestries upon the walls. It was the home of someone who'd made a great success of his life, depending on how you defined success. What it was not, was the abode of a struggling scribe.

"Where are your parchments?" asked Jordan.

Sarmillion's whiskers fell and he dug his nails into his wrist. How could he tell the boy he'd had to hide it all away in a closet so that it wouldn't stare at him in constant reproach? Only Balbadoris's long blue sasapher pipe sat on display, collecting dust on one shelf like a souvenir.

"You heard the song in the tavern," he said. "I'm not a scribe anymore." He cleared his throat. "Now, let's get down to business. Considering we've probably alienated our best source of protection, we'll have to move onto Plan B. You'll need a disguise," and he led Jordan to his closet — it took up an entire room. It made the life of a thief worth every black-gloved stolen-candlestick nerve-wracked moment.

"At home I have a drawer," Jordan sighed, "with three shirts and two pairs of short pants."

Sarmillion shrugged. "What good is life without a collection of smoking jackets?"

He considered Jordan's colouring and then selected a pair of ivory pants for the boy, and a long embroidered shirt made of silk and dyed the colour of jade. "And you mustn't go out without a headdress," he said, pulling one from a drawer.

"That way no one will recognize me," said Jordan.

"Don't be ridiculous," said Sarmillion. "This is purely a matter of style."

He adjusted the headdress, fitted Jordan with a brown belt and a woven leather bracelet, stood back to evaluate the effect, and then nodded his approval. Jordan positioned himself before the enormous looking glass hanging from one wall and studied his reflection from one side, then another.

"I don't know," he said. "Do I have to wear the headdress? It feels a little funny."

"Nonsense, it's smashing."

Sarmillion moved in front of Jordan and placed his hands on the boy's shoulders. "Twice today you disappeared, right before my eyes. The Landguards thought you ran away. Piccolo figured you'd snuck outside. But I know what I saw, and I've never seen it before. Tell me straight, now: did someone help you? Did you take a potion?"

Jordan's eyes flitted towards the rows of shiny boots and two-toned leather shoes. "I just did it — myself," he stammered. "It's my gift. I can disappear."

This boy who had for sixteen years shown no magical aptitude whatsoever, other than to make tomatoes vanish from market stalls and miraculously reappear in his pockets — suddenly he could disappear himself? Sarmillion didn't believe it for a second. "Sorcery's a dangerous game, feirhart, and disappearing is no common feat. Did you pay a sorcerer?"

"I didn't pay anyone."

"Underrats say they saw you on the Bridge of No Return ten or more twin moons ago."

The boy's face coloured. "They must have made a mistake."

"You're telling me it wasn't you?"

"No way," said Jordan. "Underrats are never right about anything."

While the boy did have a point, Sarmillion still suspected he was lying. Jordan had gotten involved in some sort of mischief. He'd bought himself a gift — only Lady Destiny knew what price he'd paid for it — but now he was here and the Loyalists, who needed a hero, might just have found one. How splendid it was when the universe cooperated with his plans.

The wild woman has brought me my redemption. She still loves me. But oh, how cruel she could be. After having scored such a coup in getting the information about Arrabel and the others from those two drunken Landguards, Sarmillion had sat down the next morning and tried to write a love poem. He imagined himself as an Omarrian troubadour. He could wear one of those floppy brown hats with an ostrich feather in it. He'd learn to play the lute. He'd sing about Grizelda.

That was the image he'd held in his head that morning, feather pen in hand, ink bottle open on the table. He'd fulfilled his Loyalist spy mission. He could do anything. Yes, he'd dipped the pen, poised it over the parchment, waited for inspiration to strike — and wrote nothing. Blobs of ink dripped onto the paper as if mocking him. The tears of a scribe. But no, they were merely the smudges of an undercat with sticky fingers.

Oh, heavy penalty. Oh, unfair conclusion. That afternoon, in broad daylight, he'd broken into the home of a well-known Omarrian merchant and made off with his collection of brass bells, which Piccolo hadn't even asked for. The way Piccolo had smiled at him — it was a greasy smile, a colluding 'you're one of us now' look that had made Sarmillion feel the need to wash his hands.

Sarmillion startled as he realized he was still standing with Jordan in the walk-in closet. When finally he spoke, his voice was soft. "I know what you mean about wanting glory."

Jordan tilted his head to one side.

"At the tavern. You told Piccolo you wanted to do something glorious."

The boy turned away.

"No," Sarmillion said, "I understand. I want it, too. I have these ideas — well, a couple of poems, actually. I've never shown them to anyone before," and he opened the bottom drawer of a cupboard and took out a slim sheaf of parchments. He started to hand the papers to Jordan, then pulled them away. "You can't read them yet, they're not ready." *They'll never be ready.*

Sarmillion couldn't meet Jordan's eyes. "One day it will be my masterpiece and I will travel the lands of Katir-Cir reciting my poetry." He left out the part about the lute and the feathered hat. Some things were private. "Grizelda will be there. Some of the poems will be for her." He swallowed hard. "Only right now I'm here, in Omar, working for Piccolo, and these hands," he held up his slender ringed fingers, "these hands have not used a feathered pen for anything except to pick locks." He fingered his most recent acquisition, a camel-hair coat. "Glory is a fickle dame, boy, as elusive as smoke. Grab her if you can. But don't be surprised if you come up empty-handed. She's a trickster. Take it from someone who knows."

Jordan busied himself adjusting his belt and Sarmillion bit his lip. "Well, then," he clapped, in an attempt to lighten the mood, "let's have a sip of fireweed whiskey to celebrate your birthday, shall we? A baptism of sorts. You're a Loyalist now."

He led Jordan to a lavishly carpeted sitting room, where he opened a cupboard and took out a tall blue bottle and two small glasses.

"Since we're going to be living together for a while," he spoke as he poured, "I'd better lay out the ground rules. I work late, sleep late, and start my mornings reluctantly, with a pipe of dried dung and a generous shot of Bloody Billy. I won't wear plaid and I won't say no to dinner reservations, but only at the Riverfront Café. I quite like that fancy new food they're serving. If you're going to lie to me, you'd better tell a good one because I've got a face full of whiskers and every one of them's a fine-tuned specially-made slag detector."

Jordan shifted and Sarmillion thought, *I know you've got a secret, boy.* The question was, did it matter?

"I live for glory, groder and Grizelda," Sarmillion continued. "Not necessarily in that order." He winked. "You see? I haven't abandoned my quest yet." Handing Jordan a drink, he declared, "Stand up, young man, and raise your glass. May the Great Light shine upon you."

"And upon your family," Jordan replied. He gulped his drink and immediately his knees gave way and he had to sit.

"Easy now," Sarmillion said. "You've had a long day. A hearty meal and a long sleep will do you good."

The undercat set about clattering and singing in the kitchen as he concocted his specialty: fish stew seasoned with a pinch of stolen sasapher and some hefty cloves of garlic.

They lingered over the meal as the sun set and the moons rose. Afterwards Sarmillion led Jordan to the guest room and leaned casually against the doorframe as the boy whispered, "A bed," with something like awe. "I've only ever slept in a hammock."

Jordan was asleep before Sarmillion had the chance to wish him a good rest. He scrutinized the boy's tanned face and unruly mop of hair. He had always fancied himself as an undercat who knew all the answers, but evidently there were questions in this world he'd never thought to ask.

Sarmillion shut the bedroom door, poured another glass of fireweed whiskey, and settled himself in a soft armchair. He recalled the day not long after the coup when he'd set off for Omar and the boy had trotted along beside him asking unusual questions about the brass door in the Cirran palace. All those rumours about that door and its connections to the undermagic: well, what if they weren't rumours? What if Jordan had acquired the power to disappear?

"I didn't just think that," Sarmillion said to himself. And he tried to unthink it, but he'd never been much good at that. Because the truth of the matter was undeniable: if they could get their hands on the undermagic, their Brinnian problem would be solved. And then that trickster, glory, would have no choice but to come knocking at Sarmillion's door.

Thirteen

THE BRASSED DOOR

WHEN JORDAN AWOKE, THE BLACK SKY outside his open window was punctuated by two true-full circles of yellow moon surrounded by an eerie orange hue. It took him a moment to remember where he was. He lay there, trying to decide if he preferred the firmness of a bed or the gentle cradle of a hammock. There was a distant hum — was it a conversation? Jordan listened. He was certain Sarmillion was speaking to someone in the sitting room. Maybe it was Grizelda.

Jordan crept to the door and clicked it open. Warm candlelight spilled into the dark bedroom. Though the other voice did not belong to a female undercat, it did seem familiar.

"Sweet sasapher," the stranger was saying, "do ye reckon he's taken some sort of brew?"

It was Mars! He and Sarmillion would be discussing Loyalist business. Jordan held his breath in order to hear every word.

"He claims it's his gift," said Sarmillion.

"I smell sorcery," said Mars. "'Tisn't regular for a boy to have such a skill. 'Tisn't wise, neither. Disappearing's a trick from the undermagic days. How could he possibly do it without help? And deceitful help at that?"

"Does it really matter how he does it?"

"Blooming bellwethers, Sarmillion, of course it does. Ain't no one disappeared in Katir-Cir for over a thousand years, and all of a sudden our Jordan can do it? We'd be fools not to ask where it came from."

"Mars, Mars — imagine the possibilities. He could get into the palace without being seen. And you know what's in the palace, don't you?"

"Indeed, I do, underkitty: scores of guards carrying clubs and whatnot."

"I mean, besides them."

"What are you on about now?"

"Go to the last door, yes the brassed door, the one that will not open with a key," Sarmillion sang in such a horrible scratchy voice Jordan nearly burst into laughter.

"How much fireweed whiskey have ye had?" asked Mars.

"It's a Rubber Band song. They say — "

"Those three flobbers? Is that where you're gettin' yer intelligence?"

"I've spent half my life in the Cirran palace, gardener! I don't need the Rubber Band to tell me what's behind that door."

"Is that so?" Mars exhaled heavily. "Explain it to a simple fella."

This was the palace secret that Sarmillion had refused to reveal to Jordan so long ago. Jordan heard the sound of a chair being pushed away, and then the soft padding of feet. Sarmillion was pacing.

"It was always guarded in Arrabel's time," the undercat said, "but the Elliott boy told me there isn't a soul around that dingy hallway anymore. The Brinnians are too dim-witted to realize what they've got."

"What was Jordan doing in them parts? If Arrabel posted guards at that door, it means it ain't safe."

"Of course it's not safe, Marsy. Nothing is safe anymore. If it were, I wouldn't be interested. It's power, pure and simple. And if we got hold of it, we could do whatever we wanted."

"I've heard 'tis the undermagic itself locked behind that door."

The undermagic. The word made Jordan feel as if he were teetering on the edge of a cliff.

"Well, then," Sarmillion said, "we're in agreement finally. Don't start wiggling your funky eyebrows at me. We're going to need something extraordinary to overthrow these Brinnians. Tell me, my shovel-bearing friend, what are our choices?"

"I can tell ye one thing, the brassed door ain't a choice. It ain't on the list. It ain't even a consideration — most particularly if our Jordan's been messing with dark magic in the first place. Now, how about ye tell me something? How can a full-time scribe disregard his traditional schooling without a second's thought?"

"What do the old tales have to do with this?"

"The Tale of the Sister Moons, Sarmillion — ever hear that one? The dangers of the undermagic, how it can darken a soul? Blast it anyway, Sister Lucinda gave up everything to hide that evil power away. 'Tis a great mystery, that brassed door, and here you are ready to treat it like it were naught but the entry to a tavern."

"What are you afraid of? Do you think the big bad Beggar King will come and steal the undermagic away from us?"

"Beware the beggar who would be king. What do ye reckon it means? King of the Brinnian provinces? 'Tis the kingdom of the undermagic he wanted all those years ago and some folks say he still means to have it."

"You can't be serious," cried Sarmillion. "The Beggar King, as I was just telling some underrats, is not an actual person.

Surely you know that. No one really believes the story about the sister moons. It's all metaphor."

Jordan's skin prickled as the odd man's words rang in his head: "Human nature works in our favour." That vision he'd had when he'd touched the brass door . . . It had felt like something opening inside him. There had been a shadow on the other side, a shadow that had called to him, and he had answered. And there had been glorious darkness, that charge in the air that he had never encountered anywhere before.

"Even if the undermagic is behind that door," said Mars, "what does it matter? What do ye think ye can do about it?"

"Don't you see?" cried Sarmillion, and the pacing stopped.

"It could change everything."

"Sure. It could make things a whole lot worse."

Sarmillion let out a harrumph. "You're not listening to me."

"Oh, I hear ye. Anyway, we got no chance of opening that door," Mars said.

Jordan was tempted to shout, "Of course you do. You have more than a chance. You have me."

"Even if we did," the gardener said, "who says 'tis wise to do it? Ain't a soul understands the source of the power ye be calling up. Wakin' the vultures. Personally I don't like the sound of that."

Waking the vultures. There was a mention of vultures in the Tale of the Sister Moons, but Jordan had never thought of them as real. They were quaint, as meaningless as the crows' feet carried by Cirsinnian traders in their pockets to ward off evil. Yet hadn't he heard wings that day he'd opened the brass door? But what could vultures have to do with anything?

"Far as I'm concerned about yer brassed door, the case is closed."

"No it isn't!" Sarmillion's cry startled Jordan.

"Great Light, underkitty, calm yourself."

"I — forgive me. I am not myself tonight. Has there been news from Ut?"

Mars let out a sigh. "Not a word, but it's early still. 'Tis a good ten days' sail for our men to get there, and then they'll need to find the place. Five miles from Utberg could be five miles in any direction, and ye know the way Uttic folk are with strangers: as closed-mouthed as the dead."

"What if we sent the Elliott boy up to the palace?" said Sarmillion. "Just to get information. There's bound to be some up there."

"Blighted billy grain, underkitty, think on what yer asking. The boy risked his life at the hanging tree this very day. Rabellus and his Landguards won't be forgetting that anytime soon. They'll be searching for him, ye can count on it. And you mean to send him right into the heart of danger?"

"He's the only one who could get away with it. Besides, he'll be a hero. It's what he wants."

"He might pay for it with his life."

Jordan thought of Theophen and how he would have given his life to protect the Holy City, and then he could stand it no longer. He burst out of the bedroom yelling, "I'll do it!"

Mars rose in surprise, and then gave him a short bow. "May the Great Light shine upon ye, young feirhart."

"And upon your family," Jordan replied.

The gardener clasped him in a hug, then stood back to look at him. "Your father was a sight this afternoon, poor fella, but I assured him yer out of harm's way."

"Thank you." Jordan smiled at him.

"Sit, feirhart," said Mars. He placed his large tanned hands upon his knees and gazed at Jordan with his bright blue eyes. "Ye need to be straight with us, now. How did ye come upon this gift of yours? I'm sure ye realize 'tis no ordinary skill. I can't lie, Jordan. I'm worried about where yer new power is coming from."

Jordan bit his lip. Maybe it would be better if he told them about this man who called himself the Beggar King. "Tell no one," the man had said.

"Didn't you say that it happened one evening in the cedar groves?" Sarmillion interjected. "You'd been eating mushrooms and you fell asleep. When you woke up, you felt different."

Mars's eyebrows rose. "I asked the boy, underkitty, not you."

But Jordan was nodding vigorously. "It's just as he says." And then he gave a theatrical shrug. "Who knows? Maybe the mushrooms were enchanted."

"Well . . . mushrooms," said Mars, appearing to give the matter serious consideration.

"Anything's possible with mushrooms," said Sarmillion. "You can't be too careful."

"Were ye ill afterwards?" asked Mars. "Did ye visit a healer?"

"No, I was fine," said Jordan. "I am fine. There's nothing to worry about."

The gardener scratched his bald head.

"You know we could use someone to sneak into the palace and find out more about the prisoners," said Sarmillion. "Would you be willing to do it?"

"Rabellus took my mother away," Jordan said. "I have to try."

"Don't give up hope, feirhart," said Mars. "We know they're in the south of Ut, thanks to Sarmillion here. We got spies down there now scoping out the conditions of their confinement. But they haven't sent word yet and time is passing. The sooner we know more, the sooner we can go down and bring 'em home. They're gonna come home, Jordan — Arrabel and Theophen and your mother, too."

"While you're at the palace, you might also go knocking on a few doors," said Sarmillion, but Mars rose and said, "Don't ye start on that nonsense. Are ye fixing to get the boy killed?"

"Mars here isn't interested in the undermagic," said Sarmillion. "If you can believe that."

"What I ain't interested in is prying something open that's meant to stay closed."

Prying? Jordan had opened that door without any effort at all.

"Now, the night may be made of time," Mars said, "but none of it belongs to us. You've made an enemy of Piccolo. Landguards come calling, he's gonna tell 'em he seen ye, and this is the first door they'll knock at."

"Where can I go?" Jordan asked. He couldn't disguise the tremor in his voice.

Sarmillion and Mars exchanged a look.

"Best place to hide something is under their noses," said Mars. "No one suspects a simple gardener. They all reckon I'm lowly and dumb. I've got a cave down near the river. We hide Loyalists there sometimes if they're in danger. I say we go there."

Sarmillion collected the whiskey glasses off the table. "I'll pack my bags."

"Ye won't be needing yer smoking jackets, underkitty."

"I don't expect you to understand," the undercat replied. "You wear overalls."

Mars slapped his hands on his thighs. "I'm a gardener. What do ye think I'd wear? Meditary robes?"

Jordan followed the undercat into his walk-in closet.

"Put your headdress on," Sarmillion said. "You'll need it."

Jordan tried to fix it the way Sarmillion had shown him but his hands were shaking too badly and it ended up a twisted mess.

"Let me," said the undercat, and he arranged it in less than a minute.

Jordan regarded himself in the looking glass. There were the same green eyes staring back at him, the same mole on his cheek, the same dimple in his chin. "This isn't going to work," he said.

Sarmillion zipped up his bag and put on a straw fedora hat. "It has to, old friend. It's all we've got."

Fourteen

CROSSING THE BALAKAN

ONLY NE'ER DO WELL WOULD GRANT Jordan, Sarmillion and Mars passage across the Balakan River. As they negotiated the dangerous bridge of uneven planks, anxious about it supporting their weight, Jordan could make out the stooped silhouette of a person standing on a distant bridge, watching them. Which bridge was he on? Jordan counted them. After Ne'er Do Well there was the glittering structure of Amethyst, but apparently no one at this hour possessed the tranquility required to use it. The person must have been standing on the next bridge, which was — but no, that wasn't right. It couldn't be.

Jordan's heart thudded above the loud rushing of the water. It was dark. He wasn't seeing clearly. He looked again. The silhouette was still there. A musty smell drifted towards him on the river breeze.

When Sarmillion murmured, "Oh, slag," Jordan's eyes widened, thinking the undercat knew, had deduced everything through his long straight whiskers. And then Jordan saw the knot of black-booted men waiting for them at the other end of the bridge.

"Get behind us," Mars whispered to Jordan. "And then use yer gift."

Jordan crouched to hide himself.

"Three Omarrians wish to pass into Cir," said one of the Landguards in a thick Brinnian accent and a mocking tone.

"On the contrary, feirhart," said Sarmillion, "on this lovely evening we are only two."

"I saw three," said another guard.

"Aye," said yet another. "So did I. He was wearing a headdress."

"Look for yerselves," said Mars.

As Mars and Sarmillion parted, Jordan held his breath, curled his fingers around the air, and heard the rush of flapping wings as he entered the now-familiar passage.

This time there were icy puddles of fetid water on the pathway. It was so dark he could scarcely see his hand when he held it to his face. He braced himself but the dark-robed man didn't appear. He exhaled a sigh of relief, and then he heard footsteps cracking the sheen of ice.

"Who is it?" Jordan called. "Who's there?"

"Little boy wearing too-big shoes," came a snide cackle, and Jordan felt a chill spread throughout his body. He had heard that before, but where?

"Little boy thinks he's a big man now."

"Who are you?" asked Jordan. "I can't see you. What do you want?"

Jordan was feeling dizzy. A stench like rotting meat hung in the frigid air. He teetered, and then remembered he was on a bridge. If he fell, there was bound to be trouble. He peered into the world he'd left behind. Sarmillion and Mars were gone, but the group of Landguards was now trying to come across.

"These damned Cirran bridges," said one. "I can't even get my foot on it. What's the point of building bridges you can't use? Answer me that."

"Clear off. Let me have a go."

Jordan watched them struggle at the bridge entrance. They looked ridiculous, hurling themselves into thin air and hitting an invisible wall.

The Landguards weren't giving up, and Jordan decided he had better concentrate on getting to Cir himself. There wasn't room to pass them safely, so he turned and headed back to the Omarrian riverbank. He would have to enter Cir by another bridge. He considered the row of structures that spanned the river. Unfortunately, even though he was not part of the world, it seemed he still had to use it to get to where he was going.

The Bridge of Resolve refused him, which was no surprise, but when Peril wouldn't allow him on, Jordan got nervous. He ran all the way back to the gleaming golden entrance of Amethyst, even though he knew he was too agitated for it to admit him. He gazed some distance away to the next bridge, the Bridge of No Return.

Jordan would sooner have swum across the Balakan, but the bridge emitted a force that pulled at him. He couldn't have gone another way if he'd tried. His feet moved him so quickly he tripped and almost fell, and soon he was facing the terrible black bridge and putting his foot upon it.

There was no one on the bridge, no one on his dim path. Whoever that silhouette had belonged to, he was gone now. And yet, Jordan felt him like icy breath against his cheek. As he crossed, something spoke to him. It was not the same voice he'd heard a moment ago; this sounded more like the man who called himself the Beggar King.

"You could be great, Jordan Elliott . . . if you dare. Are we so inclined, boy? Do we have the blood for it?"

The words burned in his throat like fireweed whiskey, they weakened his knees and made something inside him glow. "Come, come," said the voice and it drew him and he came towards it as if it were a fire and he wanted so badly to be warm, even if it might burn him. He knew that if he made it to the end of this bridge something would be decided, although he didn't understand what it was, and yet he couldn't do otherwise. "Are you worthy to cross here?" The world fell away, and he walked.

As he stumbled off the Cirran end, doubled over and breathing hard, he spied the hunchback and the undercat in the distance, their backs to him. Jordan ripped the air apart and reappeared in the world. In that instant Sarmillion turned, and Jordan could see everything on his face: the realization of which bridge he had taken, the confirmation that it had indeed been he who'd stood upon this bridge one year ago. And then, just as suddenly, Sarmillion resumed his conversation with Mars as if he'd seen nothing. As if he had decided to ignore the evidence before his own eyes.

They need me to disappear. It was the Loyalists' only chance of getting the information they so desperately wanted. The courier hawks had still not come back from Ut. It was possible the spies were dead. If the Loyalists couldn't send someone into the palace, their cause would be doomed.

He's using me. For a moment Jordan was insulted. Using people seemed to be the way of Omar. But Jordan wasn't Omarrian, and neither was Sarmillion. He wondered what Mars would have done if he'd seen Jordan coming off that bridge. How far would the gardener go to get what he wanted?

Jordan hurried away so that when Mars caught sight of him, he couldn't possibly know which bridge had granted Jordan passage.

"Great Light," cried Sarmillion, wheeling around a second time as if it were the first, and rushing towards him. "Where have you been?"

"Straighten up," said Mars. "Let me see yer face." He held Jordan away from him at arm's length. "You're as pale as the Cirran stone." Then he reached forward and plucked something from Jordan's headdress. "What's this?" He held up a small black feather.

Jordan shrugged. "Crow, I guess."

Mars brought it to his nose, then shook his head and let the feather fall to the ground. "Come," he said, wrapping an arm around Jordan and leading him off the riverbank footpath. "We'll get ye to safety. I'll make ye a draught of herbs. And then, feirhart, I think we'd best have a chat.

The cave entrance was so well hidden behind rocks and large shrubbery that even Mars passed it the first time and had to backtrack to find it. Once inside, he made Jordan lie on a bed of pillows while he set about lighting candles. They were in an elaborate cavern with blankets and carpets upon the ground and a grate in the centre for a cook fire. Herbs hung drying from hooks in the ceiling. One wall was lined with shelves, many of which held clay jars and boxes filled with Mars's plant remedies. One of the shelves even housed a row of parchments.

"Stolen property," said Mars with a lopsided grin, "thanks to our scribe."

"Former scribe," said Sarmillion, clearing his throat. "I took what I could in the early days, when a fellow could still sneak in through the back door."

"Now to work," said Mars and he opened several bottles and ground their ingredients with a mortar and pestle. In a few minutes he brought Jordan a cup full of cold brownish liquid.

"Drink," he ordered. It was gritty and tasted faintly of moss, but Jordan did as he was told and gradually some of his strength returned. For a long time Mars sat there watching him, saying nothing. His strong calloused hands rested in his lap. Jordan's breathing slowed and steadied. Having the gardener nearby was almost as peaceful as sitting in Somberholt Forest.

"'Tisn't a gift you've been given, I reckon," he said. "'Tis more like a curse. It does ye harm, Jordan. I don't know where or how ye've come upon this peculiar power but I fear for you if ye use it too often."

"What are you talking about?" said Jordan, but he knew only too well. Every time he disappeared he felt worse.

"Tell me what ye sees when ye goes away," said Mars. His eyes were trained on Jordan, who began to squirm.

Tell no one. "I don't know. It's dark, I don't see anything. Look, you're worried for nothing. When the guards showed up at the bridge, I panicked. I ran back to Omar and then lost my nerve. Ne'er Do Well wouldn't take me. I had to go all the way back to the Walkway to get here."

Sarmillion was nodding and saying, "That's a very long way."

Mars studied the far wall where the roots of a tree protruded from the dirt. "Can ye sees the world ye left behind? Can ye hear people talking?"

"Yes," said Jordan, "but ... at a distance. Almost like through a tunnel. It's not like hiding around a corner and listening in on a conversation. It's more like I'm in another place."

Mars gave him a grim frown. "You look as if ye've been with the spirits, child."

The dead side — that was what the beggar had called it. Surely that wasn't where Jordan had been. The fellow had just been trying to scare him. He exaggerated, like the way he called himself the Beggar King. It made everything sound impressive and ominous.

And yet Jordan had crossed the Bridge of No Return, and it had been both terrifying and glorious. Somehow he'd been deemed worthy. The secret glowed inside him.

"I'm tired," he said. And though he was wide awake, he made a show of flopping onto the pillows and shutting his eyes.

Fifteen

THE RIGHT THING

MARS WAS OBLIGED TO SHOW UP to work in the nearby
Balakan Gardens every morning. As for Jordan, he was under
strict orders to stay inside. He would not be dispatched on his
mission to the palace until the storm he'd created with his act of
rebellion had passed. Sarmillion feared it would be a long wait.

"Door to door searches," the undercat reported after his
second eavesdropping foray to the Cirran Common. "Rabellus
has even offered a reward to anyone who brings you to the
palace alive: a hefty velvet bag of gold groder. Less, if you're
dead."

"That's encouraging," said Jordan.

"Indeed. Considering we plan to send you there ourselves.
Oh, foolishness," Sarmillion cried, throwing up his arms. "Oh,
imprudence."

"It was your idea."

"True," said the undercat, but he was beginning to wonder if
he had gone too far. "You should see the likeness they've posted
of you. Hideous. I'd complain if they did that to me."

Sarmillion kept his tone light. In fact, for the past five days
the Landguards had been conducting a campaign of terror,
banging on doors at all hours, arresting anyone who showed the

slightest tendency towards defiance. At least the guards were ensuring that everyone found out about the boy's courageous act. They were, in their own way, spreading hope.

Every whispered word on the Common was about Jordan and the flowers he'd left at the holy tree. Arrabel's name, which had not been heard in months, was flying through the air like a Cirran dove that had been set free.

Now, all of this was interesting and important, but it was not what was keeping Sarmillion awake at night. Sarmillion's mind was fixated on the idea that the brass door could be his path to redemption.

Using the undermagic might be the Cirrans' only hope of defeating Rabellus and the Brinnians. There were fewer sources of good magic in the Holy City now that the Book of What Is had been burned, the holy tree compromised and so many of the Somberholt cedars felled and deer killed. The seers were complaining that their powers had weakened, and there was only so much sasapher Mars could filch. Even if Arrabel and Theophen returned, they would be no match for the hordes of Brinnian Landguards that now populated the Holy City. They would need the undermagic — regardless of its possible dangers — or else they would be Brinnians for life.

Sarmillion knew what he had to do: go back to his apartment to find his trusted prying bar. That sturdy tool had gotten him past many locked doors in its time. And seeing as how his apartment was in Omar, and Grizelda was in Omar, well . . .

The air was mild that night, and the moons a little more than half-full. Sarmillion dressed in his finest black velvet suit, complete with fedora. Mars had gone out, and Jordan lay napping on his bed of pillows. The undercat had just about reached the cavern door when there was rustling behind him.

"Where are you going?" Jordan asked.

Sarmillion took a deep breath. He considered confessing — everything. *It was I who gave Rabellus our precious Book of What Is, I who was the first to forsake our Cirran people. And I saw you standing at the Bridge of No Return and said nothing.*

Probably it was the right thing to do, to tell Jordan the truth about why he wanted him to go to the palace. But Sarmillion and the Right Thing had an understanding — it could show up as often as it liked, and he would continue to ignore it. He knew Jordan wouldn't understand the truth. No, Jordan would see him as a traitor.

So the undercat swallowed hard and said, "I'm off to see the little lady."

"Griswold?"

"Mice alive, boy, it's Grizelda. And yes, her, if you must know. Don't wait up."

Jordan smirked and Sarmillion remembered he wasn't a little boy anymore.

"Do you have a special someone?" he asked, grimacing at how old and fusty it made him sound. *Next we'll be exchanging love potion recipes.*

But Jordan was too busy blushing to notice. "I suppose so," he said.

"What's she like?" asked Sarmillion.

"She wears the veil," said Jordan, and Sarmillion groaned. *Another fellow who wants what he can't have.*

"You realize that's a lost cause, don't you?" said the undercat.

"Don't care," mumbled Jordan.

Sarmillion took his leave and slipped out as quickly and quietly as he could. Further along the footpath he spied Mars with his back to him, burning small piles of herbs. It sounded like he was chanting something, but Sarmillion didn't hang around to find out.

Crossing the Balakan was easy: once he'd smooth-talked the Landguards with mention of the famous Omarrian fish fry, Ne'er Do Well practically beckoned him along its uneven surface. And then, before he could fully prepare himself, he was back in the noisy colourful circus that was Omar, and he wondered, not for the first time, how he would ever adapt to living in the Holy City after having spent so much time here.

He decided upon a roundabout route to his apartment. He didn't fancy a run-in with Piccolo and anyway, the alleys and back passages of this part of town were as familiar to him as fond memories.

In the distance shone the torches of The Pit, and from the high-spirited chatter carrying across the river he realized it must be the weekend. He thought of Mojo and the cobra, and wondered if Grizelda was already there. Behind him three men were lighting a fire in a large metal bucket. At the dock were the sounds of a riverboat pulling in, the swish of oars in the water, the calls back and forth for lines to be thrown and tied off. Passengers began to disembark. They were wearing the long white robes and stifling headdresses and veils that were customary in Ut and left only the eyes exposed.

Sarmillion slunk closer to the boat and tried to listen in on conversations, but the Uttish dialect was guttural and made the words hard to decipher. Something wanted his attention here — the boat from Ut, the white clothing. Something bothered him about this scene.

He'd almost grasped it when a husky female voice said, "Hey, underkitty, what'cha doing slumming in these parts?"

Sarmillion wheeled around. "Good evening, Shasta." The underrat was alone, dressed for trouble in a short black skirt, high heels, and rhinestones everywhere. "I thought you creatures traveled in packs."

There was a glint in her eye that made Sarmillion feel like a hunk of cheese. "Marco's at the boats. He'll be back in a few minutes."

Sarmillion's eyebrows rose. "Marco doesn't seem the sailing type."

"Uttic knives," she said. "He gets 'em cheap from one of them oarsmen. Trades him for trinkets."

"Ah, well," he stammered, "I'd rather not be here when he comes back with his knives, so. . . . " Sarmillion was walking away when a hand clamped his shoulder.

"You'll stay away from that boy if ye know what's what," Shasta said gruffly. "He's trouble with bells on."

"What boy?" said Sarmillion, thankful for the dark that was an aid to liars in any land.

"The one what disappeared in Piccolo's place some days back. Oh yeah, I heard the talk about him. Word passes, underkitty. A kid don't just disappear into nothing like that. And I saw him on that bridge many twin moons ago, I know I did. It don't smell good, not at all."

The fur on the back of Sarmillion's neck bristled. He hadn't seen Jordan on the bridge, exactly, but he'd seen him get off. So what if he had crossed it? Sarmillion steadied himself. "We're not going to talk about the Beggar King again, are we?"

Shasta held her arms close as if she were suddenly cold. "Lower yer voice. He'll hear."

"Who?" Sarmillion didn't see anyone other than Uttic travelers and Omarrian shore men.

"Him!" she hissed. "Ye won't see him when he comes. They say that's his way."

"Where do you get your information, feirhaven?"

Shasta looked around before speaking. "People say he wanders at night. Appears out of nowhere. He carries little bottles in his coat, with things in 'em — fearsome things. A finger, a piece of a man's heart, I heard; sorcerer's things, for cursing. Old Willa says so, too. She says he's come back. She don't want to see, no sirree, but she sees it all the same. We can't choose the truth, can we, Sarmillion? No matter how much we'd like to."

The undercat wasn't so sure about that. The Truth was an awful lot like its good friend, the Right Thing. They could show up at the party with healthy snacks; it didn't mean you had to invite them in.

Shasta straightened and pasted a smile on her face. "Here comes Marco with his knives, in case yer wanting to know. Mind yer step, underkitty. The dark corners might seem empty, but the eye is a liar."

Sarmillion directed a nod towards the approaching leather-bound Marco and made his way swiftly out of the dockyard. The Pit was a five-minute walk away, and its flickering torchlight invited him in. But there was the Right Thing showing up at the wrong time, telling him (as it usually did) something he didn't want to hear. And that something was that maybe, just maybe, Shasta was right. Not only had Sarmillion seen Jordan too close to that bridge but he had also seen him disappear — twice. It might behoove him to find out what was behind all of this, no matter how much his educated and sensible self told him it was nonsense. This meant paying a visit to a certain door-maker who'd had his number back when he'd been a teenager.

And so, for once, he chose the Right Thing instead of the Desirable Thing, and headed down a lane that would take him through the blustering maze of the Omar Bazaar and eventually to Trades Alleyway.

The bazaar was nearly his undoing. Horse blinders would have been an asset, although they probably wouldn't have been adequate, since the place was a sensory extravaganza. He smelled freshly ground cinnamon, the typical scent of belt-dancers, and then he heard the tinkling of finger cymbals and felt a whoosh of soft-spun silk at his face. A crowd of men was already trailing the dancers, and Sarmillion's feet moved in their direction until — *Stop!*

Horse blinders wouldn't be enough. He'd need a mask to cover the mouth and nose. And gloves. And ear muffs. In the absence of any such aids to good sense, Sarmillion kept his head down and tried not to breathe until he reached his destination.

Trades Alleyway at night was like a ghost town. All the honest sounds of hard work had gone to sleep. Doors and courtyards were closed and locked. Only the odd window cast its yellow candlelit hue upon the cobblestones. Though Sarmillion knew where Willa's workshop was, he'd never been there. He'd avoided it the way a Cirran avoids a sorcerer, as if any proximity to it would set the bells ringing: stay away, danger! The closer he came to Willa's creaking wooden sign about doors that opened and shut, the dizzier he felt.

Finally he stood before the hundreds of tinkling glass chimes, clenched his whiskers, and knocked at the closed workshop door. And waited. No one answered. He knocked again, now noticing there wasn't a single lit candle in the windows. She was out. He let out the long breath he'd been holding, and began to relax. There, he'd done his best. His intentions were impeccable. But she wasn't at home, and that was that. He would go to The Pit after all and, for once, with a clear conscience.

And then a rumble of laughter erupted from within the workshop that nearly made him wet his pants. The door slid open and there stood Willa, older than he remembered but just as fearsome as ever. "I wondered when you'd be back," she said.

All along she'd known he was out there. She was waiting for him. Sarmillion backed away from the door.

"I'm sorry, feirhaven," he stammered, but Willa spat a stream of brown liquid that landed right next to his two-toned shoes.

"Never apologize!" she barked. "Come in, and have out with it."

Reluctantly Sarmillion entered the dark shed and the door slid shut behind him. Willa lit a small rusty lantern. The place was dusty and cobwebbed and smelled like the inside of a farmer's work glove. Casting around for somewhere clean to sit down, Sarmillion settled on a three-legged wooden footstool.

"It wobbles," he said as he balanced himself gingerly upon it.

"Ain't a footstool maker, now, am I? Doors is what I'm about," and she guffawed so loudly it sent a flock of night birds flapping away outside. Willa was wearing rubber boots and an overcoat that was too heavy for this time of year, though she didn't seem inclined to take it off. She turned over a large wooden bucket and sat on it spread-legged across from Sarmillion. There was no avoiding that familiar weathered face, that hair so wild it looked like it hadn't been brushed in years. She even smelled the same, of coriander and wood smoke.

"I was right about you, weren't I?" she said without smiling.

"More than you know," said Sarmillion.

"I know," she said, and Sarmillion felt the air go out of his lungs.

"How much?"

"All of it." She stared at his slender ringed hands, and he knew she was seeing the long feather pen he once wrote with, the bone-dry ground with scant patches of brown weed where once there had been a fertile garden of stories.

"It was I who gave the Brinnians our Book of What Is." His voice was so low even he could hardly hear it.

"Aye, it was." She was watching him. "Ye can't stand in the path of destiny."

No kidding. Once that mean woman fixed her eye on something she was like an Omarrian fishwife at a boot sale. Sarmillion sighed. "Can't you tell me what to do to make things right? Can't you see ahead for me?"

She scowled. "I'm not in that line of work no more, ye know that."

"Too true. You are a door-maker. And as it happens, I have a need to open a particular door that is locked."

Willa straightened. "What door?"

"Does it matter?"

"It might. A locked door would be needing a key, and I ain't in the business of keys."

"Let's just say in this instance a key would make no difference."

Willa's eyes narrowed. "That door was sealed because 'tis meant to stay closed."

"Are you not a patriot, feirhaven?"

"Patriotism ain't got nothin' to do with nothin'. You're wanting to use bad to make good. A cake don't come out so nice if ye make it with rotten eggs."

"Nonsense. This is a Loyalist venture. We shall use the undermagic for one thing only — to free the Cirran prisoners and rid our land of this Brinnian scourge forever. Then we close the brass door with the undermagic snug behind it, seal it up as good as new, and there's an end to it."

"Is that how ye think the world works, underkitty?"

"Why shouldn't it work that way?"

"Because the undermagic don't bend when ye bend it, or leastwise not in the direction yer expecting. Ye let it out and it will run from you and never come back. Ye'll be rid of the

Brinnians, maybe, but ye'll have more of a problem on yer hands than ye bargained for."

"That's your opinion, feirhaven."

"This ain't guesswork, beef-wit, 'tis a straight-up fact. You're naught but a dabbler in the magical world, and when it comes to sorcery, dabbling's the greatest menace there is."

Sarmillion glowered at her. She didn't think him up to the task. Well. "I suppose you're going to tell me some nonsense about the beggar who comes for his kingdom, are you?" Immediately Willa was on her feet, picking Sarmillion up beneath his padded shoulders and pushing him hard against the shed wall.

"Feirhaven! The suit! You'll ruin it."

"A bucket of steaming goat slag on yer damned suit! 'Tis a difficult task ye got ahead. How about ye start it by not being a fool? Open yer eyes, underkitty. You've got yourself a dangerous friend, or haven't ye noticed?"

Sarmillion was trying not to be a fool, but at these words his whiskers stood straight and his considerable eyebrows furrowed. "Whom do you mean?"

Willa rolled her grey eyes. "The boy ye hide. Have ye not seen what he can do?"

Sarmillion nodded. His voice had left him.

"Where do ye think such a gift comes from? From the Great Light? Not likely." She let go of him and backed away, but not far enough to make Sarmillion relax. "The Beggar King is back. He's roaming the streets and hunting for someone to help him. Run as fast as ye can in the other direction and take that slagging boy with ye, ye hear me? There's another way. The Great Light always shows ye a new way if ye just wait. A fool's road is wide and flat and makes for easy traveling, but that don't make it right."

She moved towards the large sliding workshop door, looking suddenly stooped and frail. "Stay away from that brass door. Tell yer Loyalist friends to find a different solution." And then she gripped the undercat hard by the arm. "Don't ye go sending that boy into the palace to feed yer guilty maw, neither. He's got no business being messed up in this and ye don't care for him anyhow."

"Now that's a dirty lie."

"Leave off, undercat!" she hollered. "You know very well what he's into. Ye saw him come off that bridge. Don't let him use his gift again, or there'll be trouble."

Sarmillion couldn't speak.

Willa released his arm. "About the parchments in yer drawer," she said almost softly. "Don't give up on 'em. Ye'll have that feather in yer hat one day." She slid the door open. "Go straight home. And mind ye stay out of trouble."

Sarmillion took his leave with whatever shreds of dignity remained to him. As soon as the door closed behind him he decided to obey Willa's orders at once. He would not involve Jordan in anything, not even a Loyalist fact-finding mission. He cared too much about the boy to put him at risk. And so, as she had directed, he went home — to his apartment, to find that prying bar.

Sixteen

GIVE AND TAKE

JUST LIKE THAT, THEY CALLED IT off. Sarmillion and Mars told Jordan they would not be requiring his services at the palace after all. So now he was hiding in the cave with absolutely nothing to do. The risk he'd taken in placing flowers at the holy tree had been meaningless. Jordan wore a path from one end of the cave to the other with his pacing.

He wrote, and rewrote, notes to Ophira, but they never came out quite right and he ended up tossing them all into the fire. If he could only sneak up to see her, just for a moment. He would have disappeared and slipped away, except for how it made him feel. Three times he had disappeared, and even now, after almost two weeks of hiding, he wasn't completely well. Just the thought of reaching into the air and pulling it back made him dizzy.

Yet at the same time he had an inexplicable urge to go back to that dark path. "You could be great." Had he really heard those words? Willa had mentioned the possibility of a great gift. Were the two connected? He had crossed the Bridge of No Return; he had been worthy — but of what?

One afternoon the courier hawk finally arrived from Ut. Mars burst into the cave with the bird on his arm, Sarmillion right behind him fussing about the droppings that might stain his bed roll.

"Unfasten the binding," Mars instructed. Jordan bent back the thin wire that held a small rolled parchment to the bird's leg. "Careful, now. Don't poke the creature."

Jordan tried to unroll the message but Mars's work-hardened hand was swift in taking it from him.

"Classified," he said. He moved towards a lantern in the corner of the cave and stood in his awkward hunch, eyes focused on the note.

"So?" cried Sarmillion.

"The prisoners are alive," grunted Mars. "That's one thing. Prison camp's five miles due northeast of Utberg, but our spies say 'tis well-hidden behind sand dunes. Took 'em a long while to find it." Then Mars said nothing. He didn't seem to be reading anymore.

"And?" said Jordan.

"That's it." He toed the dirt floor with his work boot.

"There's more, isn't there?" said Jordan.

"No, there ain't." Mars tucked the message into his overalls and exchanged a hard look with the undercat. Jordan suspected they would discuss it later when they thought he was asleep.

Sure enough, the hushed conversation came that night.

"Wanted to spare him some misery, is all," Mars said, and Jordan listened with one eye open just a crack. "Spies say there's been plenty of trouble down in that Uttic prison camp, Cirrans sabotaging all sorts of stuff, plans to escape and what-not. Rabellus has lost his patience. He's given the order: build gallows and hang the lot of them at next half-moons."

In one week. *Great Light.* Jordan clamped his mouth shut to keep from shouting. How would they ever save them?

Sarmillion was shifting from one foot to the other as if he had to go to the bathroom.

"What've ye got in yer pants, underkitty?"

"I shouldn't," he sputtered. "I mean, I'm not supposed to, but she didn't say anything about matters of life and death."

"Out with it!" hissed the gardener. "We ain't got all night."

"Oh, blast the Right Thing anyhow. We must go up to the palace and open that brass door. We've got the undermagic at our fingertips. What choice do we have but to use it?"

Mars's face darkened and his hands clenched. "I ain't got time for foolishness, underkitty. There's not a case so desperate in the world that ye need to rely on dark sorcery to help ye out."

"Well, Marsy, what do you propose we do? Send a contingent of untrained Cirran soldiers down to Ut with long sticks and bucket helmets? We don't have the men to fight an armed insurrection. We're not organized. We're a ragtag band of rebels with big hearts and no hope. And, I might add, no time. It takes ten days to sail to Ut; we have seven."

Jordan lay there with his eyes half-closed. The undermagic. He wasn't sure what exactly the undermagic was; the underside of magic, whatever that meant. Glorious darkness.

"The undermagic may be our only hope," Sarmillion said.

There was no mistaking Mars's quiet response for calm. "What if ye do open that brassed door? What if ye do find the undermagic? Ye got no idea what sort of power yer calling into this world. Wakin' the vultures; it could be worse by far than what we got with them Brinnians. Ye ever thought of that?"

Sarmillion ignored him. "The moons are new and we have nothing to lose. I'm going up there tomorrow night."

In the candlelight the enormous shadow of Mars's head shook in dissent. "I've been burning offerings to the Great Light for guidance."

"There's no time to waste, Marsy. Tomorrow night I'm going, with or without your help."

"Then more the fool are you," he snapped.

An air of foreboding hung about the three of them all the next day. Supper that evening was a simple meal of roasted eggplant and crusty bread. There was little conversation, and no laughter. Sarmillion dressed in black and waited grimly near the cave entrance for the sun to set.

"Off to see the little lady again?" Jordan couldn't help his sarcastic tone.

"Hmm?" said Sarmillion. "Oh, yes. Precisely."

"With a prying bar?"

"No, old friend. I borrowed the prying bar. I'm dropping it off on my way."

Mars was outside burning a pile of snakeweed and repeating the plea that was supposed to reverse any situation.

"A black suit?" Jordan whispered. "That's what you're counting on to hide you? Take me. I can disappear."

"What sort of silliness are you on about now, boy?"

"I could help you."

Sarmillion was about to say something when Mars popped his head in through the cave entrance and said, "I'll be needing a word with ye right about now." He turned to Jordan. "We're just going for a wander. You stay put. When we're back I'll make us some lemongrass tea."

"Sure," Jordan grumbled. He kicked at a pile of dry leaves at the cave entrance. It was his mother who was going to die — and yet they expected him to sit here like a good little boy and do nothing? Like slag. He'd crossed the Bridge of No Return. Had they? Greatness was waiting for him, but it wouldn't come knocking at the cave. It was up to him to go get it.

He rummaged through Sarmillion's bag and dressed in the darkest clothes he could find. There was no time to worry about the risk he was taking, no time to think about the Beggar King or the thin line between being a hero and a fool. He snuck out of the cave and into the fresh night air that he had not breathed in many, many days. The river water had that wonderful mud-brown smell to it that he hadn't realized he'd missed, and when he headed towards the cobbled roads of Cir, the whitewashed stone of its buildings glowed in the lamplight like a beacon.

Keeping to the shadows, dressed like a shadow himself, he proceeded quickly and noiselessly. It was late and the roads were quiet. He passed an enormous portrait of Rabellus with that devious sneer. Excitement rose inside him until he felt as if he were floating.

And then he saw his own painted face staring at him from a parchment affixed to the Porcelain Emporium. The likeness was not perfect, but it was close enough. A passerby might recognize him; a Landguard would, for sure. He pressed himself up against the nearest wall and waited for his pulse to slow down. There would be no rooftop jumping for him that night. The last thing he needed was to attract unwanted attention.

He was able to keep to the streets of the living world for the better part of an hour, and the shortcuts he chose had already brought him more than halfway up the mountain. All that time he kept his ears open for the familiar clop-clop of tall black boots.

When a strong arm clamped him around the neck and a deep voice said, "I got ye now, laddie," Jordan almost leapt out of his skin.

"Ye thought Piccolo wouldn't remember, eh? Ye thought Piccolo wouldn't come lookin' for ye? Well, ye thought wrong.

I'm going to collect my reward, and then I'm going to watch you hang from the holy tree alongside yer slubbering paps. So don't you go dying on me, scallywag. I want the full bag of groder for my troubles."

Jordan wriggled in an attempt to face him, but to no avail. "My father? What are you talking about?"

The bartender chuckled, his breath laced with enough garlic to wilt a hardy mellowreed. "You haven't heard the news? Seems someone told the authorities about a certain Jordan Elliott who did the dirty Loyalist deed up at the hanging tree, now. Seems someone mentioned his paps, a certain odious Elliott T. Elliott, who they might take instead, seeing as how they can't find his lump of a son. Seems someone even provided them with a home address. Now, I wonder who would do such a foul and underhanded thing."

Jordan shut his eyes and cursed Piccolo under his breath.

"I call this two for the price of one," the bartender said. "Ye both crossed me. Now ye both get what ye deserve."

"Where is my father?" Jordan moaned. "What have they done with him?"

"I reckon he's in prison. Maybe they'll give you a cell beside his if ye ask real nice." Piccolo found this so funny he began coughing and spat onto the road.

There was only one way out of this. But what if the Beggar King was there? Mars was right, this ability to disappear did seem more like a curse. But whatever it was, he needed it now, for there would be no bargaining with Piccolo.

"I believe I'll smoke me a pipe of dried dung while ye dangle next to yer pappy. Drink me a Bloody Billy to celebrate, I will. Pour me a mug full of . . . Hey!" Piccolo yelled, for his arms, which had been wrapped around his prisoner, were suddenly empty.

Piccolo sounded as if he were on a passing riverboat. Jordan was in the passageway now, and it was even blacker than before. It was thanks only to the dim and distant light from the world he'd left behind that he could see where he was going. Frost hardened the path and made it slippery. All around him came the call of, "Little boy wearing too-big shoes, little boy wearing too-big shoes."

Now Jordan remembered where he'd heard that phrase. It had been one of the grandmas — Mama Appollonia — who had uttered it. "Oh wretched gift." What had she seen with her glass eye? What did she know? Panic rose up his throat.

"Greetings," came a thin voice, and the Beggar King stood before him. He was now far more like a man than the shadow Jordan had first seen. His long hair was combed back, his face thin and bird-like, his black eyes as piercing and cold as precious stones. He was working at a small thin bone with his teeth.

"I used to eat sins," he said, "back when I was a poor beggar man in a faraway land and no one would invite me to supper, except to eat barley bread cursed with a dead man's misdeeds. I was starving, and folks were desperate for salvation. They told me the ritual wouldn't wear on me. They said I had the blood for it. Frankly, I prefer the Cirran songbirds. Tasty little creatures." He flicked the bone away. "Our project is progressing nicely, wouldn't you say?"

"What project?" said Jordan. "I'm not working with you."

"Of course you are," said the Beggar King. "You use my gift. You crossed my bridge. You came to me, Jordan Elliott. You might have changed your mind — I've given you ample opportunity. But it seems we are inclined to want, and now there is no going back. We have a deal. Pay up, carver's son." He smiled with yellow teeth that looked too small for his mouth, and too sharp to be human.

Jordan rubbed his arms to keep warm. "I've made no deal with you." But had he? He'd had the feeling that something had been sealed when he'd crossed the Bridge of No Return. What had he done?

The Beggar King studied him as if he were reading Jordan's thoughts.

Jordan hung his head. "You never said anything about paying you when you offered me this gift."

"You should know better. Sorcery does not come by grace. It is a transaction, ever and always. Give and take. I have given. Now it's your turn. Give me something, or I shall take back my gift. Something worthy, if you please. Something dear."

Jordan didn't have to peek into the world he'd left behind to know that Piccolo was still there. He could hear him swearing and spitting and stomping his feet. If the Beggar King took away his gift now, Jordan would hang and so would his father. Piccolo would make sure of that.

"How quiet we are, for a boy. Tell me, should I send you back?"

"Little boy wearing too-big shoes, little boy wearing too-big shoes," something cried into the darkness, and then came the whoosh of the wings of a thousand birds.

Jordan let out a long groan. "I have no coin to offer you, feirhart."

"But luckily it is not coin I desire. You go to the palace, do you not?"

He nodded.

"To open a certain door, I believe."

Jordan said nothing.

"Come, carving lad. We both know that's what you're going to do. The question is, do you have the blood for it? Eh? What do you figure?"

Jordan felt as if his blood had stopped flowing.

"What do we intend to do with an open door?"

Even if he'd had an answer, Jordan didn't think he was capable of speaking.

"Don't be a dullard, now. You've seen into that special room. What was inside?"

"Nothing. It was dark."

"Rubbish! You felt the power in that place. You know there's something in there. What is it?"

"I don't know."

"No," said the Beggar King, "but I do. And since we are working together, and we are both inclined to want, here is what you shall do. You will open the brass door, go in, and bring me what you find there. It will give you what you really want: glory." He paused. "You can do it, Jordan. There are only two others in this world who have the gift that you have. One is, shall we say, indisposed; both have refused me. But neither has a need as great as yours."

Jordan was silent. Two others who were like him?

"You know very well that you cannot do without the undermagic. Your Loyalist leader is a fool if he thinks he'll free the prisoners with nothing but a group of ploughboys. It will be precisely the thing to get them all killed. Unless the rebels have magic — strong magic — you won't free your mother. She will hang at next half-moons which is in — yes, in seven days. And my, it takes such a long time to travel to Utberg. How will you ever get there in time?"

Jordan stared at the ice-encrusted puddles at his feet.

"Bring me what's in that room," said the Beggar King, "and I will share the power of the undermagic with you. I will give you enough of it to free your prisoners. And then you'll be free of me. If you want to be, that is."

The Beggar King stepped back. "Go. Save the world. Be a hero. Glory will become you, I'm certain of it."

Jordan's head was aching and his legs were weak.

"Best be on your way while there's still time," the Beggar King said. And then he lowered his voice. "Heed me, Jordan Elliott, or you will regret it."

With that he was gone, and Jordan was alone on his long dark path on the underside of the world.

Seventeen

CARAMEL

IN HIS WEAKENED STATE, IT TOOK Jordan over an hour to reach
the plateau at the pinnacle of the Holy City. He'd fled the dismal
passageway as soon as he could, but now that he'd reached the
heavily guarded palace he had to disappear again in order to
cross the courtyard unseen.

He paused at the entrance archway to the Meditary. At this
hour the temple was deserted, other than the guard who stood
a few feet away from him. Jordan held his forearms at face-level
and crossed them before the sullen man in a Cirran curse. Then
he took off his sandals. There was no cleansing water, though,
and as he began to say the prayer it felt so powerless, like so
many random words strung together, that he gave it up, put his
sandals back on and passed undetected beneath the archway.

Jordan rubbed his arms to keep warm. The silk shirt he'd
taken from Sarmillion was no help at all. The air, which was
already frigid in his dark, dank pathway, seemed even colder
in the Meditary. Without the kneeling carpets or the orange
glow of the firestone in the central font, the room felt forsaken.

Jordan tried to remember the way to the brass door, but it
had been over a year since he'd last been here and the palace was
a labyrinth of hallways and dead ends. Unless he could find the

kitchen, he was sure to get lost. He took a deep calming breath and entered a stone hallway lit sparingly by small torches. There were no guards in sight. Every single door down the long corridor looked identical.

He followed one hallway lined with statues of famous historical figures, then another with stained glass windows, and then he found himself facing a pair of elaborate gilt-edged doors. This was most certainly the wrong way. He was about to turn back when he heard a stern male voice.

"Put down that bowl and leave off with your battle talk. I have military advisers for that sort of thing — and none of them half as fair as you, lass."

"Forgive me, my lord," a girl replied. "I am a seer, and I've been called here to perform a service. My visions have been dire, but they do not come clearly yet. You must let me continue my scrying without interruption."

Was that Ophira? How could it be? "I am needed at night," she'd said. But for this? Ophira was working for the Brinnians? He couldn't believe it — and yet, what other explanation could there be?

"I can't see when you stand so close to me, my lord," Ophira said now. But who was she talking to? "And I don't have enough oil left in my bottle. I'll have to go to the potions room to prepare more."

The silver bottle — Jordan remembered it. The grandmas had sent Ophira into the palace the morning after the coup. Wait — the grandmas had sent her. She wasn't working for the Brinnians. No, Ophira and her grandmas must have begun the rebellion that very morning. He could almost hear Mama Manjuza say, "Here is our granddaughter, the most talented young seer in Cir." Ophira would have ensured that the Landguards didn't enjoy the benefit of accurate prophecy even once. She hadn't worn the saffron robes in public back then, but who knew what she'd been wearing in these hallways?

"Confound your oils and ointments!" bellowed the man. "Come sit on the bed next to me. I've a mind to find out how soft your skin is beneath that veil."

"But Emperor, I've had visions of anarchy. I've seen Brinnian arrows fly slant, and Cirran dogs let loose. I'm working to protect you. Let me see just a little farther, and then I'll sit as close as you like."

Jordan's hair stood on end. Emperor? Ophira was in there with Rabellus?

"You weary me with your blasted Cirran magic," the man said, and now Jordan remembered that voice, that sneer on his face when he'd addressed the crowd in the Meditary one year ago.

"You're a powerful man, Emperor. You wouldn't want to lose your position in the Holy City by disregarding my warnings, would you?" Her voice quivered and Jordan dug his nails into his forearm.

"Too true," Rabellus said. "Very well, then, go off and mix your silly potions. But tell me first, is your hair scented with caramel again tonight?"

"You shall know soon enough, my lord."

He would know? What was that supposed to mean? The double doors burst open and Ophira walked out. Jordan was still invisible. He stumbled after her down the darkened hallway for about a minute before she whispered, "I don't know where you are, Jordan, but come out. I can sense you in the air."

"You're playing a dangerous game," he hissed, as he fumbled his way back into the world and stood to face her.

Ophira pulled off her veil and stared at him. "Good grace, Jordan, you're a fright to look at."

The Beggar King

"Don't worry about me," he said. His hand shook as he held onto the stone wall, unsure if his legs would support him.

"You can disappear. How?" she asked. "How is that possible?"

"You know what he's after, don't you? How does he know you're fair? Have you taken off your veil for him?"

"I'm in control of it," she said.

"In control? What do you plan to do? Douse him with scrying oil?"

"It's not scrying oil," she said quietly. "It's a sleeping draught. He knows nothing about Cirran prophecy. I've convinced him he has to drink it before I can tell his future. And I add essence of pickering, which I need to go fetch from the kitchen right now, if you please."

Essence of pickering — it was a mouse poison. Diluted in a draught it would not be strong enough to cause instant death, but nor would it be noticed, and over time it could do its damage quite effectively.

Jordan shoved his hands into his pockets. "Sorry, Phi."

"What are you doing here? Where have you been? You're as pale as a spirit."

"I need to get back to that hallway. That door — the archives, I mean."

Her eyebrows rose. "Why?"

"I can't . . . there isn't time, Phi. Please."

"There's always time. Do you know where Arrabel's potions room is?" She gave him careful directions, and made him repeat them to her. "Wait for me there. I have to prepare more of the draught, and I want to talk to you."

He recited her directions as he made his way haltingly towards the legendary potions room, stopping every ten steps to rest against the wall. Finally he stood before a small white door. With some trepidation, he lifted the heavy latch and the

165

door creaked open. Inside, he pushed the door shut as quietly as he could.

Though the small space was filled with light, there wasn't a single window cut into the white stone walls and no candle had been lit. The hundreds of colourful long-necked bottles that lined the shelves cast the only light, eerie hues that made Jordan think of being underwater, a sunlit rainbow of blues and greens and reds. His icy hands tingled as the blood returned to them.

The bottles were humming like a swarm of bees. Even though they were stoppered, Jordan could smell ground cinnamon so strong it might set fire to the heart, and a sharp ginger that immediately conjured a vision of a copper-haired Omarrian palm-reader with rings on every finger. Bunches of herbs and flowers hung drying from the ceiling. In the centre of the room stood a long stone table, and the implements for chopping, boiling and grinding, all set in careful order. Jordan couldn't help but grin; Ophira had become a potion-maker, after all.

A few minutes later, the door to the potions room creaked open and she entered, carrying her slim silver bottle, which she placed upon the stone table. She lifted off her veil, took Jordan by the shoulders and fixed him with her weary eyes. "You have an uncommon gift which must have cost you dearly. I can see by your face that it's hurting you, and so it must, for it comes from the undermagic. Tell me everything, now, or I'll take you straight to my grandmothers and they'll know it right away."

Jordan sank to the floor and rested his head in his hands. "They're in Utberg, in a prison camp, and Rabellus plans to hang them all at next half-moons. Utberg, Phi! I have no choice."

"Calm down, Jordan. Speak slowly." She sat next to him. "What are you talking about?"

"My mother, Arrabel, everyone. I can save them. With the undermagic I can do it."

"The undermagic? Who told you such nonsense?"

"He did. He calls himself the Beggar King. He's the one who gave me my gift."

"Don't be ridiculous. There's no such person."

"There is, Phi," he said. "I've met him."

"You're beginning to sound like Willa. She used to say she'd met the Beggar King in the marketplace on a Merrin day in winter." And then in a more pensive tone, "She said she saw him disappear. But no one ever believed her. Not even her sisters took her seriously."

They sat listening to the low hum of the bottles. "Willa went so strange," Ophira continued. "Grandma Mopu said she changed almost overnight. Her mother took her to healers, fed her exotic potions, but nothing worked. They never found anything wrong with her. But it was after that she swore she'd never use magic again."

Her gaze drifted with the floating light. "Are you sure it was really him? Maybe it's just a small-time sorcerer having one over on you, or a — "

"It's him." Jordan said. "I didn't know, at first. And he didn't ask for any payment for the gift, then. I took it because I needed it. I was surrounded by Landguards. They would have caught me."

She caressed his face with her smooth palms. Then she pushed herself up and moved to the stone table. "You're weak. You should drink something."

She sorted through bottles and sniffed their contents. After choosing a variety of herbs, she ground them together, and as she moved deftly around the room she sang.

Gentle flows the lazy river,
oarsman rest your paddle here.

Weary, weary, arms a-quiver,
sleep until you're home, my dear.

Her voice was smooth and gentle, a balm to Jordan's shaken nerves. She lit a fire, and when it was hot she heated something liquid in a pan on the stove.

Jordan's eyes drifted shut. If he could have curled up in this room and slept for a week, still it wouldn't have been enough.

"Here," she said when the potion was ready. "Drink. It will give you strength."

Jordan took the goblet and swallowed the warm draught. It had the sharp flavour of pine sap.

Ophira waited until he had finished, and then she set the goblet upon the table and sat beside him again. "Now, what were you saying about using the undermagic?"

Jordan watched the splinters of dancing light refracted through the colourful potion bottles. "It's the only way to save my mother and the other prisoners. They're going to hang at half-moons. I have to go to the brass door. I have to get it."

"Says who?"

"The Beggar King!" he cried in exasperation.

"And what does he want you to do, exactly?"

"Bring him what's behind the door."

"But you can't do that. That would be disastrous."

"I have to do it."

She set her hands on her hips the way Mama Petsane would have done, and said, "You can't take him what's behind that brass door. It's the undermagic, Jordan. If he really is the Beggar King, he can't have it. Not even the high priestess could possess such treacherous power."

Jordan didn't answer. All he could think about was the message that had arrived by courier hawk. Time was running out.

Ophira smoothed and re-smoothed the fabric of her robes. "It will be the ruin of Katir-Cir. He'll wake the vultures. He'll destroy every good thing in this world."

Jordan scratched his head. "But the vultures aren't real." He thought of the glass chimes his father and so many other Cirrans hung outside their doors to ward them off, and the tiny vultures carved out of onyx you could buy at the Omar Bazaar. "It's all myth and decoration. It doesn't mean anything."

She gave him a withering look. "The vulture people are the guardians of the undermagic. Whatever you believe about any of this, the undermagic is real and it was banished from Katir-Cir for a good reason. It is powerful and dark and exceedingly risky."

"Good. That's what will save Arrabel, and my mother. Isn't it worth the risk?"

"Wrong means won't bring a right end, no matter what your intentions are."

"He says I can use the undermagic once, and then I'll be free of it."

"Jordan, he's lying. If you use that magic even once, you'll never be free of it. You can't just wash your hands of it. It leaves a stain."

But he already used it every time he disappeared. It wasn't harming anyone — or rather, no one except him. Ophira's drink had restored some of his strength. His hands had stopped shaking and he could stand if he had to.

"What do you suggest, then?" he asked. "What can I do?"

"I have to go back to Rabellus. I'll advise him not to hang the prisoners at half-moons. I'll predict something terrible. He listens to me, Jordan. He'll do what I say. And then once the sleeping draught takes effect, I'll leave." She took his hands in hers. Her hands were so warm. "Wait for me here. I won't be long. We'll get you out of the palace without you having to disappear. You cannot disappear anymore, Jordan. You can't go back to him."

"What if Rabellus doesn't listen to you? And how am I supposed to put the Beggar King off? Don't you think he'll know? I promised to pay him, Phi. He's not the sort to let you off with a smile and a handshake."

"We'll go see my grandmas — tonight. We'll tell them everything and ask for their advice. And when they tell us what to do, we'll do it. All right?"

"But I'll never make it out of the palace if I don't disappear. My likeness is everywhere. The Landguards will recognize me."

"Not if you're veiled." She looked thoughtful for a moment. "I keep several sets of saffron robes in the maids' chambers. Rabellus pesters the girls but he'll leave them alone if they're wearing the veil. I think he's a little afraid of it."

"He didn't seem scared to me," Jordan said.

"I'll bring up a set of robes. No one will know it's you."

No one except the Beggar King, thought Jordan.

Ophira rose and took up her silver bottle of poison. Jordan stood to face her, so close he could smell her hair — and it did smell of caramel.

"Promise me you won't be foolish, Jordan," she said, resting her cheek against his and speaking softly into his ear. "Promise to wait here for me."

"I will," said Jordan.

She found a blanket in one of the cupboards and covered him with it, and he fell immediately into a deep sleep.

Eighteen

PRY AND PRY AGAIN

THANK THE LIGHT FOR THE SCHOLAR *Mimosa and his failing eyesight*, thought Sarmillion. It didn't hurt that the Brinnians had given up guarding his apartment, either. Mimosa had been with healers when the coup had taken place, and when he'd returned to the palace the Brinnians hadn't known what to do with him. Was he a threat, or just an elderly nuisance? They'd allowed him to go back to his apartment, but for many months they watched it, as if he were under house arrest. Finally they realized the scholar was too old, too blind and too deaf to pose a danger to anyone, so they let him be. Thus did Sarmillion find himself tiptoeing once again through the sleeping man's darkened apartment, vowing to thank him with a bottle of well-aged mug-wine.

Carefully he opened Mimosa's door and peered into the palace hallway. His heart was beating so hard he was convinced the stone walls were reverberating with it. But there was no one out there, and he was fairly certain he wouldn't meet anyone at this end of the palace. The Brinnian Landguards didn't go in for scholarship. They preferred activities that made noise and involved some measure of violence. The armory was their favourite place; also the music room where the drums and oboes were kept. Even from this far away he could hear a ruckus taking place somewhere near the dining hall. Lucky. There would be enough Brinnian noise to cover any sound he made tonight.

He decided to run up to Master Balbadoris's study. He had to see it again, if only for a minute. Noiselessly he mounted the two flights of stairs and jiggled his fountain pen in Balbadoris's lock.

The room had not been cleaned since the Brinnians had raided it a year ago in search of the Book of What Is. Sarmillion sank to his knees and picked up an overturned ink bottle. The spilled ink had dried and hardened upon the carpet into black splatters. Everything around him was dusty and cobwebbed. He had never seen a lonelier room in his life. *I'm going to bring you back, old friend.*

Very well, then, he had delayed long enough. Despite Mars's tirade against the plan earlier that evening, it was time to set off for the brass door.

As he left his master's chambers, he tried not to think of the long darkened hallways that lay ahead of him, or of the spiders lurking at their edges. If anyone caught him, they would throw him into prison. He hadn't even a spare smoking jacket with him, or his dung pipe — plus he'd heard there were bugs in the cells, large hard-shelled beetles that were too big to kill just by stepping on them.

There were few torches lit along the hallways at this hour. The scant light made the shadows long, but Sarmillion was thankful for the darkness. Once he heard the sound of boots upon stone, but he was able to press himself into a doorway and — naturally — he'd worn black. The walls grew closer, the torches fewer, and Sarmillion swore he felt a tickle of spider legs on his calf, but he gripped his prying bar and carried on. Soon enough, a terrible little thought poked its head around the corner and stared at him: if it were just a matter of prying open that brass door, then why hadn't anyone done it before? There were, as far as he could tell, two answers to that question. One, they had tried, and it hadn't worked. Or two, no one would dare, because the risk was too great.

But of course, he hadn't tried yet. Sarmillion had honed certain skills over the past year, and he wasn't proud of them, but there was no denying them either. He'd never met a door he couldn't open, and he'd never yet been caught. He tightened his grip on the scratched metal bar and said, "We'll do what needs doing."

By the time Sarmillion reached the brass door, his hands were so slick with cold sweat that the prying bar almost clattered to the stone floor. The place shouted its emptiness — which was convenient, but also unnerving.

There were the runes engraved into brass. Sarmillion didn't need to reread them to recall what some wise person had written, but his fingertips passed across them all the same:

Beware this door, beware your soul! May this door never be opened, or the beggar shall be king. Think twice and thrice, for if it be opened, this door can never again be shut.

Ominous, to be sure, but Sarmillion reminded himself the warning had never been tested. It might be a whole lot of slag. In any case, he was opening this door for a just cause. That had to count for something. He picked up his prying bar, jammed it into the seam where brass met stone, and heaved.

The door didn't budge. He tried another angle, and yet another, but the brass door remained stubbornly and incontrovertibly sealed. He kicked it, and swore at it, and pried and pried again. Leaning against the stone wall to catch his breath, Sarmillion heard footsteps. He panicked, dropped the bar and scurried to hide in a nearby doorway.

He listened. This wasn't the heavy clopping of Landguard boots; someone else was here. Sarmillion's heart was making so much noise it was hard to hear. Mice alive, who else knew about this? Only Mars. But he was with Jordan, back at the cave. Or was he? Surely Mars hadn't changed his mind.

But perhaps the gardener didn't trust him. Would someone else show up and steal his redemption? *It's mine*, he thought. *It's mine and I want it.* Oh, unfairness. Oh, cruel timing.

As the footsteps drew closer, Sarmillion could hear two voices: one male, one female. He couldn't make out the words, but he could hear the anxiety in them. And then he spied them as they came near, their veils and long robes. Veils? But he'd heard a male voice. Men did not take the veil in Cir, even if their vocation forbid marriage. Who in the name of dried dung was hiding beneath that silky shroud? The two strangers stopped before the brass door, which was when Sarmillion realized he'd left his prying bar there.

One of the veils picked it up and then said, "Sarmillion. Come out. I know you're here."

Sarmillion's chest tightened. That was Jordan's voice! What was he doing here? But was he here? The undercat rubbed his eyes, and looked again. He had heard Jordan, he knew he had, so he crept up behind the saffron-robed creature and said, "Aren't you supposed to be in bed?"

The person wheeled around. "I don't always do what I'm supposed to," he said wryly.

It was Jordan — gone sideways. *It's not my fault.* Sarmillion had told Jordan to stay home. He couldn't help it if the boy wouldn't follow the rules.

"The prying bar didn't make it back to your friend's place, I see," said Jordan.

"Evidently not." Sarmillion put out his hand for it but Jordan made no move to give it back.

The other veiled intruder touched Jordan's arm and said, "We don't have time for this, Jordan. He'll never open the door with that thing anyhow."

This must have been the impossible girlfriend.

"I don't believe we've met," the undercat said to her. "Sarmillion here, former scribe to the scholar Balbadoris, currently residing in Omar and usually up to no good. Except for tonight."

"I am Ophira," she said, and offered her hand.

"The adopted daughter of the Seers of Cir," added Jordan.

Sarmillion muttered, "Sweet sasapher." The boy enjoyed a challenge.

The undercat regarded Jordan suspiciously. "Curious outfit you're wearing. If you don't mind my saying, it doesn't work for you." He scowled. "What sort of tomfoolery have you gotten yourself into now?"

"I'll explain later."

"Well then, pass me my prying bar and let's get down to business."

"I don't think so, Sarmillion."

"I thought you told me earlier tonight you could help."

"He can't help you with this, feirhart," said Ophira, which was when Sarmillion understood just how poorly the veil did its job. The longer you spoke to a woman who wore it, the more time you spent imagining what lay beneath it. What face might have been sculpted by that voice? What light in the eyes?

"I can," said Jordan, "but . . . "

"But you won't," said Ophira.

Sarmillion could sniff out weakness like a home-cooked meal. "We'd both be heroes, you know. Glory, girls, and groder. In whatever order you fancy."

"I know," said Jordan, "but . . . "

"We must help them," said Sarmillion. "Arrabel, your mother, Balbadoris. We could save them all. This is the only way." *Not true.* Willa had told him there was another way. But it seemed a poor way, a sitting-around-and-doing-nothing way, when it was action that was required.

Jordan was shifting his weight from one leg to the other as if visibly weighing his options. "But Ophira says . . . "

Sarmillion wagged a long ringed finger at him. "They'll say anything to get their way, Jordan. It's best you learned that early. Forgive me, feirhaven," he said to Ophira, "but it's true." He turned back to Jordan. "If you're not here to help, then what the deuce are you doing in this hallway? You haven't come this way by accident, I reckon."

"We're going to see the grandmas," said Ophira, "and this is the safest route out of the palace. We'll hear what they have to say about this brass door, and I can guarantee you they won't recommend that Jordan open it."

"I don't think I like your tone, Missy," said Sarmillion. "The undermagic will help bring back the high priestess and her people — including Jordan's mother, I might add. I don't frankly care what your grannies have to say about it. We must open it."

"We can't," said Jordan.

"Think about what you're saying. The prisoners are scheduled to hang in seven days."

"Phi took care of that." He looked at his veiled girlfriend who seemed suddenly to have transferred her attention to something at the other end of the hall. "Right, Phi? You told Rabellus not to do it. You said he would listen."

She gave a mumbled response that Sarmillion knew from years of experience with women meant she hadn't kept an important promise.

"What did you say?" asked Jordan.

"I said, he refused me."

"But you told me — "

"Would you have me compromise my honour, Jordan? I might have bought their freedom at that price, though I doubt it even then. His mind is made up. I'm sorry."

"You could have mentioned this before," he said.

"Well," said Sarmillion, clapping his hands, "there we are. Half-moons in seven days, Ut a ten-day boat ride away. What do you figure? Unless we have some kind of magic to help us bend time to get there, it's hopeless."

"The grandmas can help us," said Ophira, sounding less sure than before. "We have to go. I don't much like the idea of getting caught down here."

"Slim chance of that tonight," said Sarmillion. "Didn't you hear the party in the dining hall? We have plenty of time to sort this out. Now, I don't fancy dithering with a bunch of old ladies over something as important as this. Jordan, if you know something about opening this door, then tell me. Make your father proud."

There was silence, and then Jordan said, "They've taken him."

"What do you mean?" said Sarmillion. "Taken him where?"

"Prison."

Ophira was shocked. "How could they? What has he done?"

Jordan shook his head. "Nothing. It was Piccolo's doing," he said to Sarmillion. "They've taken him because they can't find me."

"Piccolo," Sarmillion said. "That rogue."

"Do you know where the prison is? I need to see my father. I said things to him that . . . " he faltered. "I never got the chance to apologize. If I'd known . . . "

"No, Jordan," Ophira said. "They don't let anyone visit the prison, not even in those robes. You'd have to disappear to get in, and that's the one thing you must not do."

Sarmillion's eyebrows rose. *Must not disappear?* "Right. What's really going on here?"

"He's watching," Jordan whispered hoarsely. "He knows we've come here. He's waiting for me. He wants me to bring him the undermagic."

"He? He who?"

"Come on, Sarmillion, you saw me walk off that bridge. You've seen me disappear. You know I wasn't born with this gift. And it was you who said it: a sorcerer would never give away such a gift for free. Well, you were right. Now he wants his payment, and if I don't open this door and bring him whatever's behind it, he'll come after me.".

"He wants you to open this door?" Sarmillion's question came out in a squeak. "The sorcerer you bought your gift from is the Beggar King?"

Jordan nodded.

His common sense was up in arms. "There's no such thing," it shouted. "He's just a metaphor." But Willa, too, believed it. So did Balbadoris. Hadn't one of his famous questions been about ridding the world of the Beggar King? Sarmillion couldn't even recall the answer because he'd always believed the question to be ridiculous.

"The Beggar King," he said. "King of the undermagic. And you figure hiding behind a veil will save you?"

"Now you understand why we're going to see the grandmas," said Ophira.

Sarmillion held his head in his hands and groaned. "Willa warned me you weren't supposed to come near this door. You, above all. She warned me, and I didn't listen."

"Do you think I want to open it for him?" said Jordan. "I want to save Arrabel, same as you. We just need to find another way. And the seers might be able to help us. They're our only hope. Work with us, Sarmillion. You're a palace scribe. You know the prayers and spells almost as well as Arrabel does. We'll need your help."

Sarmillion pressed a pointed tooth against his bottom lip as he considered this. "Three of us traveling together? I don't like it. We'd be better off splitting up."

"Fine," said Jordan.

"And I'll take that bar now, if you please," said Sarmillion, holding out his hand. "It has sentimental value." Jordan passed it to him.

"We'll meet up in the Alley of Seers, then," said Ophira, "at Mama Petsane's blue door."

They wished each other safe passage and Sarmillion scurried down the dark corridor before Jordan or his girlfriend could have any ideas about tagging along. He'd performed enough burglaries to know that working solo was the only way to go. As soon as you had to rely on someone else to keep quiet or not drop something, you had earned your leg irons.

He wasn't keen on a meeting with seven old ladies — or rather, seven minus Willa — especially not old ladies who could read your mind. He had too much classified information stored away in his. No, he didn't like this idea at all. Willa had known what he'd done from the second he'd arrived at her workshop. Though of course, she was the youngest of the sisters. With any luck, the others had already gone senile.

Nineteen

FOOLISHNESS AND JABBER-BLABBER

THE VEIL BROUGHT WITH IT A peculiar anonymity. Jordan felt as if he could get away with anything. It was easier to see through than he would have expected, though it was generously scented with a maid's cloying lavender perfume. He and Ophira stood before the library archives door.

"How can you stand this thing?" he said, tugging at the smooth fabric.

"It has its advantages," she said. "It makes Rabellus think twice — despite what you might believe." She tilted her head sideways. "You make a fine-looking girl, Jordan."

"Shut up." He rotated the door handle one way and then the other.

"It sticks," she said.

"No. It's locked. We'll have to find another way out."

Jordan tried to ignore the brass door nearby, though it glowed brightly in his peripheral vision. As they hurried back down the darkened corridors in search of a safe exit, they could hear shouting and the sound of a dish crashing to the floor. A Brinnian party.

"You'd better go on ahead," said Ophira. "I'll follow in a few minutes. Keep your head down and your mouth shut, and no matter what, do not disappear. You must promise me. Go to Mama Petsane directly. Don't try to go to the prison to see your father." She fixed her eyes upon his through their veils.

"I won't," said Jordan. She squeezed his hand, and he pivoted on his heel and set off in the other direction because it was the only way he could make himself let go.

Soon the halls grew lighter and the shouting and music louder. It took every bit of his self-control not to run. He thought of his father, sitting alone in a cell, probably cold and cramped and hungry. Rescuing him seemed as impossible as bringing home his mother from Southern Ut. *You could do it — if you used the undermagic.*

A Landguard was approaching. Jordan tensed, on the verge of panic, but the guard passed with nothing more than a small bow. Jordan almost laughed. He could get used to this sort of freedom. He entered the Meditary at the northern archway where another guard sat slumped in his chair, fast asleep.

As he made his way out of the temple, there was a rumble in the sky. Enormous thunderheads had appeared above the Holy City. Thunder clattered, and a bolt of lightning illuminated the night sky. A moment later, a driving rain began. The cobblestones grew so slick Jordan slipped several times on his way down the mountain and towards the Alley of Seers. Around every corner, in every darkened doorway, he feared only one thing — that *he* would be there. What could the Beggar King see from his darkened path? But Jordan knew the answer to that: he saw everything. He must know Jordan was planning to defy him.

The rain made the veil cling to his face. It was so uncomfortable and hard to see through now that it was wet, that he almost lifted it, but stopped himself. *He cannot find me. He must not.* Thunder roared, and lightning lit the whitewashed stone of the city with unnatural brightness. He was fifteen minutes away from the Alley of Seers — almost safe.

And then he rounded a corner and there stood Piccolo, huddled with two underrats in the doorway of a smoke shop.

"Oy!" called the one whom Jordan recognized as Jack-Jack. "Pretty lass. Come in out of the rain."

"You'll spoil yer swanky veil," said Piccolo with a leer. "Now wouldn't that be a shame. We'd have to peel it off ye to see what's underneath." The three of them whooped and guffawed.

Clearly not everyone respected Cirran tradition. Jordan kept walking, shoving his trembling mannish hands into the pockets of his robes.

"Lassie," called the leather-bound rat named Marco, "Come share a glass. We've got mug-wine aplenty, and a spare pipe of dried dung."

Jordan was about to shake his head when from somewhere behind him a man said, "Greetings."

His knees went weak with terror. *Don't turn around*, but he couldn't stop himself. There was the Beggar King wearing deep black robes. His long hair was wet with the rain, his skin pink, his lips a living red. Jordan was stunned. He couldn't move. *He knows*. He had to. A simple veil, saffron robes — how could these be enough to fool a sorcerer?

But the Beggar King merely smiled and said, "Forgive them their rudeness, feirhaven. They are not accustomed to dealing with ladies."

Jordan forced his head into a bow. *Go, now. Get away*. But he couldn't make his legs work.

"He looks like that Brinnian feller we was talking about before," Jack-Jack said. "Oy!" he called to the Beggar King. "Yer the one what sells them little boxes of salty nuts, eh? We could use a little box of salty nuts right about now, eh Marco? Eh?"

The Beggar King's eyes were trained on Jordan. "Might we have a word, feirhaven?"

Jordan looked up, his entire body quivering beneath Ophira's robes.

"I seek a boy by the name of Jordan Elliott."

"That rascal," Piccolo grumbled. "Ye won't be having him, not if I gets him first."

The Beggar King didn't take his eyes off Jordan. "Might you know where to find him?"

Jordan shook his head.

"Tell me, feirhaven, what is a shrouded lass doing out at this hour on such a stormy night?"

Jordan cleared his throat, trying to keep himself from speaking, when someone grabbed him by the arm.

"There you are, Claudelle," said Ophira. She faced the others. "Excuse my sister, she sleep-walks. I've been up and down the streets looking for her. I hope she hasn't caused you any concern."

"None at all, feirhaven," said the Beggar King. And then he said, so quietly Jordan was not even certain he heard it, "Heed me, friend, and soon, or I will carve you like one of your father's pieces of wood."

"I swear he's that merchant we was talking about," Jack-Jack was saying. "I fancy a little box of salty nuts, I do."

Ophira pulled Jordan around the corner. "Don't say a word," she murmured, "just keep moving."

Finally they reached the Alley of Seers and Sarmillion wasn't there.

Jordan stood before the bright blue door and cried, "Mama Petsane! Let us in."

"Shh," said Ophira. "She knows we're here. She'll come."

It felt like ages before the door finally opened. There stood round Mama Petsane in a long flowered night-dress, her cheeks reddened with anger at having been awoken, her jaw jutting out as second sight raced after first.

"Jordan Elliott," she said. "What in the name of the cedars do you be thinking, showing yourself here at two in the morning wearing those robes? Ach, Ophira, you're a drowned mess. Look at ye both. What you been up to?" And she grabbed each of them by the sleeve, hauled them inside, and sat them at the kitchen table.

Grabbing her long stew spoon and waving it in the air, she growled, "I smell mischief and it be a foul soup. Out with it, now. And take off those robes, Jordan, ye look like a damned fool."

He lifted the wet fabric off his face but Mama Petsane wasn't stopping for breath quite yet. She screeched at Ophira. "What're you thinking about, dressing him in saffron robes? Have ye lost your senses, girl?"

Ophira took off her veil. "He had to hide, Mama. I can explain."

Jordan held up one hand, which was still shaking. "Let me. I'm the one who got myself into this mess."

"Yeah, yeah, you're a fugitive. I seen the renderings. Damned Brinnians can't draw."

"Mama," Jordan said, holding an image of the Beggar King in his mind. "Can you not see it?"

"See what?" she shrieked. "All I see is a boy what thinks he's a girl."

"Him," said Jordan. "Can't you see him?"

"What's he on about now?" Mama Petsane asked Ophira.

The stairs creaked and Grandma Mopu appeared in a frayed brown housecoat. When she saw Jordan, she hooted. "My second sight must be failing me. I would never have predicted you taking the veil."

"This be no time for foolishness," Petsane snapped. "Explain yourselves." And the spoon came down on the table with a thunk that made both Jordan and Ophira jump.

"Tell her about the Beggar King," Ophira said. "Tell her what you told me."

"Phht!" said Mama Petsane. "Ain't no such person."

"He gave me a gift," said Jordan.

"Thank the Light someone did," said Mopu.

Petsane's face creased in suspicion. "What gift? What're you talking about?"

"Jordan can disappear," said Ophira. "I've seen him do it."

"Oh yeah?" said Petsane. "Show me."

"I can't," said Jordan.

"You wear yer lies like a coat that don't fit, boy. Talk to us straight."

"Mama, he's hiding from the Beggar King," said Ophira.

"What Beggar King?" said Mama Manjuza as she hobbled into the room, with Appollonia following close behind.

Appollonia said, "What's Jordan doing in those robes?"

"Ain't no such thing as the Beggar King," said Mama Petsane. "I heard all them stories a million times. 'Tis a sailing man's tale, nothing but foolishness and jabber-blabber. You telling me you can disappear? Do it, then."

"I can't," said Jordan. "He's waiting for me. He's asked for . . . payment." He hesitated, wondering how much he should reveal to the grandmas. He'd expected their anger, but he'd never anticipated that they wouldn't believe him.

"What kind of payment?" asked Manjuza, hunching over the worn wooden table and studying Jordan as if he had sprouted horns. "Does he take tomatoes? Let me talk to him. I'm good at bargaining."

Appollonia's rocker had been moved nearer to the woodstove. The old woman settled herself into it and creaked back and forth. Jordan addressed her. "Mama Appollonia, you told me. You said it on my birthday. 'Little boy in too-big shoes, he find his gift.' You said it was wretched, and you were right. You must remember."

"Ach, she don't see nothin' with that glass eye," said Mama Petsane, but Appollonia had gone quiet and thoughtful, and slowly the room settled until all you could hear was the chair rocking and her soft humming. She grabbed Jordan's hand and closed her eyes.

Mopu said, "Open the door. There's a wet undercat coming to see us."

"An undercat? Mind the silverware," warned Mama Petsane, moving stiffly to the door.

"Good evening, feirhaven," said Sarmillion. Jordan winced at the forced charm. It might fool Omarrian tavern folk but it wouldn't go far with the grandmas. Thank goodness he'd left his prying bar elsewhere.

"I should've known there'd be an undercat mixed up in this foolishness," said Mama Petsane, wielding her stew spoon like a weapon. "State yer business or be on yer way."

"It's all right, Mama," said Ophira. "We asked him to meet us here."

Sarmillion was a sorry sight as he entered the dimly lit kitchen, his black suit jacket dripping with rain, his fur disheveled. He removed his fedora, and water splashed from its brim onto the kitchen floor. Mama Petsane glared at him.

"My apologies," he stammered. "Didn't mean to interrupt your little soirée."

"I know you," said Grandma Mopu. "You were a palace scribe." The twinkle in her eye made Jordan nervous. Grandma Mopu was called the Monkey-Maker for a good reason. "What are you writing these days, undercat?"

"A one-way ticket to success, feirhaven," simpered Sarmillion.

"Is that what they call prison these days?" Mopu said. "Actually I think hanging's the punishment for your sort of crime."

Jordan's eyebrows rose. "Grandma Mopu," he said, "Sarmillion's a friend."

"A dangerous friend," she replied.

Ophira said to Mama Manjuza, "We need to speak to you about the undermagic."

"Here comes more jabber-blabber about yer Beggar King," said Mama Petsane.

"On the contrary," said Sarmillion. "Just last night I was down in Omar at Willa's workshop and she said the Beggar King was right here on the streets of — " He stopped mid-sentence. Every eye in the room was on him. Jordan gave a sharp shake of his head and Sarmillion said, "Oh, of course, well, I don't generally hold with anything Willa says. I mean, she says so much and means so little, isn't that so?"

"Yes," said Mama Petsane, "it is. Now here is what I'll say about yer beggar man. There was something fishy about Willa's illness when she was but a young woman, and the fishiest thing was how all the blame for whatever went wrong in her pointed little head landed square on the shoulders of a man who don't exist."

"Don't you get started on that old tale, now," said Mopu, rising to her full height. "Not even the healers could figure out what was truly the matter with Willa."

"But I'll tell ye something else," continued Mama Petsane, her stew spoon raised. "If our Willa says a beggar's coming to be king, you can count on one thing: ye won't be seeing any such person on these streets or any others — ever." Whack went the spoon onto the table and Jordan didn't need a translation, it meant 'end of discussion.'

Just then, Mama Appollonia shrieked, and her rocking chair moved so fast Jordan was afraid she might take flight. "He opened the door," she cried, her good eye closed. "He felt the undermagic," and her long gnarled index finger shot towards Jordan and poked him in the stomach. "He knows the man what lives half a life. He's made promises. He owes him." The rocker slowed down, and then she let out a long contented snore as if she'd simply been in the middle of a dream.

"Is this true?" asked Mama Manjuza.

Jordan let out a long breath. "That's what I've been trying to tell you."

"Tell us again," said Mopu. And Jordan did. He told them about the gift he'd accepted, the man who called himself the Beggar King, the brass door, and Rabellus's plans to hang the prisoners in seven days.

"We must stop him," Jordan said desperately. "But I can't see any way other than to use the undermagic."

"Horse manure!" said Mama Manjuza. She pointed her hairy chin at Sarmillion. "You a scribe, uh?"

"Yes, feirhaven."

"Then you must know yer Book of What Is like ye know the twin moons."

Mopu's face went wide and sunny as she said, "Oh, he knows it." And all four women stared at the undercat, and he backed away until he was in the corner of the room.

"Tell the truth," said Mopu, "or we'll curse your feather pens."

"All right!" he cried. "I'm guilty. I did it."

"Did what?" Jordan glanced at Ophira in confusion.

"I'm the one, I gave it to them. I mean, they knew I had the keys, they would have tortured me if I didn't give them up, and Willa knew, she knew I would do it even when I was fifteen, she said so but I didn't understand and maybe if I had — if ever a prophet could speak clearly in her blasted life — it might have stopped me. I mean, how was I to know?"

"Sarmillion — " Jordan interjected.

"And if it was foreordained," the undercat went on, "does that mean it was really my fault? Oh, confusion. Oh, poor judgment. I mean — "

"Sweet sasapher!" said Jordan. "What are you on about?"

The undercat stood before everyone and hung his head. "The Book of What Is — the book Rabellus burned. I was the one who gave him the keys to Arrabel's onyx chest." He let out a long sigh. "I wish I could say I'd done it for some higher purpose, but there was none. Those black-booted Landguards took me to Rabellus, and I was afraid. I gave in before they could even threaten to pull out my whiskers. I'm a coward. There it is. That's why I wanted to open the brass door and save Arrabel and the others — to redeem myself."

The room was quiet.

"Tell me I'm a blackguard, a traitor. I'm ready for it."

"How about you start on your redemption right now?" said Mopu.

"Yes, of course, I'll do anything, just say the word," rattled Sarmillion.

"Do you know any of the Prayers for Desperate Situations?"

"Feirhaven," he said, rubbing his jeweled hands together, "I know every one of those prayers by heart."

Mopu said to Ophira, "Fetch the scribe some parchment and ink. I believe he has a feather pen in his pocket, though it has not been used for writing in some time." As Ophira went to do her grandmother's bidding, Mopu faced Sarmillion. "For shame, using a pen to pick locks. Now, sit down and do the work that the Great Light made you for." She turned to her sisters and said, "So. What do you propose we do about a gathering?"

Petsane frowned. "Don't need one."

"Come, Sister, you know the power packed into such words when they're spoken by a full family gathering. We can't afford to be petty any longer. The lives of our Cirran folk are at stake — including the high priestess and Jordan's mother."

"All right, then," Petsane spat the words out. "Bintou and Cantare can be woken. That makes six. 'Phira will be the seventh."

"She don't qualify," said Manjuza.

Petsane scowled at her. "She be close enough."

"No," said Mopu. "We'll need Willa. Someone must go to Omar to fetch her."

Petsane put her hands on her hips. "I ain't inviting that harpy into this house."

"She's our sister," Mopu yelled.

"She don't even wear the saffron robes no more," said Petsane.

Appollonia's good eye and glass eye were pointing in opposite directions. "She knows what's what," she said with her glass eye. "She ruined my good shirt," she replied, her good eye wide with indignation. "Spilled jam all over the front of it!"

"That was fifty years ago," said Mopu. "We're supposed to see into the future, not wallow in the past."

"I tell you one thing I don't see," said Mama Petsane, but Ophira put a gentle hand upon her arm and asked if she would please make some of her famous billy grain biscuits to help everyone through the night.

"They're famous?" asked Petsane. "Who says?"

Manjuza nodded. "An old lady could use a cup of mellowreed tea to go with fresh biscuits," and she rose and followed Petsane to the stove.

Jordan came to sit at the wooden table where Sarmillion had begun his work. Ophira and Mopu joined them, while Appollonia rocked in the corner.

"What if these prayers don't work?" said Jordan. "People have been burning offerings and reciting incantations and it hasn't done a bit of good." He rested his head in his hands. "The trip to Ut is at least ten days by riverboat."

Sarmillion put down his pen. "There must be a faster way across that blasted land than downriver."

"The nomads are quick on horseback, but you can't trust them," said Mopu. "They're thieves and kidnappers."

"What if we rode down ourselves?" asked Jordan.

"Through the desert?" Mopu pressed her lips into a thin line. "You'd never make it. The windstorms down there are strong enough to bury this house in sand. They say a traveler unaccustomed to the landscape of Ut can go mad inside of a week. No, we must put our faith in the Great Light. Arrabel has always relied on the power of Light."

"Arrabel isn't here," said Jordan.

Manjuza and Petsane were arguing over how much shortening to use in the biscuits. Appollonia had fallen asleep, both eyes apparently appeased by the promise of food.

Mopu spoke quietly to Ophira. "Go now, while they're distracted. Leave by the roof. Run. Come back with Willa as fast as you can. I'll try to calm them down while you're gone."

"Fifty years of hatred hardens a heart into stone, Mama," said Ophira. She put on her veil and was rising from her chair just as Petsane wheeled around and said, "Where ye off to now?"

"You should rest, Jordan." Ophira kicked him under the table and he feigned a great yawn. "Can he lie down in the guest room, Mama?"

"Yeah, yeah, but we be waking him the minute we get this business sorted out. You ain't gonna weasel yer way out of this one, boy."

"Show him which room it is, 'Phira," said Grandma Mopu, "cuz I don't want him messing up mine."

Jordan followed Ophira up the stairs, tripping on his robe. Ophira led him to the guest room, which was dark and smelled of dried moss. She lit a candle and it sputtered and hissed.

"Do you want me to come with you?" he asked.

"No," she said. "I'm just going straight there and back."

He settled himself into a hammock and she knelt before him.

"You opened the brass door," she said. "Why didn't you tell me?"

"I thought you'd be angry."

"I could have helped you. Warned you, at least." She paused. "Did you look inside? Did you see anything?"

Glorious darkness. Jordan remembered the sound of wings, and a shudder passed through him.

"Arrabel told me once that it was the undermagic, right there," Ophira said, "and that if you looked, it would open something inside you that is very hard to close again."

Jordan picked at the hammock's rope weaving.

"I saw him there, on the street, Jordan. I heard what he said to you." She took his hands in hers. "You can't risk seeing him again."

"I know," he said. "Will you be all right? Do you think Willa will come back with you?"

"Yes, and yes," she said.

He leaned towards her and kissed her on her veiled lips.

She kept her head bowed a moment longer. "Rest," she said. "I'll be back in no time." And she slipped out the door and was gone.

Twenty

SHADOW UPON DARKNESS

"CARVER'S SON."

Jordan sat up and the candle in his room went out.

"Have they left you alone?"

There was no one else in the room. The bedroom was on the second floor, with only one window and no balcony. But someone was there. Or were they?

"They scribble and scratch on their parchments, Jordan. They think they're doing something useful with their busy work. Only you can do something useful. Do you not think it's time to act? Or will you sit here with your hands clasped and your blood ebbing — and do nothing?"

Jordan was on his feet now and at the window. There was no one. But on the street something moved, and he spied a dark shape stealing off into the night.

"Come, carver's son, the time is now. The wanting will not leave you. Wanting requires having. You can have. Get out of there now, while you can. Once they realize you're alone, they'll come for you. And then they won't leave your side for a second."

The storm had passed and the moons were out, mere slivers in the darkness — two sly eyes, one darker, a knowing wink.

"Half-moons rising," came a great call like that of a Heralder. It startled Jordan. Suddenly he could see the Cirran prisoners lined up on the sand awaiting their turn at the gallows, barefoot and thirsty and chained together so that a person knew by the tug on his leg when the one ahead of him had taken the rope and broken his neck. The desert sun baked the skin of the dead, which gave off a putrid stench. Jordan heard a loud buzz of flies. They were already thick on the bodies, clustering around the unseeing eyes. And in the sky, a shadow of crows circled.

"The magic of a thousand thousand years," said the voice. "You could save them, carver's son. How do you sit idle? Half-moons rising, boy. Best not to tarry."

A thousand thousand years. Mountains were a thousand thousand years old. So was the undermagic. It would have to be enough to save them. It was all he had.

Jordan put on his veil and took the small door that led out onto the roof. Hiking up his saffron robes, he leaped from one rooftop to the next, stole up staircases and climbed lattices, until he was standing beside the palace kitchen windows.

Two guards stood nearby, their backs to him. He slipped by them without any effort. The kitchen was deserted at this late hour, though the bakers would begin work before sun-up. He took the gloomy corridor at a run, breathing hard, not caring anymore who saw him. He caught the hem of his robes so often that he finally pulled them over his head and cast them off.

At last, there was the brass door glowing before him. He knelt and pressed his hands to it, and it warmed him, moving beneath his palms as if it were breathing. Resting his forehead against it, he closed his eyes and let the warmth flow through him, the wanting running in him now like a river. His fingers traced the runes engraved on the door, and he leaned away, for this time — somehow — he could read what they said. "Beware this door, beware your soul . . . "

"They'll say anything to get their way, Jordan," the voice drawled. "Anything." A click sounded, and the door fell open, and Jordan stepped inside.

This was darkness, glorious darkness, and there were no walls capable of containing it. Jordan stood in front of a stone table, upon which sat a large candle. He clasped it. How odd. It didn't flicker or hiss in the manner of regular candles, nor was there any melting wax.

"All that fuss, for just a candle," the emptiness said.

His skin crackled and his bones hummed, and the darkness bent the sounds around him until they broke into echoes.

"We'd both be heroes, you know." That sounded like the undercat.

"Sarmillion?" Jordan called.

A piece of parchment sat on the stone table, the paper so yellow and frail it looked like Time itself. Something was written upon it in the old tongue.

"Allow me," said the Beggar King, and in the darkness the words rang out: "You, light-bearer, shadow-caster, you bear the candle that wakes the dark side of the world."

A great rushing sound came at him, like the fluttering and screeching of enormous birds.

"I can't breathe," Jordan said in a gasp. He tried to drop the candle back on the table but the air was so heavy he couldn't move his arm or even open his hand.

And then the air opened like a ragged seam and he could smell the familiar dankness that told him he was no longer in the world of the living.

"Little boy wearing too-big shoes, little boy wearing too-big shoes." The chant rose all around him.

Twenty-One

A MERRIN DAY IN WINTER

SARMILLION SPREAD SEVERAL BLANK PARCHMENTS ACROSS the kitchen table and set up his ink bottle. He'd forgotten how many rituals he relied upon before beginning a project. Every one of them was critical. Everything had to be done just so or his thoughts would come out crooked. Methodically he blew upon each of his fingers.

"What you doing that for?" asked Manjuza.

"A little before-work ceremony," he said, fidgeting with his jacket collar. "It reminds my dear fingers to dance."

"Oh." Manjuza pulled out a chair and sat next to him. "I know a few of them desperate prayers myself," and she stretched out her large-veined, weathered hands and blew so hard upon them she coughed. "Fetch me a feather pen, Mopu." And while the biscuits baked, she set to work scratching out prayers beside the undercat.

Eventually Bintou and Cantare wandered downstairs, drawn by the smell of food. Bintou settled herself onto a divan and began to knit, while Cantare lit candles and sang. No one needed to explain to them what was going on. *How peculiar and convenient it must be to live with a family of prophets.*

Sarmillion and Manjuza had been working for close to an hour when the front door burst open and in came Ophira, breathing hard, with Willa right behind her. Willa in her stained overcoat and rubber boots, a wide-brimmed hat upon her head, her hair springing out from beneath the brim. She stood in the entrance like a stray dog unsure of its welcome.

Petsane was busy taking another tray of billy grain biscuits out of the oven, but the moment she saw Willa she set them down and blurted, "Oh, so ye've come here to tell us how you been right all these years and we're just a bunch of toadstools? Well, I ain't listening. And don't be asking me to say I'm sorry for the years gone by, cuz — "

"I come to help," Willa said. "Ye don't want my help? Fine, I'll leave."

"No!" cried Mopu. "Willa, you know how Petsane gets. Ignore her."

Willa shifted her feet in their big boots. When her eyes lit upon Sarmillion, she said, "You! I tell you what to do but ye don't listen, eh? Not much point asking for help if ye ain't prepared to do the things what'll help ye."

"You stained my good shirt!" Appollonia cried, her good eye open. Then it fell shut and the glass eye took over and she said, "Shut up! Here's the sister that knows what's what. Here's the one that helps."

"I always thought you'd be better off with two glass eyes, Polly," said Willa. She looked at Petsane. "Ye gonna let me stay or are ye shoving me off again?"

Petsane put her hands on her hips. "Ye can stay, for now. So long as ye don't spill nothing."

Willa removed her hat and hung it on a hook and Petsane curled her lip with distaste.

"I need ye all to sit down with yer mouths shut and yer ears wide," said Willa. "There's something I been wanting to say for a very long time, to every one of you."

As the women assembled themselves on various chairs and divans, Sarmillion tried to make himself small at the kitchen table. He did not want to be asked to leave. After years of being a scribe he could sense a good story shaping up — or a disaster, which amounted to the same thing — and he wasn't about to miss it.

Willa looked as if she wanted to hide behind her rumpled hair, but she planted herself in the centre of the large room and began to speak.

"On a Merrin day in winter was the first time I seen him disappear, but it weren't the first time I seen him. That day was long ago. I weren't much more than eighteen myself when I been out gathering mushrooms in the woods of Somberholt, like I often do. I walked a long time that day and then it got dark, and I got scared, because I couldn't find my way home.

"Soon enough I was hearing a noise — stone on stone, banging out a rhythm, and I ain't never heard such a thing before. It was late and I was confused and thinking it was the Trades Alleyway in Omar, or some such. To a young girl, confusion comes easy. To a girl who's lost, even more so. So I followed the sound, reckoning on help, till I came to a grotto. And there amongst the rocks sat a small man dressed in black who seemed neither spirit nor living. Long sharp nose made me think of a raven, a dark bird of wisdom and sorcery. Upon one rock he was banging another, over and over. He didn't see me. I don't reckon he saw much of anything.

"I started thinking maybe he's a time-keeper, cuz I heard stories about them, though I hadn't known them to live in the forest. And the banging kept on and on, loud and hard, so hard it made sparks.

"And then I saw the blackened place where he'd lit a fire, and scores of dead birds strung up from branches. And I could just see the sister moons up between the trees, the lighter and the darker, and he was staring up at them and I knew which one he was watching. "He's tryin' to wake the vultures," was what I was telling myself, "He's tryin' to wake those black-winged guardians of the undermagic," and oh how I wished for one of my sisters to be there with me because now I was petrified. And then he saw me, and he asked me to come to him. And I ran. I ran so fast, I didn't even care where, and finally I found my path, and I took it home. But I guess I wasn't fast enough. He came to me later, many years later, in the marketplace, on a Merrin day in winter."

Her voice became a low growl. "He told me he was the Beggar King and then he disappeared right before my eyes. Told me to tell you all about it, and so I did, I told it to my family because I trusted 'em and I knew they would help me if I were in trouble. But that's not what ye did. Ye called me crazy." Her bottom lip trembled and her eyes filled. "He figured it'd be like that, that there wouldn't be a soul in the world who'd believe what I said.

"It was the brass door he wanted. He knew I could open it if I wanted to. He offered me anything. Offered me the undermagic. Scared me half-silly, it did. But I wouldn't take nothing from him. I decided then and there, I wouldn't practice any magic, ever. Cuz I knew it wouldn't have taken much for him to get hold of me. One taste of that sort of power and yer done for.

"That was what ye called madness. That was what left me changed, what had Mumma dragging me off to healers and whatnot and them finding nothing wrong with me. You didn't listen," she said, pointing a finger at each of her sisters in turn.

"You didn't believe any of it. Left me to myself. Sent me yer damned fruit baskets. Blast ye all to the depths. And now he's come back and found himself another one, a willing one, one with more need of his gifts than I ever had."

"Oh wretched gift," moaned Appollonia.

Willa scratched her head and wood chips fell onto the floor. Petsane glared at her but Willa didn't pay her big sister any mind. "He wants his kingdom and he means to have it, no matter what the cost." She stopped and scanned the room as if something had suddenly occurred to her. "Where's the boy? Who's been set to watch over him?"

They all looked at one another.

"Blasted bells," she exclaimed. "No one's keeping an eye on him? Go and fetch him, 'Phira, right away. Ain't safe leaving him alone, not with that sorcerer roaming the streets."

Ophira took the stairs two at a time.

"He's gone," she hollered. She stood at the head of the staircase. "I left him in the guest room. He wasn't supposed to go anywhere. He promised me." And she covered her face and wept.

Willa fixed on Sarmillion. "Has the boy been up there tonight?"

"Where?" asked Sarmillion with an innocent pout.

"Ye know damned well where. The brass door. Has he been back since we spoke?"

"Well," said Sarmillion, "he might have passed it by. But I had nothing to do with it, I can assure you."

Willa stared at him until sweat formed on his brow. "I never met a more careless undercat in all my life."

"He didn't follow the rules," said Sarmillion. "It wasn't my fault."

"You encouraged him, didn't ye? Isn't that yer fault? Told him he needed the undermagic, that there was no other way — when I told ye there was."

"Yes, well, that might have been a small mistake on my part."

Petsane elbowed her way to the centre of the room, the stew spoon high. "What do ye mean by a small mistake, underkitty?"

"I told him," Willa said. "I warned him well, so don't blame me."

The undercat pressed a pointed tooth against his lip as Petsane stood next to her little sister and shook her head. "Ye can't trust them undercats for nothin'. I could have seen it coming. Now we're into it with both boots on."

"But I've almost finished writing out the prayers," said Sarmillion. No one seemed to be listening.

Ophira had found her way down the stairs and grasped Willa by the arm. "I can go after him. They let me into the palace without question. I know where he's gone. Maybe it's not too late."

Willa gently loosened her grip. "That ain't our way, dear 'Phira, to go running after things. A seer thinks things through, and then she sees. At least we got our gathering, and that's something."

"I've done a good job, remembered all the words and everything," said Sarmillion.

"How about ye do yer thinking with a billy grain biscuit?" Petsane said to Willa. And she went to the stove, cut a hot biscuit in half and buttered it, and brought it to her sister.

"Not all magic is the undermagic, Sister," said Petsane in a hushed tone. "We got good power at our fingertips, power we can use to help folk. You, too. Ye got to take back what ye were born with."

"I been so afraid of it," Willa said.

Petsane patted her gently on the back and said, "Foolishness, girl. You got a good heart. We all know that. Even if ye do wear them damned boots."

The two sisters studied each other openly now and Willa swallowed hard.

"Bring the candles over here, Cantare, and start singing," Petsane said. "We got a long night ahead."

Twenty-Two

JUST A CANDLE

WHEN JORDAN OPENED HIS EYES, HE was on the dirt path and the candle was no longer in his hand. He coughed and almost gagged. There was an intense smell of garbage, or maybe it was a decomposing animal, he couldn't be sure. As his eyes adjusted to the scant light, he could make out the black skeletons of bare trees. They lined either side of a track that was slippery with greasy-looking water.

"On your feet, boy. They're waiting. Quickly now. They've waited a thousand thousand years for this."

Jordan stood, and had to grab hold of the Beggar King's arm to keep from falling over. The older man laughed. "It's like high altitude," he said. "You'll grow accustomed to it. Before long, it will be the world you left behind that will sicken you."

Above them were no moons or stars, no light at all. Ahead lay darkness. The living world was far behind, like a dream Jordan had had but couldn't quite remember.

"Let go my arm, now. Stand on your own two feet and be a man. That's why you're here, isn't it, carver's son? You're a Loyalist. Buck up." He wrenched Jordan's hand away and Jordan stumbled to the side of the path and retched.

"You milksop! Are we going to flinch, then, when it comes down to it? You disappoint me, boy. You told me you had the blood for this. We'll make a man out of you before the night is done. Any wood can be turned if you push hard enough."

Jordan's feet seemed to know where they were going even while he didn't. Every step forward was frightening; every step blind, yet sure. He did not walk the path, yet it moved beneath his feet.

The darkness was now so thick it was a stifling blanket, but it brought no warmth. There was frost in the silent air and Jordan could see every puff of his breath.

Once when a horse had died at his Uncle Eli's farm, its death had somehow gone unnoticed, and flies had gathered and the crows came and the living horses stayed on the far side of the pasture. His father had warned him not to look but he had to, and there was a rancid stench of decay that had taken him days to wash out of his clothes. It had been there, too, on Jordan's sixteenth birthday when he'd placed sasapher flowers at the holy tree and said a prayer for a dead man whose eyes had been plucked by crows.

The Beggar King stopped. "Here is your Cirran mystery of death — not quite the way they teach it to you in school, eh boy? The truth is pitiless and it lasts forever."

Jordan's sandal-shod feet were sinking into freezing mud. He sensed a crowd nearby but it took his eyes a moment to make it out. At first he thought they were vultures, but then no, they were more like people, lined up single file. Soon he could make out bald red heads with a fringe of long hair, and on their backs beneath tattered black robes were bumps that might have been wings. And yet they were people: two arms, two legs, bare human feet. And each held an unlit candle.

"They've slept for an unconscionable long time," said the Beggar King. "The Great Light has not been merciful to these poor folk. Look how they're drawn to our steady light — like moths," and it was true, the vulture people drew ever closer and Jordan could smell oily feathers. Some of them reached out and touched him with sharp claw-like hands.

"They want life, Jordan. In exchange they will allow us a share in the undermagic, for they are its guardians. It's a fair bargain, wouldn't you say? They serve us, we serve them. You always serve something in life, isn't that so? Whom do you serve, carver's son?"

Jordan tilted his head in confusion.

"Watch. I shall light their candles and wake them. See if they do not give you the power you desire. Then you can decide how to answer my question."

One by one the vulture people came to the Beggar King and he lit their smaller candles with his bigger one until the entire place glowed with unmoving light. Jordan now saw that he was standing beside a river so wide he could scarcely make out the far shore. Objects floated in the water. He couldn't tell what they were until a bloated human head bobbed up and went under again. And then he knew — they had come to the River of the Dead.

A vulture person approached, holding an unlit candle towards him.

"I can't — I can't light it," he said.

"He's giving it to you," said the Beggar King. "It's the undermagic. It's your power. Take it. Go save your people while there's still time."

The candle shook so badly in Jordan's hand the Beggar King could not even light it.

"Not a man yet, I see," said the sorcerer, his small black eyes glowing in the candlelight. "Hold still." And he gripped Jordan's arm so tightly to steady it Jordan cried out in pain.

Once the candle was lit, Jordan's sickness abated immediately. He stood for a minute, while his lungs eased, and just breathed.

"What are you waiting for?" cried the Beggar King. "Move along. And keep that candle hidden in your pocket. Don't let anyone see it."

"But . . . "

"It won't burn you, carver's son. It's not that sort of light. Safe passage," he said with an odd smile, as Jordan returned to the world.

Twenty-Three

A Yellow Square of Cake

With the lit candle in his pocket, the world changed. Jordan could see the hard-shelled beetles that hid between the cracks of stone in the palace walls. He could hear Brinnian Landguards singing their drinking songs all the way over in the dining hall. He set off down the corridor at a run, reveling in the sweet effortless flight of his feet over the rough stone floor. Somehow he'd have to get out of the palace unseen. It wouldn't do any good if he were captured now, after all this. No sooner had Jordan formed the thought when before him appeared a door which opened onto a deserted courtyard.

"Command it, and it shall be done for you," said a voice inside him. Jordan laughed. *Very well. Take me to the Omar Bazaar.* And it happened, he was in Omar. The light from a still-open tavern formed a shimmering rectangle on the cobblestones.

"Great Light!" As soon as he spoke those words, his lungs felt tight and he gulped for air.

"Take me to Utberg," he sputtered. "Speed my journey and bend every natural law to get me there at once." In an instant, his feet were sinking into dry brown sand.

He took a minute to rest, doubled over in cramps. It felt as if he'd been squeezed through a small hole. He was standing in a bleak, barren landscape made of sand dunes and broken only by the occasional patch of rough yellow stubble that might once have been grass. Not a single tree could be seen in any direction. In the endless early-morning blue sky, not one bird.

"They say a traveler unaccustomed to the landscape of Ut can go mad inside of a week," Grandma Mopu had said, and now Jordan understood why.

"Utberg, I said," he spoke into the emptiness, but nothing happened. "The prison camp. Where are they keeping the Cirran prisoners?" Perhaps that was where he was, five miles northeast of Utberg. Now what? He chose a direction at random and set off with long, swift strides.

The furrows and stubble made him feel as if he were walking across the face of an old man. He scrambled up one dune, down another, as the sun rose higher and the heat grew more insistent. He learned to stay away from the yellow grass, for the snakes hid in there, and they were long and colourless and as silent as thoughts. Jordan's ears were alert to other movement too, for he remembered Grandma Mopu's warnings about the bands of nomadic thieves.

Finally he saw a familiar silhouette: one lone black tree, leafless and pressed against the sky as if branded into it, upon a hill that rose higher than the others. He increased his pace until he'd reached the top and leaned against the dead tree to catch his breath.

And there, stretched before him, was a substantial view of the landscape with the blue waters of the Octavian Ocean shining to the south. Sunlight gleamed off metal roofs at the shore. It was a town. He also saw a trail through the sand and dry grasses that seemed well traveled.

He picked his way down, while crows perched upon thorny bushes fixed him with their black beady eyes. After an hour's descent, he found himself on the outskirts of the town, where the clay houses had rounded roofs that didn't look strong enough to withstand a rainstorm, if ever it rained here. A street shimmered in the distance and Jordan could make out two Brinnian Landguards.

He reached the centre of town, which consisted of one dusty main street with a stone barrier on the ocean side and market stalls made of sheet metal along the other. It was a busy place, and every single person milling about was dressed in uniform. Jordan glanced at the clothes he'd borrowed from Sarmillion and realized he would have to change.

He closed his eyes, imagining himself into Brinnian black, and felt at once the transformation in the fabric. The uniform was hot and itchy against his skin. He sighed in relief, reached into the pocket of his trousers to make sure the candle was still there, and continued on his way.

The late morning heat shimmered off the metal market stalls and lifted a rusty blood-stench of raw meat to Jordan's nose. He sauntered along the street in an attempt at Brinnian bravado. At a nearby stall, two soldiers were fingering with their soiled hands the lightweight white fabric from which most Uttic clothing was made. An older woman in a white kerchief and long white robe who stood behind the table was watching them, her bright blue eyes glowing in a sun-beaten face. A couple of undernourished dogs sat behind her.

"You gonna buy or no?" Jordan heard her say.

The men chuckled.

"No buy, no touch!"

That only made them laugh harder.

She raised a long thin stick in warning and the dogs behind her backed away. As the guards leaned into each other, Jordan caught a glimpse behind them of a small child sitting on a wooden stool in the shade, wearing a loosened headdress and long white robes. The gentle dark eyes might have belonged to a boy, but only Uttic girls wore the tiny jewel pierced into the side of their nose. Hers was a ruby. But it was her hand that kept Jordan's attention. In her tiny dark-skinned hand she held a yellow square of cake with crimped edges. It was one of Tanny's sasapher cakes. He had to bite down on his lip to keep from crying out.

One of the soldiers took a corner of the white fabric for sale and used it to wipe his sweating face.

"Leave off, friend," Jordan snarled in his best attempt at a Brinnian accent.

Both guards glared at him. The woman lowered her stick.

"Fresh face," said one in a gust of mug-wine breath. "A young'un. You'll sing a different tune about these lowly folk before long, *friend.*"

Both men reeked as if they hadn't washed in a month, and one was now blowing snot from one of his nostrils onto the dusty ground near the clean white cloth. An image came to Jordan's mind of boils, red and oozing. The undermagic flowed through him with a jolt, jerking his arms up, and suddenly the two men screamed, clutched their faces, and ran off.

The Uttic merchant woman was staring at him, eyes wide with fear. Jordan turned back to speak to the child, but she was gone.

"Your little girl," he said to the woman. "Could you please tell me — "

"Leave this place," she hissed, and then said something in Uttish that Jordan could not understand.

"I won't hurt you," he said in a soothing tone. He took a step toward her and she moved back. "Please — that cake she was eating. Where did she get it?"

But the woman just stared at him, worrying the thin stick in both hands. Jordan was certain she understood what he was asking. His hands balled into fists. He could make her talk. It wouldn't take much — she was already afraid, and she'd seen what he could do. He was about to will it into being, but then he stopped himself. The woman was cowering behind the table in terror, holding one of the dogs against her while the other growled at Jordan from a corner of the stall.

No, he decided. He would find the child himself.

Beyond the market was a maze of narrow streets that were strewn with garbage and lined with small clay huts. The girl was nowhere to be seen. *Find her.* As he moved effortlessly down darkened alleyways he felt so light his feet skipped over the ground. He was almost disappointed when he came to a crumbling clay hovel and knew he had to stop.

A torn piece of coloured fabric served as a door. Pushing it aside he poked his head in. The little girl stood pressed against the skirts of a tall woman who had the same wide dark eyes. When the two of them saw Jordan's uniform they backed against the far wall of the room.

Jordan held up his hands to show they were empty. He took one tentative step forward. "I'm not a soldier. Here, take these." He drew from his belt both the dagger and the long black stick that were part of the Brinnian attire, and laid them on the floor.

"Nothing good comes from those uniforms," said the woman in a thick Uttish accent. "Speak your business and then leave."

Jordan bowed and said, "Your little girl was eating a cake today at the market. It was a special type of cake that I know is not native to Ut."

"What do you know about our country?"

"Very little, feirhaven, but I know about this cake. It comes from my land."

"Oh?" the woman said flatly. "And where might that be?"

"The Holy City of Cir," said Jordan, and he saw the woman's shoulders relax slightly. "My mother is a baker. She was taken prisoner one year ago with many others from my land. The Brinnians brought them here. I've come to free them."

She studied Jordan. "Your mother is Mistress Tanny."

At the sound of her name Jordan sank to his knees and covered his face with his hands. He couldn't speak. He felt a rough hand touch his, and he let his own hands drop and looked up.

"You've seen her?" he asked.

"My daughter and I go to the camp to shine the boots of the Brinnian guards." The woman frowned with distaste. "It's a poor job but we are poor folk and it is how we live. They are pigs, those men. They . . . " but she didn't finish her sentence. "One morning my daughter wandered into the kitchen and there was Mistress Tanny. They have her cooking for the Brinnians. I don't believe they care if the prisoners starve, but the guards must eat. Of course she only agreed to cook for them if she could also prepare meals for her own people. That morning when my daughter saw her, she gave her one of the small lemon cakes she was making. She's been giving them to her ever since."

"Not lemon," said Jordan. "The cakes are made with sasapher. I wonder where she got it."

"She has a garden. It was one of her demands, if she was to work for them." The woman stroked her daughter's hair. "She is kind, your mother. She has often fed us when we were hungry. Here," and the woman took down something from one of the shelves and handed it to Jordan. "One of hers." It was a small square of sasapher cake.

Jordan took a bite. Here was that flavour with the mud on its feet and courage in its belly, and it wanted something from him, oh yes. He held the sweet piece of cake on his tongue before swallowing it.

"Could you lead me to her, please?"

The woman pushed the Brinnian weapons towards Jordan with her foot. "Come back tomorrow at sunrise. The midday sun is too hot for such a journey."

She took Jordan to another one-room home — her brother's — which was empty while he was away working on the fishing boats. There was dried fruit in the cupboard, and a hammock hung in one corner. Jordan knew he should rest but he couldn't sit still for long. His legs should have been tired but they ached to move and his chest felt broad under the black uniform. He was eager to use his new strength upon the people who had kept his mother captive for so long.

"I do hope the undermagic will come when you call for it," he heard the Beggar King's taunt. "The prisoners are unarmed and it will take nothing for the Landguards to subdue them. I doubt they'll mind hanging them a few days ahead of schedule."

"What?" Jordan gasped.

"The undermagic is not a mongrel mutt, friend; it doesn't always come when it's called. And it will want feeding. Mind you don't let it go hungry for long."

Feeding? Jordan's eyes flitted from the grimy jars sitting on one shelf to a long tattered coat hanging on a hook. He told himself this feeding issue was nothing to worry about, but his eyes wouldn't stay shut and the night dragged on.

When he rose at dawn, the woman was waiting for him.

"You must go in front of me," she said. "It's not right for an Uttic woman to lead a Landguard. They will know something's amiss. I'll whisper the directions from behind you. Also, you must walk the way they do, as if with every step you're killing something."

"All right," said Jordan. "Which way?"

"Straight ahead," she said, and he set off, forcing his feet down hard, an arrogant swagger in his hips. Behind him came the quiet instructions to turn here, follow this road, now head east. Before long they had left the town of Utberg and were back in the bleak dunes. Jordan could already feel the rising heat.

It wasn't long before the landscape was playing tricks on his eyes. Once he thought he saw a vulture person rise out of the sand, her robes long and black and oily. Once a raven followed him, and Jordan could feel its eyes pulling at the centre of his back, while the wanting swelled inside him. He heard the name of the Beggar King, heard it and then forgot it, and then heard it again.

The sun was high in the sky when Jordan finally asked, "Is it far?"

"Not much farther," the woman said, yet he could see no prison, no sign of life at all besides the sun-dried bones of animals in the sand. They crested a large dune and below it a valley came into view, a city of tents surrounded by barbed wire. In the distance he could see a group of people working, though he could not tell at what. He was sweating under his black uniform.

"Mind how you go," the woman said. "They've littered the sand with shards of glass. Many times we've cut ourselves."

When they arrived at the gate, the guard nodded to Jordan, then sniggered at the woman. "Mine could use a shine today, Missy," he said with a leer. As soon as they had passed, Jordan thought one word — sickness — and saw the guard stumble to the ground, his face almost green, his arms folded over his belly.

After they were out of earshot of the guard the woman said quietly, "The kitchen is to the right. It's the big tent, at the end." Jordan walked, and she kept talking. "Don't knock. None of them ever knocks. Just barge in and demand something to drink."

Jordan blanched at the powerful smell of urine. There were Landguards everywhere. "Sickness," he murmured as he passed them. Some doubled over in pain, but many simply continued without complaint. If his new powers failed him now, he'd be doomed. Every one of the Landguards was armed.

It will want feeding. "All right then," Jordan said to the air, "take what you want."

They approached the kitchen tent. Outside there were large clay ovens, as well as the impossible sasapher garden blooming yellow in a patch of fresh black soil. Jordan pushed at the canvas flap of door, clomped onto the rough wooden floor and shouted, "Give me a drink of water."

There were three women chopping vegetables at a rudimentary table, their backs to Jordan. He recognized his mother, her small plump body, long blonde hair pinned up. His knees threatened to give way, but then he saw a Brinnian guard sitting in the corner with his feet up on a table, watching, and he forced himself to stand straight.

One of the other women said in a snide tone, "This fellow would like a cup of water."

"Mind that smart mouth, girl," snapped the guard.

"Water!" Jordan barked. "Now!"

It was Tanny who leaned forward and pumped some rusty liquid into a rusty cup. Then she turned and came towards Jordan, her head down. Her freckled skin was burnt by the sun. Jordan willed himself not to move. She stood before him, looked up, gave the smallest cry, and dropped the cup.

"What's wrong with you, woman?" cried the guard, his boots landing on the floor with a thud as he pushed his chair away and stood. "Can't you keep hold of a damned cup?" He stomped over to Tanny with one arm raised as if he might strike her. Another woman was already hurrying to fill a second cup as Tanny knelt to wipe up the mess.

Instinctively Jordan bent towards his mother and helped mop up the water.

"In the name of all Brinnian lords, soldier, that's woman's work. Get up off your knees and show some respect for your regiment."

Jordan stood and glared. "I have no respect whatsoever for your regiment, soldier. I am Cirran born. My name is Jordan Elliott, the carver's son." A small shiver went through him. "I have come to free my people."

"I think not," said the guard, whipping the dagger from his belt. But just as quickly Jordan pointed a finger at the guard, and the man thrust his dagger into his own chest.

Twenty-Four

THE FULL PRICE

TANNY, STILL CROUCHED ON THE FLOOR, stared wide-eyed at her son. "What darkness have you brought to this place?"

Jordan smiled. "A power strong enough to free you all."

The Landguard's blood pooled on the wooden floor. Jordan helped his mother up and they held each other for a long moment. Then she pulled away and studied his face. "What have you brought, my son? Tell me. Your eyes — something isn't right."

"I've brought something for Arrabel. Don't worry. I'll give it to her, and she'll know what to do with it. I'll be fine."

"Tanny, let him go," said one of the other women.

"But you're alone," said Tanny. "How will you get to her?"

"He won't be alone," said the Uttic woman. "We've waited a long time for the chance to rid our country of this Brinnian plague. I passed the word last night to the men. They're preparing to storm the camp gates as we speak. They'll help you."

I won't need help. But Jordan kept that thought to himself.

"They're holding Arrabel apart from everyone, in a cell underground," Tanny explained quickly. "Leave from the back of the kitchen tent and then keep left. There are two guards posted outside her cell. Great Light, I don't know how you'll get by them." She placed a hand on Jordan's cheek. "You are changed. It's not just time that has touched you. There's something else."

"I'm fine." Jordan was bounding towards the back door when Tanny yelled, "Wait! Your uniform. The Cirrans won't know you. You'll be in danger."

"I'll change," said Jordan.

He turned to one of the other women. "Go spread the word to Theophen and the others, now, while surprise is still on our side."

The bright sun nearly blinded Jordan as he left the tent. The black Landguard uniform he wore drew in the stifling midday heat, and beads of sweat trickled down his temples. In his mind he chose a white suit of Uttic fabric and commanded the change, but the change did not come.

Jordan's eyes darted from the rows of tents to the barbed wire barriers farther away. Thanks to the sickness he'd inflicted on some of the guards, Uttic soldiers had already burst through the north and south gates of the camp and were felling Brinnians with their arrows. An arrow flew past Jordan's shoulder and he cursed. A second arrow grazed his leg.

He had no choice; he would have to disappear. He reached behind him and tugged at the air, taking himself out of the Uttic camp and back onto the dark path, but he found it was dark no longer. The vulture people and their candles milled everywhere around him, some alone and others clustered in small groups. Farther away on a platform near the riverbank sat the Beggar King. He was perched not on any simple chair but upon a golden throne, his eyes fixed on Jordan.

"It will want feeding, carver's son. It is inclined to want, just like you. Have you anything to give it?"

Jordan shouted, "Give it what it wants. I can't afford to be without it now."

"As you wish."

Jordan used his hidden path to find his way to Arrabel's tent. The world he'd left behind was now in chaos, with Brinnian guards running in every direction. Some languished near the gallows at one end of the camp, while others struggled to flee. Many were so sick with Jordan's curse they could do nothing to save themselves. Theophen's men had gathered planks, hammers and anything else they could use as weaponry. There were the hard, heavy sounds of wood making contact with human limbs. Jordan heard cries of pain and the sound of bodies hitting the ground. In the distance he could hear Theophen issuing commands.

When Jordan arrived at Arrabel's tent, there were two wooden chairs sitting at the entrance but no guards. He re-entered the world, snuck inside the tent where it was cool and smelled of damp sand, and nearly fell into an enormous hole in the ground.

"My lady?" he called down into the opening.

"Who's there?" Her voice was clear and strong.

"My lady, it's Jordan Elliott, Tanny's son. I've come to set you free." He spied a rope coiled in one corner of the tent. He fastened one end to a metal bar that must have been intended for that purpose, then dropped the rope into the dark hole and shimmied down.

It was so dark in the underground cell that, without thinking, Jordan pulled the candle from his pocket so that he could see. Arrabel was in a corner, her arms and legs fastened with ropes, her blue robes stained and torn, her long blonde hair in a tangle. She was staring at him with terror in her eyes.

"Don't worry," he said, fingering the black lapel of his uniform, "this is just a disguise."

"Where did you get that candle?" she asked. Her words were almost inaudible over the grunts and calls of battle that sounded above them. "Jordan, what have you done?"

"It was the only way, my lady. Nothing else would have saved you in time. Watch." And with his gaze he made the ropes fall away from her limbs.

In an instant she was on her feet. "Do not use that detestable power on me."

Jordan shoved the candle back into his pocket.

"Give it to me at once."

He took a step away from her. "No."

"Jordan. Give it to me."

"Listen to the battle above us. That's thanks to the undermagic. I was only able to get here before half-moons because of it. Don't you see? Nothing else would have worked."

"You don't know the price you've paid for it."

"I felt ill, at first. That was the price, and I was willing to pay it to save my people."

Arrabel stood rigidly straight. "Is that what you think?" She grasped his arm, covered his eyes with her hand and said, "Look!"

At first Jordan saw only darkness, but gradually it gave way to visions that faded in and out, one after the next: crows, as far as the eye could see, darkening the whitewashed stone of the Holy City; vulture people lurking in the shadows; yellow finches dropping from the sky. And the seven seers gathered together, chanting the prayers for desperate situations over the inert body of Ophira.

"It needed feeding," he heard the Beggar King say. "You told it to take what it wanted."

Jordan's knees gave way and he sank to the ground. "I didn't know," he cried.

"It was the Beggar King who came to you, was it not, Jordan?" asked Arrabel.

"Yes." His voice was small.

"He'll say anything to make you do his bidding. And he will never reveal the full price of what he provides until it's too late."

"Is it?" he rasped. "Is it too late?"

"I can't say. We'll have to return to the brass door. I cannot make promises. No one has ever brought the undermagic back to Katir-Cir. The runes upon the door itself say that once it has been opened, it can never be shut."

Arrabel's blue eyes were steely. "It was Sister Lucinda, our bright moon, who wrote those words, Jordan. Her warning was meant to be heeded. It took all of her power — her very life — to seal that door."

"But maybe we could use this," he held up the candle. "Couldn't it heal Ophira? It certainly brings sickness quickly enough." And he winced, for he had said more than he'd intended.

"The undermagic is what's making her sick, Jordan. It does not have the power to heal. This is a magic that brings curses, and twists the world into the shape of your desire. It chooses darkness. Only the power of the Great Light can heal." She put out her hand. "Give me the candle."

Jordan held the candle before him. He did not give it to her.

"We are all inclined to want, my friend. But the Great Light provides, if only you ask."

"Cirrans have been praying for a full year for you to come home, and nothing has happened."

"Are you so certain of that?"

In one movement she knocked the candle from his hand. "It can't touch my skin," she said. "I'll have to find something to contain it."

Jordan was doubled over, holding himself tight at the elbows. Every part of his body ached. Sweat formed on his face and he clenched his teeth.

"I know a potion that might help," she said. "It requires sasapher, which your mother has in her kitchen garden." She stroked his head. Her hand was cool against his face. "You know, I had such a terrible premonition about you on the day of the coup."

He had scarcely the energy to nod, but he remembered how she had looked at him that day so long ago, on his fifteenth birthday.

"That was the day I first saw him," he breathed.

And while the battle clashed above them he lay down in the sand and she began to sing, a soft sad tune that made Jordan think of falling leaves and a north breeze. He rested in the gentle light of her gaze.

Twenty-Five

THE SEVEN SEERS OF CIR

THE POSTERS AND ANNOUNCEMENTS WERE PLASTERED on walls all across the Holy City declaring that a Half-Moons Festival would be held in a few days at the palace. There would be feasting and mug-wine and contests, and sometime that afternoon Emperor Rabellus would make a grand statement. Sarmillion didn't know what this would entail, but he feared the worst. Jordan had been gone for four days now, disappeared from the guest room of the seers' house. And it was entirely his fault.

He'd encouraged the boy. Blast it anyway, he'd damn near begged him to open that brass door. "We'd both be heroes. Glory, girls and groder. It's the only way to save them."

He cringed at the memory. That night — the night it had all happened — Willa had stood there, her eyes blazing. "I knew ye never cared for the boy," she'd said. "Yer a selfish undercat, right down to the bone."

Sarmillion had left the Alley of Seers with his head down and his heart heavy, and had hidden in The Pit, drinking Bloody Billy's and listening to Binur charm the cobras. He'd burrowed into his grand apartment, and even went shopping — the known cure for every ill, though he'd come home empty-handed. The truth was, he did care about Jordan. That was the trouble.

This was no metaphor haunting the Holy City streets, he had to admit it now. All his scribing wisdom and fancy words and pretty little ideas — oh, fat-headedness, oh, conceit! There was evil in the murders of crows that blackened the sky. The nights bore the evidence of imbalance in the moons themselves, one now unmistakably darker than the other. Sarmillion had thought the stories of ghoulish vulture people appearing with candles were sheer nonsense, until last night when he'd seen one himself. He'd been a fool, a pretentious, hot-aired pumpkin head who had never truly believed in the undermagic until now that it prowled the city streets.

What could he do? He had to do something.

He spent that night at the Elliotts' empty house, setting lanterns in every window and hanging two more sets of glass chimes outside. He tried to coax green out of what had once been wild-evergreen ivy, but no amount of watering could undo this curse. The new growth of poisonous stinkweed choked even the stubborn peppermint plants.

The next morning, Sarmillion awoke at dawn — an hour he usually only saw if he'd happened to stay out all night — and headed out. The sun rose with a shadow across it, barely brightening the whitewashed Cirran stone.

"Be gone!" a butcher cried, as crows flew at the meat he was setting out at the market, but they paid him no heed.

Down the road Sarmillion spied a tall, bearded man dressed in brown robes, walking at a determined pace and talking to himself. The robes bespoke a tradesman, but there was no mistaking the clipped stride, the aristocratic tilt to his nose, and the way the fellow's expression soured as he passed the agricultural stalls. He acted as if he expected someone to throw flowers in his path or touch the hem of his garment. And why not? For this was none other than Emperor Rabellus himself. Emperor Rabellus, disguised as a commoner.

No jewels? No fanfare? *What in the name of dried dung is he up to?* There was only one way to find out. The undercat followed him.

Eventually it became clear where he was headed, to an alley where the doorways were closely set, and the air was already heavy with prophecy and the scent of frying fish. It was the Alley of Seers, Sarmillion's own destination.

There they were, all seven of them in veiled saffron, sitting on their front stoops. Mama Bintou held her knitting on her lap but she just stared straight ahead. Next to her sat Mama Cantare, humming a mournful tune. Appollonia's eyes were fluttering open and shut as she discussed something heatedly with Mopu the Monkey-Maker, while Willa and Petsane were engaged in a passionate argument about which healer should be summoned next. Manjuza sat with her veiled face to the darkened sky.

The undercat tucked himself into a shadowy corner and watched.

Emperor Rabellus strode right up to Manjuza and then stood there. Probably he was waiting for her to offer him one of the Brinnian greetings, "Glorious Rabellus," or, "Emperor be praised," but she kept gazing up into nothing as if it was by far the more interesting view.

"Feirhaven!" he barked.

"Eh?" She pressed a small bony hand to her face and peered at him as if he were a curious specimen of lizard. "Well, if it ain't our fine Mister Mucky-Muck, the man what pretend to be king, wearing his slumming clothes."

His face reddened.

"You come about the girl," said Mama Bintou, and her knitting needles clattered to the cobblestones. Rabellus's face contorted as he tried to come to terms with the fact that these women really could see what others could not.

"I have no idea what you're talking about," he said.

"Sure you don't," said Grandma Mopu.

He huffed and said, "I would prefer to have this discussion in private."

Manjuza waved away his concerns. "Our visions are like meadows to us, Mister Mucky-Muck. We all tramp about on them in our bare feet. Ye got no secrets here."

"Where is she?" he said huskily. "She was supposed to come to my chambers. She hasn't been there these several nights."

"Ophira has taken ill," said Grandma Mopu, "and has suffered many days of fever. You will not disturb her. In any case," her eyes hardened, "you don't seek her for her prophecies."

"You come about the girl," Grandma Bintou said, "when you ought to be coming about the undermagic."

Rabellus stiffened. "Don't speak of such absurdity around me," he said. "There is no magic, and there is no undermagic. But, as it so happens, I'm also here to inquire about this," and he waved his hand vaguely at the sky. "You are creating chaos."

"Us? We're the ones causing a rumpus in this city?" said Willa.

"This thing you've brought on, this is the work of charlatans. Seven crotchety con artists who use trickery to call birds and kill plants and make foolish peasant folk believe they see vultures that are part-human. Fah! You will cease and desist with this claptrap or I shall throw you in prison. You're spoiling the mood for my festivities."

Mopu chuckled. "Spoiling the mood, are we? Ah yes, I'd forgotten, everything in the Holy City is about you now. The universe revolves around the emperor. Careful, big man. This world will make a monkey of you yet."

"Guard your tongue, feirhaven," Rabellus growled. "I control this city now."

"Even the crows, Mister Mucky-Muck?" said Manjuza.

"The devious birds," said Willa. "Messengers of death. They come to Cantare."

"Praise the birds!" sang Cantare. Her short hair stood so rigidly on end it made the top of her veiled head prickly. Her singing was wretched but three crows responded all the same, flying over and landing on the steps next to her.

"But watch this," she said. "Praise Emperor Rabellus. Praise our Brinnian leader."

Rabellus cringed at her voice but seemed impressed when a hawk came out of nowhere to land at his feet. And then, as if it had been shot with an arrow, it slumped to the cobblestones in a dead heap.

Rabellus pressed his thin lips together. "So you do call the birds. Are you really such fools as to prove me right?"

Manjuza smiled. "Not fools, just old women who see farther than you. What do ye figure on a dead hawk at the feet of Mister Mucky-Muck, eh Petsane?"

The heavyset woman barely fit on her front steps and was already sweating despite the early hour. "Who can say?" she chortled.

Rabellus shifted his feet. "If you know something, you are obliged to tell me. I am the emperor."

"He is the emperor," said Mopu, puffing out her chest.

Petsane waved her meaty hand in the air. "We don't need to tell you nothing, big man."

"I got something to tell him," said Appollonia. Her glass eye shone so brilliantly even through the veil that Rabellus had to look away. "Doom, she travels by riverboat."

The other women grunted their agreement.

"What in the name of Brinnian good sense is that supposed to mean?" said Rabellus. "This is fraud. I ought to throw the lot of you in prison."

"Praise perplexity," sang Cantare. "Praise the mysteries of this world."

"He's gonna throw us where?" asked Willa.

"Prison," said Bintou.

"Ach," said Petsane. "I'd like to see him try."

Rabellus stomped one foot and said, "Where is the girl? I demand to see her."

"She is dying, big man," said Mopu. "And unless you leave this city with all of your black-booted toads and restore our high priestess to power, she will die."

"I'll send my finest physicians," he declared.

"Quacks, all of 'em," said Bintou.

"I will have her healed by sundown, and then you will resolve this bird matter at once. Tomorrow — " Rabellus cleared his throat, "I mean to make an announcement of great significance, and I want the mood to be right. This bedlam in the streets will make me seem like an addle-head."

"He's worried about what he looks like!" said Petsane. "Maybe ye should've thought of that before. Scores of Cirran folk hanging from our holy tree — ye should be ashamed."

"There's blood on yer hands," said Manjuza. "The vulture people will smell it before long. They'll come for you. They have a fondness for murderers."

"Mind you keep yer doors locked," growled Willa.

"Murder, murder," several of the women chanted. This had the general effect of waking up the neighbourhood. Doors opened, and people came out to the Alley of Seers in their nightclothes.

"Confound these fortune-tellers!" Rabellus sputtered, and then shouted at Manjuza, "Your people died because they couldn't follow the rules."

The prophetess stood, and though she was small and elderly she seemed anything but frail as she faced the emperor, hands balled into fists and pressed against her hips. "Don't you be treatin' us like buzzards and then expect our help, feirhart. If ye want to set things right, you'd best be willing to look the truth right in the eyeball. There's evil on our streets, a dark magic that's beyond any power we got. Our high priestess could help, but she ain't here, is she?"

"It's your spells and drivel that have done it," snapped Rabellus.

"You're the one in charge," said Bintou. "It must be your fault." And all seven women laughed.

"Your high priestess left this city by choice," he said, speaking each word with precision. "She abandoned her people. How can I be held responsible for her cowardice? She might have stayed, if she'd cared to."

"Foolishness and jabber-blabber," cried Mama Petsane. "Ye turned yer knives upon our lady and sent her to the desert to die."

The crowd moved closer. Everyone was listening.

Manjuza, who was still standing, now raised a finger and pointed it at Rabellus's chest. "You've trampled Arrabel's traditions into the dust. Bring back our priestess. Then maybe we'll talk about the undermagic."

Rabellus's eyes narrowed. "I could take you away right now for the way you're speaking to me."

Manjuza trained her small black eyes on his. "Go ahead."

Rabellus grabbed the seer's arm. There was a moment, a knife's edge of hesitation, when he might have shaken off this confrontation. He eyed the crowd of Cirrans.

"You're coming with me," he hissed at Manjuza.

Immediately the other grandmas rose and formed a circle around him. Petsane pulled a long wooden spoon from her saffron robes and waved it at Rabellus.

"You so spineless, you arresting old ladies now?" she said.

But Manjuza shook her head and said, "Sit, sit. Let destiny take its course."

Rabellus's face fell. "What do you mean by that?" He scanned the other women's faces. "What does she mean by that?"

"If only you knew, eh?" said Mopu.

Willa strode over to the emperor in her great galumphing rubber boots and growled, "Leave the Holy City now, while you still can."

Rabellus turned and walked away. He led the seer by one arm so gently you'd think he was helping her cross the street, while the eyes of the six other grandmas burned into his back. And the gossiping crowd didn't miss a thing.

When he judged that Rabellus and his captive were a safe distance away, Sarmillion crept out of his hiding place.

"Go away, underkitty!" hollered Mama Bintou. "We've had enough excitement for today."

"Our mighty emperor just took Manjuza away," said Grandma Mopu.

"I saw," said Sarmillion. "It was unjust. The people won't stand for it."

With one of her large hands, Mama Petsane clutched Sarmillion's arm. "Spread the word," she said. "Tell everyone what ye seen here this morning. And then tell them to come to that high-falutin' party Mister Emperor's got planned. Tell them that at half-moons, the hawk is gonna die."

"Okay, right away, whatever you say." Sarmillion clapped enthusiastically, hoping this would encourage the woman to let go of his arm, which she finally did.

"So?" she said. "What're ye still doing here? I tell you what to do. Go do it."

The undercat cleared his throat and pressed the toe of one shoe against the cobblestones.

"He's worried about the boy," said Mama Bintou. "But he doesn't want to tell you that on account of he feels guilty."

Sarmillion was about to explain that he wasn't selfish at all, merely short-sighted at times, and that he was ready to go anywhere and do anything to bring Jordan home. But then he caught sight of Petsane's stew spoon and felt Willa's grey eyes on his face, and it occurred to him that this knitting grandma had just read his mind. Appollonia's eyes were crossed and Mopu was bouncing from one foot to the other like she wanted to hang something upside-down, and the singing grandma was poking at the dead hawk like she might just make a sandwich out of it.

Bintou pointed a knitting needle at Sarmillion. "You got a jumbly mess in that head of yours," she said. "I can't make kitchen curtains out of it."

"I'm, I'm . . . " Sarmillion stammered. "Jordan's been gone for days. I'm sorry about what happened, I really am. Isn't there something I can do to help?"

"Ach, come back later," said Petsane. "You're getting on our nerves and we got a sick girl to tend to." And then came a piercing cry from behind one of the doors and three of the grandmas were up and inside even before the sound had stopped ringing in Sarmillion's ears.

Mopu had a grip on Sarmillion's bicep. "Come," she said. "Come see what that brass door has done to our girl."

Sarmillion entered a room of blinding lantern light. It had the claustrophobic smell of sickness to it. There was the impossible girlfriend lying on the divan, blankets pulled to her neck.

"She won't be kept in a darkened chamber. She insists on being down here in the light," said Bintou.

Sarmillion was horrified at the change in her. Her skin was white, her eyes ringed with dark circles, and she looked skinny and frail. Without warning she gave another shriek of, "No!" and then went so still Sarmillion feared she had passed on, right then and there.

"Get a cold compress!" Mopu commanded. When he came back from the kitchen with the cloth, his hands were shaking.

"We been speaking the prayers you wrote," said Bintou. "But we might already be too late. We're in great need of our high priestess."

"What can I do?" Sarmillion said, backing away from the grandmas.

It was Appollonia who answered from her rocker. With her good eye closed, and her glass eye shimmering in the light, she said, "Put the undercat in Manjuza's chair and make him write the spells for haste. Arrabel's coming, and she's with Jordan, but she ain't coming fast enough. He can say the spells with us in Manjuza's place. Bid him sit."

"We can't do that, Sister," said Bintou. "Our word isn't powerful enough to move the river, and he's not kin."

"Not kin, no," said Mopu, "but his bond with Jordan is strong."

"We must try," said Cantare. "If Polly says it's so, we must try."

Before anyone else could argue, parchment and pen were thrust at Sarmillion, and he was sitting at the kitchen table wracking his brain for the spells that might help. He scribbled them down, dipping his pen into the ink so rapidly he left sprays of black upon the parchment.

"Mind yer mess, now, underkitty or we won't be able to read nothing," said Willa.

When it was done, Sarmillion waved the parchment dry and tried to ignore the moans that were coming from the near-dead girl on the divan. The six remaining seers gathered around the battered wooden table. Sarmillion took Mama Petsane's sweaty hand in his left and endured Mopu's man-like grip on his right.

"You begin," said Bintou to the undercat. "Customary incantations, you know how it all goes. And don't be skimping out on even one word, and don't be saying any of them like you don't mean 'em. Understand?"

Sarmillion nodded, and began with the opening incantations to the Great Light, which he knew by heart. When he came to the spells for haste, he spoke each word with care.

"Precipitate, facilitate, nimble-footed, wings on wind," he said, thinking of Jordan and High Priestess Arrabel. Arrabel was coming, Appollonia had said, but how? On the river? Could these simple words really make it flow faster? Could they bring Jordan back, too?

The spells ended and they all fell silent, but no one let go of Sarmillion's hands. As his eyes closed, he swore he could feel something flow through all of these arms and clasped hands. It was a river and it was moving quickly.

Then Appollonia said, "Go to the place with the snakes. Be there tomorrow, at daybreak."

Petsane let go of Sarmillion's hand, and waved one arm in front of her. "Yeah, yeah. Go to Omar, then. Now, get out of our way so we can help our dear 'Phira."

"Omar?" he said with a squeak.

"Remember the riverboat," Appollonia said. "Go to the boat."

"Now, git, and spread the word about our Manjuza like Mama Petsane told you to, before we chase you off," said Grandma Mopu. "We've got curses in our pockets," and she jiggled her robes, which was enough to set Sarmillion scuttling on his way.

The next morning, when he saw a group of Uttic travelers disembarking from a riverboat in their ghostly white robes and headdresses, he knew he had seen this all before — even though it was only happening now. It was like someone had taken time and bent it backwards.

While the group climbing off the riverboat looked for all the world like tourists, Sarmillion recognized them. A year of harsh desert living had darkened their skin and traced its sharp fingers around their eyes. They wore their Uttic headdresses in the traditional fashion, covering everything except the eyes. No one would know them. The eye was indeed a liar, and today it would lie to everyone. But he knew who they were.

The grandmas had given him a job that for once he was qualified to do — spread gossip. He didn't much understand how this would help, but he'd have to trust them. He recognized the erect and proud bearing of his priestess, and hurried to meet her.

"My lady," he said softly, "the seers require your most urgent assistance."

She said nothing, but her eyes were fixed on a point on the far horizon and she strode quickly past him.

The undercat glimpsed the stout and stalwart shape of the true commander of the Landguards, Theophen. At last he spotted Jordan's green eyes and moved towards him, his heart swelling with gratitude and blissful relief.

Twenty-Six

THE NEW COMMANDER OF
THE BRINNIAN GUARD

CITIZENS FROM OMAR AND ACROSS THE Cirran provinces
flooded the palace courtyards. *Even a group from Ut has come*,
thought Jordan with a wry smile. Emperor Rabellus stood on
a platform observing the contests, surrounded by Brinnian
flags, his jeweled breastplate dull in the weak sunlight. This
was probably not the scene he would have chosen to survey.
The grassy courtyards which had once been brilliant green were
now yellowed and dry. Over the past few days the flowers and
shrubs on the palace grounds had shriveled and died. In their
place grew thorn bushes and clumps of poisonous mushrooms.
There was a persistent stinking haze that hung at the top of
the mountain, compounded by the afternoon's incessant heat.
Waves of crows darkened the bruise-coloured sky.

Nevertheless, the emperor tried to put on a good show.
Trumpets blasted fanfares. The scent of roasted deer competed
with the putrid smog, and merry cries came from the off-duty
Landguards who were already knee-deep in mug-wine. The
emperor looked gaunt and pale. Ophira's poison was taking its
toll — it might even have done the job, eventually, if she hadn't
fallen ill.

Rabellus planned to announce the deaths of Arrabel, Theophen and the others, deaths he'd had confirmed when a courier hawk had brought him a scroll that read, "It is done." A hawk sent to him by Theophen. In truth, not a single Brinnian remained alive in the prison camp near Utberg. And not a single Brinnian in the Holy City knew about it.

Jordan stood in the centre of the blazing courtyard. Everyone wandered restlessly from the various games to the banquet tables, and yet they all kept their eyes on the emperor. A group of his school friends swept past him and he almost called to them but stopped himself in time. He imagined himself picking up one of the bows, shooting an arrow into the haystack. Laughing along with the other boys.

Jordan's arms and legs were aching. He had not tried to disappear since he'd found Arrabel, but he heard an echo of wings in his ears and knew he could do it. The Beggar King was with him still.

"Are you all right?" his mother asked him from her place at his side. "Maybe we should move into the shade. You don't seem well."

He took her arm. Despite the sasapher potions Arrabel had prepared for him he was dizzy when he stood, dizzy when he lay down, nauseous almost all the time. Slowly and gingerly he walked with his mother to stand beneath one of the canvas awnings set up along the edges of the courtyard assembly.

"Try your luck with the hammer throw?" said a Landguard.

Jordan was about to say no, when an odd procession caught his eye and he saw him — Elliott T. Elliott. Tanny gasped and grabbed Jordan's arm, for her husband's hands were tied behind his back and he was being led across the grounds by two hooded Landguards. Behind them followed another pair of hooded guards leading Mama Manjuza, and behind them another with the chief healer, Malthazar. There were other prisoners as well but Jordan didn't recognize them.

"Where are they taking them?" Tanny said. "I can't even bear to look."

Jordan glanced towards the blackened hanging tree, which was thick with crows, but the guards weren't heading in that direction. They disappeared through a door, into the east wing of the palace.

"It won't happen," he said to his mother in a low voice.

The crowd of Cirrans on the palace grounds had grown larger. "They're here because of you, you know," Tanny said to Jordan.

"They're here because of Manjuza," he countered.

"No. Manjuza's arrest made them angry, but I've heard the talk. It was the flowers you left at the holy tree that gave everyone hope, when so many were on the point of giving up. What you did was very brave."

Jordan frowned. He wondered what his mother would say if she knew what he had brought to Arrabel, the candle she now carried concealed in the pocket of her Uttic robes. They would have to go back, he and Arrabel. Jordan would have to open the brass door one last time and return to the other side.

"And then we give back the candle, and what's done is done," Jordan had said, before they disembarked from the boat that had ferried them from Ut.

"No, Jordan," she had said. "You'll have to extinguish the bigger candle — the one you took from that room."

The candle that wakes the dark side of the world. "But he has it," Jordan had objected. "How will I ever get it from him?"

Ceremonial drums brought him back to the afternoon with a jolt. The trumpets blared and Emperor Rabellus approached the archery fields followed by a pair of Landguards who struggled to carry Theophen's enormous bow. The Uttic tourists standing as a group at one side of the assembly seemed to straighten at once, but Jordan hoped that only he had noticed.

"Rabellus won't really try to use that bow, will he?" Jordan said to his mother. "He'll make an ass of himself."

But no, the emperor left the bow in the archery fields and climbed the stairs to his platform to speak.

"Cirrans, and those of you from foreign lands, we have come together for these Brinnian contests in celebration. And what, pray, do we commemorate on this day of half-moons rising? Far away in the land of Ut, a group of people whom you know well has been living in hiding. A group whom you counted on, but who has let you down."

At this, the Cirran people mumbled and stirred, and the Landguards put their hands upon their daggers. Rabellus, however, was sailing his speech through boisterous winds, enjoying the rise and fall of his own voice.

"I bring you great tidings. The traitor Arrabel, her chicken-hearted commander Theophen, and all of the other cowardly palace folk who abandoned you are no more. Brinnian rule has once and for all embraced these lands. Your high priestess has breathed her last."

The cheers came only from the off-duty Landguards, most of whom were drunk. The Cirrans were dumbstruck.

"But we, too, shall have our hangings." He waved towards the palace's east wing and called, "Bring out the prisoners." Two hooded Landguards emerged, escorting Mama Manjuza. She shuffled and hobbled as if she were lame, and there was a collective gasp.

Elliott followed behind her, tall and proud and fearless, and Jordan lurched instinctively, but his mother held his arm and said, "Wait. Wait for the right moment."

He could stop everything. One move, one last disappearance, another candle — the vultures would give it to him, he was certain. And then he felt his mother's eyes on his face and he knew who they would strike in return.

"Trust in the power of the Great Light," Arrabel had said. But where was that power?

"We will all bear witness to the terrible fruits of rebellion," Rabellus declared. "But first, to the contests. Let us see who can wield Theophen's infamous bow, now that he and his men are dead. Whoever is capable of hitting the mark shall be named the new commander of my Brinnian guard. He shall win the right to preside with me over the executions. Come one and all; everyone can try his hand."

The target was set its customary distance away as an unruly line-up of Landguards formed. A couple of Circassic farmers shuffled forward but not a single Cirran joined the line. And no one in Uttic dress approached, either.

The shooting began. Many of the Landguards couldn't even nock the arrow. One of the farmers managed it, but then his arrow wobbled pathetically into a haystack. Jordan could hardly concentrate. He kept glancing at his father and wishing he would turn in his direction.

"Come now," said Rabellus. "Cirrans, Cirsinnians. What about you Uttic folk? Is there none among you willing to try your hand?"

One of the Uttic tourists stepped forth reluctantly.

"Here's an eager young buck," boomed Rabellus from his platform. "Have a go, Son. We'll drink a cup of mug-wine to your success."

Jordan could scarcely breathe. All the Uttic 'tourists' had weapons beneath their robes, except for Jordan and Arrabel. They would go directly to the palace as soon as the opportunity arose. But his father. . . . Jordan hadn't counted on that complication. He spied Arrabel on the outskirts of the crowd near the sun tower, a meeting place they had agreed upon earlier. He shook his head emphatically and hoped she saw, and understood, that he couldn't leave his father here to die.

The Uttic man picked up the bow as if it were a harp. Those who didn't know would have assumed he had never held a bow in his life. Those who did, knew it was music in his capable hands. He pretended to struggle with the arrow, taking so long to nock it that the crowd grumbled its impatience. And then, so quickly that no one even knew how it had happened, the Uttic man swiveled, took aim, and shot the arrow into the heart of Emperor Rabellus. Theophen threw off his headdress and strode towards the emperor. Rabellus looked up, his face smoothing from shock into recognition.

"You!" he cried, and then he collapsed and died.

Cirrans who had been milling about peacefully now had knives in their hands, their blades flashing as they pursued the open-mouthed Landguards.

"Go to him," Tanny urged. "You know what he's like. He won't fight."

But as Jordan moved towards his father, he saw Elliott give the Landguard next to him a sudden and debilitating kick, and then a Cirran man was beside him, freeing his arms. Elliott and the other man worked swiftly to unfasten the other prisoners' restraints.

"I have to go," Jordan said to his mother. "You shouldn't stay here. It won't be safe."

"But where are you going?" she said.

He kissed her cheek and ran towards Arrabel, who stood poised and still, her white Uttic robes shimmering with light.

Twenty-Seven

AN URGENT QUESTION

SARMILLION DODGED A CIRRAN IN ROSE-COLOURED potter's robes wrestling a Landguard to the ground. He was looking for his beloved Balbadoris.

"Master, is that you?" he called towards a stooped man dressed in white Uttic robes. "Master, we must get you out of harm's way."

"Nonsense," roared Balbadoris. "Give me my walking stick. I shall be known for generations to come as the scholar who fought off enemy soldiers with a limb of burnished oak. You shall write it all down and draw up the illustrations."

"Well then," said Sarmillion, "I'll stand and fight with you. Let's brandish our weaponry and have at it."

Except when Sarmillion reached into his pocket and pulled out a small rusty billy knife he didn't feel quite so brave. Quietly he stuffed it back in and stood next to Balbadoris as a burly, bearded Landguard ran towards them with a long sharp sword.

"That's it, Master, you can take him!" Sarmillion said. "Now, balance your weight on both feet. Jab him with your walking stick, feirhart. Knock the sword from his hand."

Balbadoris lifted his walking stick high in the air and brought it down on the Landguard's arm so hard the man fell in a heap. Sarmillion ran towards the downed soldier and kicked him in the stomach.

"There!" he cried. "How do you like that, you steaming pile of goat slag?"

A quick check to make sure he hadn't damaged his two-toned leather shoes, and then the undercat trotted along behind Balbadoris who was swinging his walking stick at the Landguards in their path. Some of the Uttic 'tourists' had scaled the palace walls and taken up sentry in the towers, where they were picking off Brinnians with their arrows. In one corner of the melee Sarmillion saw the saffron-robed seers conjuring fireballs and hurling them at the Brinnian platforms. Crows screamed into the sky, taking flight from the holy tree, which would not allow them to land on its branches anymore.

But as the battle roared on, something irked him. He couldn't put his finger on it. It was something to do with what Master Balbadoris had said about his walking stick. It made him think of those notorious questions the scholar used to ask him to keep him on his toes — Master Wickellhelm and his walking stick with the perching birds. And then for some reason his eye sought out Jordan. Where had the Elliott boy gone?

He spotted Jordan at the sun tower — with the high priestess herself. They were dodging the crowds in a rather shifty way, it now struck him, and heading towards the palace. The palace! Blast those two, they were going back to the brass door, Sarmillion was certain of it.

What in the name of the twelve bridges was Jordan up to? Surely he wasn't going back to see the Beggar King. He was under strict orders to stay away from that miscreant. But maybe — was it possible he was going to try to fight him? Balbadoris had just given a Brinnian Landguard a good rap across the shoulders and was standing there wearing a proud frown.

"Master," said Sarmillion, tugging on Balbadoris's robes as they both looked down at the unconscious brute at their feet. "How would one rid the world of the Beggar King if ever the circumstances arose?"

His bristly white eyebrows rose. "Do you dare to jest at a time like this?"

"No, Master. In fact, your answer to the question is rather urgently required."

"Sarmillion, how many times have I told you?"

"Several, as it turns out, but I should like to hear it once more."

"Very well, then, my undercat scribe, perhaps you should mark it in ink upon your robes." His voice rose dangerously. "You drown him in the River of the Dead!"

"That's it!" And without another word Sarmillion ran towards the palace, zigging and zagging around fallen Landguards and dead crows. He had to tell Jordan this important bit of information. But making his way through this mess of battle without getting himself killed was the first challenge; getting into the palace was the second. It was all taking an unconscionable long time.

Oh, sad endings. Oh, cruel irony. He'd finally gotten hold of something true and real and helpful, and now he would never reach his friend in time to tell him.

Twenty-Eight

DARKNESS AND LIGHT

THE ENTRANCE TO THE MEDITARY WAS still guarded.

"We can't enter the palace here," Jordan said. "Come with me," and he led Arrabel around to the low kitchen windows that had once served as his chief means of stealing sasapher cakes from his mother. But when they peered in through the unshuttered frames, they saw Brinnian cooks and scullery maids chopping carrots and shouting to each other about how many biscuits still needed to be baked. The battle outside had not reached them yet.

"Let me take you through my potions' room," Arrabel said.

"But there's no way in except through the palace."

"I'll find us another entry," and she took Jordan's hands in hers and began to sing a slow and tender song.

> Lay your cares upon my shoulder,
> soft the wind is blowing.
> When you rise, you will be bolder,
> soft the moons are glowing.

He thought of Ophira, who was gravely ill because of him.

"Jordan," said Arrabel. She had stopped singing. "You must empty your mind of worries or we won't be able to pass."

He shut his eyes and as she sang once again he tried to focus on her voice, which was like a river flowing past a sweet meadow of sasapher, past horses grazing peacefully in the early morning sun. When finally he opened his eyes, he stood before the blue and yellow potion bottles with their otherworldly glow.

"How did you . . . ?"

"There is a good and true magic in the Holy City too, remember?" Arrabel placed her hands around a tall blue bottle, lifted it to her lips, and drank from it. "Wisdom," she said, handing it to Jordan. "Drink. You, too, will need this."

Jordan took a sip. It was cold, and the liquid inside sweet but with a bitterness that made it hard to swallow.

"We must go," said Arrabel, and they left the potions room and crept towards the brass door. The halls were empty. As they passed a large window whose shutters hung off its hinges, they heard a man cry out and then saw a black-clad Landguard rise from the ground and charge at his Cirran attacker. They moved on reluctantly.

"Are there enough of us?" asked Jordan. "Do you think we'll overpower them?"

It was a moment before Arrabel looked at him. "We have surprise on our side, and that's one thing. Their leader is dead, and that's another. But then there is you, and that's something else altogether."

The halls grew narrower and darker, and only their footsteps and breathing sounded in the damp silence.

When at last they arrived at the door a chill broke out on Jordan's skin.

Arrabel stood very still. "The Beggar King came to me, too. When I was your age, and waiting for my gift. He sensed my connection to the Great Light long before I did. That is what's required, you know."

"What do you mean?"

"Anyone capable of great goodness is also capable of great evil. The Beggar King is no fool. You must not underestimate him. He sees farther and more sharply than most folk do."

"I don't have any connection like that to the Great Light."

"Are you certain of that, Jordan?"

He picked at the sheen of frost on the walls. "He tried to persuade you to come to him, then."

Arrabel nodded. "He wants a partner, the willing participation of a good and decent soul. That's what means everything to him, that you choose to follow him."

"But you didn't go," said Jordan.

"I came to this door, just like you did. But what I read upon it frightened me. Lucinda wrote those words a thousand thousand years ago. Never has there been a man or woman more infused with the Great Light than she. The light of her moon has guided me on many a dark night. She knew him — the Beggar King. She gave her life to warn folk away from him and his sorcery. How could I dismiss that?" She fixed Jordan with her severe blue eyes. "And he frightened me."

"What did he offer you?"

"He could have offered anything, I wouldn't have gone. But no one has faced him with a need as great as yours was." She bowed her head. "Do you understand what we're about to do?"

Jordan didn't reply. He removed his Uttic headdress and then took a deep breath.

Arrabel reached into the pocket of her robes and brought out a bundle of purple velvet cloth that she carefully placed between them on the stone floor. Jordan clenched his fists. Inside the cloth was his candle. He could see the glow at one end.

"Before you open this door, I must tell you," said Arrabel, "I am loathe to lead you back to this place. But the candle was given to you. You're the one who must return it."

"But the bigger candle, the one he holds — how will I ever get it from him?"

"You'll find a way. You must. Everything depends on it, Jordan." She grasped his arm and in a flash he saw Ophira, her pale face, her lips now tinged with blue. "Remember the Light — always."

Jordan's brow furrowed. "I don't know what you mean by that."

"You will." She held out a trembling hand toward the door. "Do it now — before I lose my nerve."

He fell to his knees and leaned against the brass door, dreading what was to come. And yet, when its power surged through his body he relaxed into it and the door clicked open beneath his weight.

Arrabel picked up the velvet bundle and gave it to him. She drew one last breath from the living side of the world and then took his arm, and he understood that she would not be able to come into the darkness unless he escorted her. They stood close together in the black space as Jordan reached into the air and drew it aside like a curtain. When the sound of wings filled the area around them, they stepped out of the world and onto the path that now glowed with the steady light of thousands of unearthly candles.

Jordan had not seen this many vulture people before. Where had they all come from? They stood shoulder to shoulder as far as he could see. Arrabel's grip tightened on his arm.

They set off on the long walk towards the River of the Dead where the Beggar King had established his throne. The mud was slick beneath their sandals, and the vultures along the path had begun to chant in an indecipherable babble.

"They are announcing our arrival to their king," Arrabel explained.

"Why must they carry candles?" Jordan asked.

"It's the only light they have left," said Arrabel. "That is the exchange they've made, their souls for power."

As they came to the river, Jordan couldn't help but remember what the Beggar King had said. "So this is the mystery of death," he murmured.

"Is that what you think, Jordan?" said Arrabel.

"You've come at last," cried the Beggar King. His hair was combed and neatly tied back, his robes a grand black velvet, his throne golden with a crown to match. And in his hand, the great candle that Jordan had won for him.

"I had hoped you would come back, carver's son. And I see you've brought a guest. A friend, as it were."

"I am no friend of yours," said Arrabel.

"No need to be rude, Priestess. We might have been better acquainted in your younger days if you had willed it, though I believe there will still be ample time for that. Now," said the Beggar King, "what are we inclined to want today? World peace? A cure for death by magic? It is fortuitous that you come to me, for that crack in the darkness you call your Great Light does not seem quite as forthcoming."

Jordan felt Arrabel tense beside him.

"Do you like my throne?" asked the Beggar King. "You could have one just like it. The Holy City could be yours, Jordan Elliott, if you wanted it. She won't have a choice in the matter," he flicked his chin towards Arrabel. "Cirrans would worship you. You could live forever. Glory at last, for the boy who pined for it."

"Look behind him," Arrabel said to Jordan. "See what he's paid for it."

There was a shadowy simpering figure lurking behind the Beggar King's throne. "Who is it?" Jordan asked.

"The soul of his best friend," she said. "Son of a butcher. A dabbler in the dark arts."

"He didn't have the blood for it," said the Beggar King. "But I do. And so do you, boy."

"The guilt weighs heavily upon the Beggar King," said Arrabel. "He'll never admit it, but nor will he ever be free of it."

Far, far away on the horizon Jordan saw a pencil-thin line of what might have been sunlight. "That's it?" he asked. "That's the light I'm supposed to remember?"

"Stand away," said Arrabel, with authority. She closed her eyes, put her arms straight out in front of her and spoke an incantation.

"Come out, conjuring of darkness. Flee savagery, and reveal the true beating heart of our world."

Jordan staggered, and had to catch himself to keep from falling. The darkness slid away, as if it were shedding its skin. The river became clear and shimmering blue, lined with rocks, and upon them were beautiful pink-shelled creatures, green barnacles, and yellow-headed snails. Through the water Jordan could see the tips of glorious flowers, their long white petals streaming past him.

The muddy ground upon which he stood was now a meadow of yellow sasapher flowers. Their rich lemon scent filled the air. He was enveloped in a gentle light.

Jordan was incapable of speech. Behind him were the vultures with their pitiful candles — such a paltry light it now seemed — and there was the Beggar King gloating on his throne.

"Listen," and Arrabel put her hands over his ears. Jordan could hear singing coming in waves and he recognized the voices of the Seven Seers of Cir — Manjuza's coming from the prison, and Arrabel's, too — and he saw Ophira lying upon the couch with the covers pulled to her chin, her body wrapped in a glowing light.

"The undermagic is not the only way, friend," said Arrabel. "In order for shadow to exist, there must first be light." She unfolded the velvet cloth and bid him to take the candle. "You must go to him." She embraced him quickly. "Remember the light," she whispered. And then she pushed him towards the Beggar King's throne.

"Carver's son!" cried the Beggar King. "You've come to kneel before the one you serve at last, eh? We've come to the nub of it, boy, haven't we? I told you. We all serve something. Whether you realize it or not, it hardly matters. We all make our choices."

"I haven't come to kneel," said Jordan. "I've come to return the candle that was given to me. And then I'll take back the one you hold."

The Beggar King laughed. "What do you fancy this is, boy, a library? Did you think you could give me the undermagic on loan? Are you a man? If so, you're a foolish one. But I'll teach you your place before long. I didn't choose you just to let you go."

Strong wet hands grabbed him and forced his arms behind his back. The candle he'd been holding fell to the ground. He gazed into the vacant eyes of the vultures, and his mouth went dry. A wild energy made his limbs jitter and there was that pulsing again in his chest. *I could be prince of this glorious darkness.*

The vultures holding him forced him to face the Beggar King.

"You've developed a taste for the undermagic," said the sorcerer.

Jordan focused on the thin line of light on the horizon. At first the sound he heard was faint, but then it grew clearer, the Seven Seers of Cir speaking the prayers for a desperate situation — for him. He could hear his name, could feel a new strength rushing into his arms. In the distance, the river glowed and the line of light shone like a beacon. The vultures loosened their grip on him and backed away.

The Beggar King was on his feet. "What have you done? What sort of power do you call upon? Kneel, or I shall force you to your knees."

"You couldn't do it if you tried," shouted Jordan, and he leapt forward to grab the candle from the Beggar King's hands but the sorcerer was quick, and the heavy candle came slamming down hard on Jordan's back.

Jordan yowled in pain.

"You will learn to kneel!" roared the Beggar King, and he fell upon Jordan, throwing him to the mud. The blows rained down on him and Jordan struggled beneath the weight of the man.

Jordan heard someone calling from very far away. "Drown him in the River of the Dead. You must drown him, Jordan! That's the only way."

He edged towards the river, his feet slipping in the mud. All the while the sorcerer thrashed at him with the heavy candle. When at last they were beside the water, Jordan clasped the man's legs and they fell together into the frigid river with a splash. Jordan landed on the Beggar King and held his head under the water, but it bobbed up again. Jordan went under with him, his eyes filling with black water. The man's hands seemed to be everywhere.

Jordan thrust himself up into the air and landed hard on the sorcerer, and he felt a sharp pain in his chest. He coughed, winded, and for a second he lost hold of the man. The Beggar King came up for air and Jordan went for his head again, holding him under longer, and longer. The sorcerer kicked and thrashed, and at last went limp underneath him.

The candle! There it was, floating, still unnaturally aglow, in the river. He swam towards it, struggling in his long Uttic robes.

The vultures crowded together along the riverbank. As Jordan climbed out of the water, the candle in his fist, they shrank away from him.

"It's gone out," Jordan said quietly, staring at it.

"He's dead, he's dead, the Beggar King is dead," the cry went up, yet the beaked faces closest to Jordan were silent and blank with shock.

"Long live the Beggar King," screeched others in response.

One by one the vultures turned from him and shuffled away, and all Jordan could see for miles was a line of candlelight receding into the darkness.

"The world was hard on him," said Arrabel. She'd startled Jordan. He hadn't realized she was beside him. "He was a sin-eater once. You have to have the vocation for it now, of course."

You have to have the blood for it.

"For whatever he did wrong, we must have mercy," said Arrabel. She put out her hand and Jordan gave her the heavy darkened candle. "Let me dispose of this."

As she moved away from him, Jordan sank onto one of the nearby rocks, his back to the river, feeling the weight of all that had happened. Above him shone the twin moons. Had they been there all along? If so, he hadn't noticed them until that moment. He gazed up into their light the way he once had from his rooftop patio.

But now Jordan had the peculiar feeling that he could see the sisters themselves in the moons. There was the darker Maelstrom with her long black hair, her eyes furious slits. He heard someone say, "It will find a way to come back, boy. The undermagic always finds its way."

Jordan also saw another woman, Lucinda, with flowing hair and gentle eyes that were the blue of the sea. Light shone through her as if she were a prism, scattering colour everywhere.

Arrabel appeared at his side.

"I've seen the sister moons," Jordan said, his eyes wide.

Arrabel nodded. "You've been touched by both light and darkness." She offered him her hand and helped him up.

"Come, let's leave this place and reclaim our Holy City."

Twenty-Nine

GOAT STEW

JORDAN AND ARRABEL PULLED THE BRASS door open, staggering into the dim light of the palace hallway. Arrabel slammed the door and bent to trace her finger around its edges, murmuring something under her breath. Wherever she touched, a fringe of frost formed. Jordan became aware of the clipped sound of someone pacing, and then the footsteps came to an abrupt halt.

"Sweet sasapher, you're back! Is it done, then? Is he dead? I thought you'd never show up. Could you hear me shouting? I came as quickly as I could. Oh blast it anyway, I — "

Jordan clamped Sarmillion in a hug. "It's done," he said. "And I did hear you, and thank goodness because I couldn't have done it without you."

Sarmillion's chest puffed out and his eyes were shiny. "You realize they'll write songs about us, don't you? You realize we'll be famous. Glory, groder and Grizelda," he exulted.

Jordan's face darkened, but Sarmillion seemed oblivious.

"Very well," the undercat clapped. "I'm off to meet Master Balbadoris in his study. Time to tidy up, and then it's back to work. We're going to reassemble the Book of What Is, see if we can't create a little magic." He set off down the hall at a good pace, talking to himself about his apartment in Omar and how

256

he had no intention of giving that up no matter what Balbadoris might say about it.

Jordan regarded the sealed brass door as if it were a python. Arrabel was watching him.

"It will get easier with time," she said.

They set off down the long dark halls of the palace. Jordan was still wearing his Uttic robes, but somewhere along the way they had dried out. Arrabel now bore the bright blue garb of the high priestess, with beads and buttons and many-coloured feathers — and it was pressed and shining, not the shabby mess she'd worn in her prison cell. She walked down the halls like someone who has just arrived home after a long journey, running her hands along the walls, reveling in the familiar.

They arrived at the Meditary. As they were taking off their sandals to pass beneath the archway, a Brinnian Landguard called out, "You there!"

Jordan faced him. "Put down your dagger, feirhart," he said. "It's over."

When the guard saw Arrabel's robes, his face paled and he hastened away. Arrabel stood before the Meditary's central font and placed her hands upon the orange stone that had for an entire year given off nothing more than a dull glimmer. Beneath her touch it blazed back to its customary glow.

Outside, the palace grounds were littered with bodies. All of Rabellus's raised platforms had been flattened or burned. Against the far wall of the courtyard stood a long line of Brinnian Landguards, hands tied behind their backs. There was Mars helping the healer, Malthazar, tend to the wounded, feeling for broken bones and bandaging gashes. Some Cirran citizens were already busy white-washing the stone buildings that had borne Rabellus's portrait.

Near one of the fountains Jordan made out the tall stoop-shouldered form of Elliott T. Elliott. Next to him stood Tanny, her Uttic headdress removed, her round tanned face angled towards her husband. Jordan ran to them and as Elliott caught sight of him he gasped his name and they came together in a tangle.

Jordan held his father by the arms. "When I'd heard they had taken you away . . . it was my fault. I'm so sorry. And then this afternoon when I saw those guards, I thought . . . "

"Shh," said his father. "I'm fine now."

"May I take him from you?" Arrabel asked when she joined them. Then to Jordan she said, "Come, we have something important to do."

She led him towards the holy tree. Wherever they passed, the grass became green again. As they stepped onto the mosaic stone pathway closer to the tree, Jordan heard the sound of wings. His heart rose into his throat, but he forced it down. A finch lit in one of the branches.

Someone had already taken down the bodies that had hung from the tree's twisted limbs. When Arrabel bent towards a thorn bush, it transformed into pink flowers. She returned with two bouquets and handed one to Jordan.

"Phinius," he said. He inhaled their powerful scent, thinking of Sarmillion. "It's the flower of the sages."

"Flower of insight. I thought it might be fitting," said Arrabel. "Now, do you remember the words we'll need?"

He grinned. "I said them only a few weeks ago."

"Blessed is the Great Light, light of all lands of Katir-Cir, light of our path," they recited together, placing their bouquets beneath the tree. Cirrans who had been bustling around them sensed what was happening and stood still. Before long there was silence across the grand expanse of the palace grounds.

Then Arrabel said, "Get ready now," and she pulled Jordan back.

The entire tree burst into flames. There was a collective gasp, and then applause. The fire lasted a full minute. Jordan had never stood this close to the burning tree before. The intensity of the heat made his whole body glow with warmth. He watched the flames shift from orange to red to blue, and then abruptly go out. People were hugging each other and offering the Cirran greeting with a bow and three fingers pressed to their forehead.

"Now," Arrabel whispered to him, "I believe something weighs heavily upon you. You have served well today. Go to her. Give her my fondest regards and tell her I will be down to see her later."

Jordan gave a solemn bow, and stumbled away from the now blackened tree and down the steep road towards the Alley of Seers, his heart pounding.

When he burst through Mama Petsane's blue door Mama Appollonia nearly shot out of her rocker and through the ceiling.

"Blasted billy grain, Jordan, why you always be waking old ladies?"

Mama Petsane was at the woodstove, stirring a cauldron of goat-meat stew. "You ever hear of knocking, boy?" she said without turning around.

"Where is she?" he panted, and in the same moment he saw Ophira stretched upon the divan. Her skin was almost translucent, but her eyes were open, and she managed a small smile.

"Jordan," she said weakly.

He came over and knelt beside her. "You're all right." He stroked the hair away from her face. Her cheek was cool. "I was so worried."

"Her fever broke a few hours ago," said Grandma Mopu as she came down the stairs carrying a fragrant basket of dried sage. "It was the strangest thing." She regarded Jordan. "There she was thrashing about as if she were possessed by the darkest curse, and shouting your name. And then — it just stopped."

"We be thinking the dear girl's dead." Petsane held up her stew spoon. "I would've come after you, ye rapscallion, I tell ye that."

Ophira's eyes were on Jordan. "Is he gone? For good?"

"He's gone."

Jordan looked at his hands. They were covered in scratches and one of his fingers was swollen and blue. Mopu patted him on the shoulder and handed him a bundle of dried sage. She distributed the other bunches to Petsane and Appollonia.

"We have to smoke the sickness out of this place," explained Mopu. She opened the front door and all of the window shutters, then lit each of the sage bundles on fire. The women made their way around the room, waving the aromatic sage smoke into every corner, but Jordan wouldn't budge from Ophira's side.

"Give me that, then," and Mopu took the sage from him, bumping him playfully with her elbow.

"While I was there, at the River of . . . " he struggled, "I heard — "

"What did ye hear?" interrupted Petsane. She glared at him.

"Nothing," mumbled Jordan. "I guess it was a desperate situation."

"So it was," said Appollonia, fixing him with her good eye. "So it was." Her glass eye seemed to be pointed at his shoes. "I reckon you've grown into 'em now."

Mama Cantare came through the front door calling, "Praise freedom. Praise the blue sky." Behind her came Bintou and Willa leading Mama Manjuza each by one arm.

"I told you she was making a goat stew," said Manjuza. "Didn't I say that's what was cooking?"

"Take off those damn boots, Sister," said Petsane when she saw Willa. But Willa didn't take them off, and Petsane finished smudging the room with sage smoke. Willa looked over at Jordan and gave him a satisfied nod.

"I already told your parents you'd be here," Mama Bintou said to Jordan. "I invited them for supper. They'll arrive in nine and a half minutes, unless they stop to pick some eucalyptus which . . . they are doing right now. Twelve minutes, then."

Jordan went into the kitchen to fetch a glass of cold water and brought it to Ophira, helping her to sit up and bringing the glass to her mouth. She took small bird-like sips.

"I'm feeling a little hungry," she said faintly.

"Then we'll set a place for you," said Mopu. She was practically dancing as she placed wooden bowls around the battered kitchen table.

That evening the conversations started and ended in mid-stream. Everyone had too much to say. In the distance came the shouts of celebration and the music of flutes and lyres. Jordan ate his fill of goat stew, keeping close to Ophira and basking in the sound of her gentle voice.

And yet, something hummed beneath the surface of the evening, beneath Jordan's thoughts, under his skin. It was the memory of those vultures, thousands of them, each with a lit candle, retreating single file into darkness.

He dropped his napkin and as he bent to pick it up, he tested the air, pulling with just one finger — and it gave way. He could still do it. It was like learning how to nock an arrow. You didn't forget.

On the walk home, Elliott smoked a pipe filled with dried sasapher while Jordan chewed on a long stalk of mellowreed.

Tanny was strolling with her hands in the pockets of her yellow baker's robes, breathing deeply of the night air.

"You've become a young man," she said to Jordan. "Hard to believe you'll be taking your robes next week."

Robes. Jordan sighed. He still didn't know which ones he would take. Arrabel had told him not to worry, that she had given it great consideration.

Elliott observed him with a furrowed brow. "You're pale."

"I'll be okay," said Jordan. He gazed up at the twin half-moons, shut like two eyelids. You couldn't really look at the light one without seeing her darker sister.

Thirty

ROBES

ONE WEEK LATER, JORDAN STOOD BEFORE Mama Petsane's blue door wearing his short pants for the very last time. From behind the closed door she yelled, "Ach, Jordan, it's open."

He entered the kitchen. All seven old women were seated around the table, and Mama Bintou was knitting.

"Big day," said Mopu the Monkey-Maker. "Any guesses?"

"Potato peeler," said Jordan. "Pipe carver. Chicken butcher."

"Praise the chicken butchers," said Cantare.

"At least we know he won't be wearing saffron," said Ophira from the divan.

Jordan was still. Only his eyes moved towards where she sat. When he realized she was wearing the dark green robes of a potion-maker, his jaw dropped. "But I thought . . . where are your prophet's robes?"

"There's only seven seers in this family, boy," said Willa.

"No need for another," said Mopu, and she flashed a smile at Ophira. "Girl's gotta get a real vocation, now."

Ophira's face was still ghostly pale but the colour had returned to her lips.

She stood and asked her grandmas, "Can I go up to the holy tree with Jordan?"

"Off ye be, then," said Petsane. "We ain't ready to leave yet. Don't steal nothing along the way, Jordan. Those days be over now. And mind ye walk slowly. 'Phira ain't strong enough for cantering up the city streets quite yet."

There was a gleam in Mopu's eye.

"Give me a hint," Jordan whispered as he passed her. "What colour will they be?"

But she shook her head and said nothing.

Outside the sky was a clear bright blue. Not a single crow, as far as the eye could see. Gone were the poisonous mushrooms and thorn bushes. Instead flowers bloomed in every pot and along every alley and from every rooftop. They even sprouted between some of the cobblestones.

All the portraits of Rabellus had been painted over, and the Brinnian flags taken down. In their place flew the Cirran doves. Some Cirrans had called for Arrabel to hang the Brinnian prisoners. Others felt they should languish in prison until they died. But after much deliberation, Arrabel decided to send the remaining soldiers home, led by a contingent of Cirran Landguards all the way to the mountain pass.

"They'll just turn around and come back," some folks said.

But Arrabel promised that was the one thing they would not do. A strong weave of spells would guarantee it.

Jordan took Ophira's hand as they wound their way uphill. He welcomed the slower pace. At least he wasn't the only one taking robes today. Some of his school friends would be alongside him, in front of the crowd. And Sarmillion would be there.

He paused near the Cirran Common and stood before Ophira. A chicken stopped its pecking at the cobblestones and squawked at him.

"When you got sick," he began, and then thrust his hands into his pockets.

"Jordan, you don't have to explain anything," Ophira said.

"Yes, I do. That night, I went back to the brass door. I took him the undermagic. He said it would need feeding but I never dreamed — if I had known . . . "

"It's okay." She cupped his face with her hands. "It's over."

"But that's just it." Jordan lowered his voice. There were groups of people milling about the market stalls, most of them headed up to the ceremony at the holy tree, where, amongst other things, he was about to be celebrated as a hero. "It's not over."

"The Beggar King is dead," said Ophira.

Long live the Beggar King. That interminable procession of unnatural light. Where had the vultures gone? And how long before they came back?

"The undermagic." Jordan faltered. "There was no way to get rid of it, Phi."

Ophira fixed him with a grim expression. "You mean the vultures," she said.

Nearby a set of glass chimes tinkled as if moved by the breeze — but there was no breeze.

"He woke them," said Jordan. "And I helped."

"But this city has come back to life," said Ophira. "And so have I. Wouldn't it all be different if the vultures were really awake? You killed the Beggar King. You put out the candle that mattered. Wasn't it enough?"

"Maybe," he said. "Maybe it was."

They resumed walking. The afternoon was warm, but the stifling humidity of the past weeks was gone. As they reached the palace plateau, they stopped so that Ophira could catch her breath. Groups of Cirrans were sitting on blankets on the grass, some on benches or by the fountains, some in the olive grove. Flowers overflowed around the holy tree as if today were the feast day, and Jordan could hear someone playing a sweet tune on the mellowreed flute.

He kissed Ophira lightly. "I'd better go over with the others," for he could see a group of young men and women waiting off to the side of the tree, their faces solemn. He took his place beside them and wished the day were already over. A moment later Sarmillion joined them dressed in freshly pressed scribe's robes. He squeezed Jordan's arm.

"My," he said, his eyes darting from one end of the crowd to the other. "Oh my."

The assembly went quiet as Arrabel made her entrance, flanked by crimson-robed mystery keepers, as well as the young girl chosen to be robe-bearer for today's ceremony. Jordan tried to spy the colours in her arms but each of the robes was well covered in its black silk bag. The high priestess stood beside the holy tree. The sunlight made her hair shimmer, and reflected off the many beads and buttons of her robe.

"My dear friends," she said, gazing into the crowd as if singling out each person. "How overjoyed I am to be here."

She spoke of the coup, of the Brinnians' brutality, of the terrible necessity of accepting imprisonment in order to prevent the slaughter of scores of innocent Cirrans. When she spoke of Jordan's heroic part in the battle at the Uttic prison camp, he didn't realize at first that she was talking about him. He noticed that she left out certain details about the brass door and the undermagic. He tried to catch her eye, to let her know he was grateful for her discretion, but her attention was on the crowd.

She called upon Sarmillion, awarding him a medallion of honour for service befitting a scribe.

"My lady," he said, his head bowed as he accepted his award. When everyone applauded he looked as if he had settled beside a warm fire. Jordan noticed a white-furred undercat amongst the crowd wearing an elegant turquoise dress covered in sequins, her eyes trained on Sarmillion.

A tall, broad boy was called forward to accept his farming robes — brown, streaked with yellow. As acting scribe for the ceremony, Sarmillion took up a peacock-feather pen and ink to inscribe the boy's name and vocation into the book of civil records.

Two girls, one after the next, accepted the emerald robes of scholars. That afternoon there was also a new metal worker in Cir, and a gardener, and a bone-setter. And then it was Jordan's turn.

"Jordan Elliott," said High Priestess Arrabel. He came to stand before her, certain his legs would give way.

"Today you take your robes," she said. "These robes mark your departure from childhood, and your entrance onto the path of Cirran adulthood. Son of a carver, son of a baker: stand tall and declare your gift."

The entire mountaintop fell silent, but for the chirping of songbirds.

Jordan looked at the furrowed surface of the holy tree. "I have none," he said.

"You have shown cleverness, and great courage," said Arrabel. "Strength, and also stubbornness. But above all, your experience has won you an understanding of this world that few will ever be graced with. Mystery has two sides, and we must see them both."

Jordan tried hard to read her kind, wise eyes but they revealed nothing.

"I am told you've been known to spend more time in Somberholt Forest than in our Cirran classrooms. Is this so?"

Jordan chuckled nervously. "I guess so."

"You have a deep connection to trees."

He thought of his father's suggestion to keep the cedar groves, how insulted Jordan had been by the notion mere weeks ago. Now it occurred to him that spending his days surrounded by the good and healing magic of the cedars would be a pleasure. "I do love trees, my lady."

"Good." She reached over and touched the blackened bark of the holy tree. "This one in particular will need your attention." She stepped forward and announced, "Jordan Elliott, on this day I declare you to be keeper of the holy tree."

His forehead creased. "But . . . there's never been such a keeper."

"It's an oversight I've been meaning to correct for some time."

The young robe-bearer had removed the black silk bag and was thrusting leaf-green robes into Jordan's arms and then somehow the robes found their way over his head. They were as soft and light as a breeze. Just above his heart was embroidered a tree with black twisted limbs.

"I will do my best to merit this honour, my lady," he said.

She held him by both shoulders. "You've proven yourself worthy already."

Sarmillion's pen scratched upon the parchment but he looked up from his work long enough to catch Jordan's eye and give him a wink. The nearby mystery keepers came over and shook his hand, and then he was swept into the crowd. Even in such a din he could hear Grandma Mopu's guffaws.

"You'll have to learn your tale of the holy tree by heart," she said, patting him on the back. "Prayers and incantations, too. My word, boy, you'll even have to wield a shovel!"

Ophira gave him a congratulatory kiss and whispered, "Green suits you." And then his parents were before him. His mother clasped him in a teary embrace and kissed him on both cheeks. Elliott T. Elliott rested a hand upon the green fabric of Jordan's robes and murmured, "Well. Keeper of the holy tree. Who would have thought it?"

Jordan was surrounded by people offering him good wishes. He slipped one hand into the pocket of his robes and realized with a start there was something in it. He pulled out his hand and stared in disgust. In it was an oily black feather. He dropped it and stamped it into the grass with his heel.

The seers were in a deep discussion about whether or not a guard should be set at the Bridge of No Return. No Return. Well, that wasn't quite true. He had returned and he had no intention of going back.

He went to stand by one of the fountains, where he had an unimpeded view of the beautiful white city below. His eye followed the winding streets all the way down to the glittering river and the twelve magical bridges that spanned it. Commander Theophen came to stand beside him.

"It was worth fighting for, wasn't it," said Theophen.

"Yes," said Jordan. "It was."

Michelle Barker's short fiction has been published in journals across Canada. She has also published non-fiction in magazines, newspapers and literary reviews, and she won a National Magazine Award in personal journalism. Her poetry has been published in literary reviews around the world, including the *2011 Best Canadian Poetry* anthology. A chapbook of her poems, *Old Growth, Clear Cut: Poems of Haida Gwaii,* was published by Leaf Press in 2012, as well as a mini-chapbook, *Glimpsing the Stars,* with The Centrifugal Eye. She has worked as an editor and leads creative writing workshops.

Barker is studying for her Master's degree in creative writing at UBC's optional-residency program. She lives in Penticton with her husband and family. This is her first novel.